ELEVEN NEW GHOST STORIES

First published in 2014 by DPN Books

© David Paul Nixon

Cover design by Marie Bussiere

For my father

With thanks to the Velkys and Mrs Goddard
for their time, encouragement and patience;
to Mr Donaghy and Mr Lownds for their web skills;
to Ms Gordino for her design skills,
and to Ms Bussiere for the cover.

Read the latest New Ghost Stories content on
davidpaulnixon.substack.com and
www.newghoststories.com

You can follow the project on Twitter
@newghoststories and download the New Ghost Stories
Podcast from most podcast platforms.

CONTENTS

INTRODUCTION

Do I believe in ghosts?

A few years ago that wouldn't have been a difficult question: A resounding "no" would have sprung from my lips with barely a moment's thought. I love a good ghost story; I even watch some of those ropey documentaries on the less-respectable TV channels. But a believer – I most certainly was not.

Now things are more complicated...

My strange journey started almost three years ago. I was on the London South Bank, having just seen a Hitchcock classic at the cinema, and was killing time before returning to see a screening of The Innocents – *the* classic cinematic ghost story. By luck and coincidence as I walked out in front of Charing Cross station I crossed paths with an old school friend, someone I had not seen in years.

We took the chance to catch up and settled down in a nearby pub. I explained that I had a few hours before the film started and I ended up telling him the plot, as he had not seen it, though he was apparently a fan of horror.

At some point, as we started to trade our favourite scary tales, he said to me that he knew someone who had experienced the real thing. A relative who had actually seen a real ghost and had a real story to tell. Naturally, I was sceptical; I knew people who had seen ghosts, but these were always stories that had taken place during their childhood and lacked credibility, transformed as they were into fascinating anecdotes, ripened for ear-catching conversation. Yet he was insistent, and if I wanted I could hear the story straight from the horse's mouth.

After a few pints, this became something of a gauntlet thrown down and I felt obliged to pick it up. A few weeks later I found myself in an unfamiliar part of suburban London going to visit a man who, as it turned out, was firstly, not expecting to see us, and secondly, didn't want to tell us the story.

If this seems like a humorous situation, I can state quite categorically that it wasn't. He *really* didn't want to tell it. He was afraid we might laugh, that we might scoff. This was something quite serious to him; something he didn't like to talk about. Unfortunately, this made it all the more fascinating to hear. I'd only really accepted the invitation out of kindness, now I really couldn't wait to hear what the man had to say.

We managed to persuade him after a while; swore that we weren't about to laugh at him or mock him, that we really just wanted to hear what he had to say. He didn't want just to tell us the story though; he wanted to prove it! Prove that he wasn't making it up. There was this contradiction within him; a wanting to be believed but also a fear of being laughed at.

So we listened intently. What struck me about his story, and what caused me to really embark on the journey that led to me starting this book, is just how affected he seemed to be by what he had experienced. It seems like an obvious thing to point out doesn't it? But when you hear a ghost story, you always take it as a roller-coaster ride. Some frights and some chills, a bit of fun and a bit of a scare. You don't really take it seriously.

Yet, when I heard this story, I was taken aback by how serious it really was. It wasn't a bit of fluff told in low-light with a sense of relish. This was a defining moment in this man's life, and not a good one; a painful one.

I found the urge to tell his story almost irresistible. He was uncomfortable with the idea at first, but slowly I was able to talk him around. This was his chance to put his side of the story across, to present what had been a great tragedy in his life, without judgement, for others to discover. For him to just tell it like it is – people could either then take it or leave it.

And that's how I decided to approach the idea; I sat down with him and a microphone and just let him tell it, recording every word. This was useful for several reasons, not just for capturing his words but also it allowed me to scrutinise them. Though I found nothing suspicious about him or his story, I nevertheless wished to be certain that he was telling the truth, at least as far as he knew it.

I could detect no great diversions from the story he had told me before, no signs of great exaggerations or flexible facts. And as for his evidence... Let's be clear that this did not amount to categorical proof of supernatural occurrences, but it did establish a certain number of facts, dates, locations; proof that certain events had happened, even if their cause could not be concluded.

Having heard his story again, I felt even more strongly that he was sincere, that he was no great fantasist or exhibitionist. And for his part, it seemed that we had in some way helped him to get these matters off his chest, given him some small sense of catharsis.

And this is where my journey started. As I sat at home transcribing his words, I wondered who else out there had a real ghost story; a story that preyed on their mind that they had perhaps kept hidden, reluctant to tell their friends or family for fear of ridicule or worse.

I took small steps at first, just a mere few blog posts and forum entries. The early response was overwhelming – a mixed blessing to say the least. I had given out an open invitation for any joker, loon and nutcase to vie for attention. I was bombarded with the ridiculous, the stupid and the mundane; everything from tales of creaking doors and gates to the attacks of full-grown bogeymen.

But I stuck with it. My first storyteller confessed to have spoken to a few others online about his experiences and said he knew of a few he felt were serious, sensible people like him who had experienced something out of the ordinary, but also feared ridicule or the attentions of the over-enthusiastic amateur ghost-hunter.

Some of these became my first subjects and gave me confidence that the whole project was worth undertaking and worth the work.

It has not been easy picking through the heavy correspondence, trying to separate the honest voices from the dishonest ones. I have come dangerously close to being fooled and wasted a great deal of time chasing people who it turned out could not be relied upon; who if not lying outright, were being obviously very liberal with the truth.

I have applied some technique to my recording of the stories that follow in this collection. I can't say that I have been very scientific; I have tried simply to approach each case with my best judgement. I have asked for every story to be told twice, sometimes on paper, ideally at least once on tape, so that I could compare and examine their words, searching for any reason to doubt them.

I have required some kind of evidence as the minimum criteria for any sustained contact with anyone claiming to have a story to tell. This evidence could be anything from receipts to train tickets, emails, photographs; just small things to ascertain dates, locations, anything to tie down certain facts and to deter tellers of fiction. In some cases I may have refused to speak to people with honest stories because they lacked any items of proof. I sincerely apologise if I have offended anyone, but this has been a difficult process with many a trap to fall into. I have simply had to be ruthless.

What I present here are 11 stories from amongst the many hundreds I have heard and attempted to investigate. These 11 stories represent what, as far as I can tell, are the most truthful accounts amongst those I have heard.

Truth is a slippery thing and upon reading these stories you will undoubtedly feel this also. There are extraordinary things written within these pages; things I could not believe. Things that go beyond what goes bump in the night...

You may be sceptical; you would be foolish not to be. Yet in each case I have done my best to probe each subject, question them and challenge them. They have remained firm in their convictions, backed up much of what they have said and proved themselves within a certain reasonable doubt to be rational, sane people.

You will probably come to doubt this. And this in turn will be revealing; what these stories may say about the tellers, if they are not true, is almost as fascinating as the possibility of them being entirely factual.

What follows then are the edited transcripts of interviews or the written accounts of 11 subjects, printed here with as much fidelity as possible. I have avoided editing them unless absolutely necessary. I have removed any interruptions or any great diversions from the story, but only with great reluctance. I have striven to offer the complete testimony of each subject as authentically as possible.

Ensuring the confidentiality of each subject has been paramount to me throughout this whole project. Certain names or locations may have been changed or simply omitted to help protect their anonymity. The people who tell these stories did so at great personal risk and I am extremely grateful that they have put their trust in me.

It is possible with the tool of the internet to investigate, to form hypotheses and to put great effort into tracking down these individuals. In one case the teller of the story will be so easy to ascertain that masking it was virtually pointless. Yet I saw no reason to offer them any different assurances than any other subject. Nevertheless, I must ask and implore you to leave these people alone and not to attempt to uncover their identities. Frankly, they have been through enough.

What these stories tell us about the supernatural, about life and death, the universe... I cannot say. This project has made me simultaneously both more sceptical and more of a believer. Sceptical because of all the countless hours wasted listening to lies and dross and delusional behaviour. But in these stories there are 11 people who speak with a genuine pain. Their stories cannot so easily be explained away.

Does that mean I believe in ghosts? I think until I see one face-to-face, I will always be a sceptic. But do I believe there are things that exist in this world that defy explanation and our understanding?

You bet I do...

A RHYTHM OF SIX

He was excited at first. After all, he'd just made his name – and a fairly substantial amount of money – selling a script about ghost stories to a producer. Now the flat he'd used the money to buy apparently had a ghostly apparition of its own.

Well, not so much an apparition; more a noise. I felt certain he was talking crap. He told me it made a tapping noise. As someone who lives in an old Victorian tenement with piping more than a hundred years old, I wasn't buying it; just turning on the central heating was like unleashing a symphony of slow spoon players. The incessant clicks and clacks could go on all night.

It was then that he moved his coffee cup and tapped out a rhythm: *tap t-t-t-tap tap*. That's the noise it would make. It could happen at any time, day or night, coming from somewhere in the flat. "The rhythm of six" he called it. Always the same, never different. It would come from somewhere far away, never near where he was. And as soon as he went looking for it, it would stop.

I didn't believe him, and he knew I wouldn't. So he invited me over to come and see for myself. I was a little sceptical, not just because I didn't believe him, but because I thought that this might be some pretext for him to try something.

We had been close friends once, but then, after quite a long time of us being friends, he had got drunk and announced his "love" for me. It was quite definitely not what I wanted to hear. I'd never really thought of him as someone I'd want to go out with. I was seeing someone when we became friends, and I was seeing someone when he suddenly said he was in love with me.

I suppose I'd always found him a bit too much work. He was fun to spend time with, to talk to, but he could get pretty clingy. He barely let his last girlfriend out of the house – he liked your undivided attention because he wasn't very confident. And if you ignored him or didn't pay enough attention to him, he could get a bit sulky and offish.

I'd known worse, gone out with worse, but he never really seemed my type. I'd enjoyed spending time with him, we were decent friends – I thought. He'd made a bad lunge for me, and held on too tightly and a bit too long when I told him to let go. It wasn't a side to him that I'd seen before, and I didn't like it.

We didn't talk for a long time after that. And it was only when we started living nearby again, about a year ago, that we patched things up. Things were good between us, but he didn't have many friends in the area, so I saw him quite a lot, and knew he wanted a little more from me. It was a bit obvious.

I went along with it any way, I thought we had to get past this awkwardness – and I did genuinely like him; we'd had good times. A nice inexpensive night in with him and his DVD collection actually seemed nice, as long as he didn't try anything.

Anyway, we got take-out – pizza and chips – and put on some movies, a mixture of the good and bad. But not with the sound on loud – he didn't want me to miss it if we heard the tapping. I really didn't give a toss about it, and just went on eating and drinking and talking.

We were half way through taking the piss out of Keanu Reeves in Point Break when he suddenly cried: "There it is!"

"What?"

"The tapping." He grabbed the remote and stopped the movie.

"Did you hear it?"

I had the feeling I might have heard a knock or something, but I didn't want to over-play its significance. But Craig was adamant I had heard the ghost.

"It could've just been the pipes."

"It's June, the heating's off and none of the taps are on."

I wasn't buying it, but I could see that this was no joke. He honestly believed something was going on. He was getting all worked up; what mysteries could his home be hiding? Who had lived here before? What had happened to them? What kind of restless spirit lived here?

It was a bit sad how quickly the sceptic had become a convert. He'd started to really believe the kind of things he was writing about. I teased him about it; he admitted his imagination was running away with him, but he promised me that there was something, and that he wasn't just making it up. I told him he should contact that fool on the telly, the one who goes into people's homes to talk to the dead. He laughed at the suggestion – at least he hadn't become a complete believer.

We finished watching Christopher Lee in The Devil Rides Out at about half-past midnight and there was still no sound from the so-called ghost.

It was then that he said I should stay the night – it almost always made some noise in the night time. Considering our past, this was something I did not really want to do.

But it was tipping it down outside – typical British summer weather. The thought of staying made me a bit uncomfortable, but the lazy part of me was already thinking: it's wet, it's a bit of a walk, you're pretty drunk and you can't afford a taxi. Besides, it was probably safer to stay here than go out into the streets this late when clearly plastered.

He sensed doubt on my part, so he said, "I'm not going to try anything; I'll put up the fold-up bed in the library, you can lock the door if you want to."

So I consented and he set up the bed for me. His library was in the small second bedroom. As he put the bed up, I couldn't help notice just how much stuff he had based around the occult. Books about witchcraft, hauntings, pagans; all the classic ghost story authors: M.R.James, Poe, Le Fanu, Stoker... and suspicious things by sinister folk like Aleister Crowley and Anton LaVey. I didn't believe in any of this stuff, but to be surrounded by so many tomes about nasty things was a little bit unsettling. It also made me wonder whether he'd fallen under their spell just a little, and had started to be swept up by it after all.

I didn't sleep well, but I put that down to the booze. I phased in and out; hard to know how long I was sleeping. I woke myself up properly and tried again. I ended up reading DVD sleeves in the moonlight. There was probably every Hammer Horror known to man, multiple versions of The Amityville Horror – even that movie they banned after the Jamie Bulger murder (bootleg of course).

I got up after a while to get some water. I moved in the dark to the kitchen and put on the light after a little searching. I grabbed a glass and turned on the cold water tap. The water was massively over-pressured and it spat out with a thump, hitting the bottom of my glass with enough force to splash onto my t-shirt. I turned it off quickly, swearing loudly, before wiping myself down with a tea towel – Craig had warned me about the tap earlier.

As I tried to wipe water up from the counter, I heard something. It was the slightest sound of tapping; not loud, but it was there.

I scoffed – it was the pipes after all. That idiot! I turned on the over-pressured tap again – it splashed heavily against the dirty dishes in the sink, getting me wet once again. But I turned it off quickly and waited for the sound of knocking.

I was sure I'd got it, but then nothing happened. I waited for more than a minute. I was so sure I'd found the source, but nothing was heard.

That didn't prove anything though; the tap was still probably the most likely explanation. I filled my glass with water from the hot tap instead. I waited a little then too, but there was no sound.

I started to walk out of the kitchen, and then I heard it:

Tap-t-t-t-tap tap.

I stopped still. That wasn't the sound of a pipe; it sounded like someone tapping on a wall or a table. Quite clearly in a rhythm; no clumsy clunking or banging.

I immediately assumed Craig was taking the piss, so I walked quickly out into the hall to see if he was there. It was empty and dark. I looked both ways, down to the bedroom at the end of the hall, and back across the landing to the living room. All seemed quiet and empty.

What had he said? It always stops when you go looking for it... Now it was giving me the willies. I felt a shiver and suddenly thought it would be best to go back to my room and hope the dark words of the occultists might protect me.

I walked forward a little, past the door to the bathroom. There it was again, behind me:

Tap-t-t-t-tap tap.

It came from the landing, I was sure of it. I spun around and saw a figure – I almost screamed, but after a second realised that it was the hat-stand.

I exhaled and shook my head. I chuckled slightly at myself and turned back towards the library.

There it was again: *tap-t-t-t-tap tap.*

It was from the stair bannister, creeping along the surface, getting closer to me with each tap.

I inhaled quickly – then it came again, from the bathroom door right next to me:

Tap-t-t-t-tap...

...TAP – right on my shoulder! Like someone poking me hard in the back.

I span around in a fright and tripped over the end of the rug in the hallway. I fell over backward with a screech, throwing my arms up in the air. My glass of water splattered dramatically over the wall. The glass, by some miracle, didn't smash – it landed with a thud on the carpet and rolled up to the door of Craig's bedroom.

I tried to get up, but as I scrambled to my feet all I did was roll the rug up under me. I stumbled again and fell back on the floor with a thump.

The door opened and Craig came out into the hall: "What the hell's going on?"

"It touched me," I screamed. "The thing touched me!"

He took me into the living room and, rather quaintly, thought that what I needed was some warm milk to calm me down.

He accused me of imagining it because I was drunk. I almost hit the roof: "I felt it! It touched my shoulder. You expected me to believe you; now you won't believe me!"

He said I should calm down: "All it did was touch you. That's not so bad."

"He didn't touch me, he poked me!"

"Well, how do you know it's a 'he'? Maybe it's a 'she'?"

"Oh you'd love that wouldn't you? A jealous she-spirit who wants you." Sounded like the kind of thing he'd try to make a story out of.

Despite my distress he was clearly very excited. I'd experienced it too, so there was no question now. It was real! He was suddenly in his element. It was time to research, find out about the house's history, who'd lived there before, what crimes had taken place in the area – maybe unsolved?

He'd missed something obvious: "What about the people who live downstairs?"

"There's no one – it's been empty since I got here. Maybe this is why it's not for sale – there's no sign. I bet it's something that happened in the house below."

It struck me instantly that he was very much in his own fictional world. That he was actually living out one of his own stories and that he was going to approach this like a work of fiction. I tried to point this out, but he said he'd studied ghost hunting and knew what it was that psychical researchers do when they hear about phenomena.

I didn't dare point out that most of that was made up too – guesswork that lent itself to mankind's natural capacity for making sense of things by making a story. But then I thought, well, what if it isn't all nonsense? I had just been poked in the shoulder. And I hadn't imagined it – I wasn't that drunk, surely?

I didn't sleep well the rest of that night as you can imagine. I kept having this unpleasant feeling that I was being watched. I think I was just being paranoid. But there was something in that house; something had touched me. I knew it. I didn't wait around for breakfast; I walked home and climbed quickly back into my own bed for comfort.

I didn't see Craig for a week or so after that. This wasn't deliberate – the thing at his place hadn't scared me that badly; I just had accountancy exams coming up and needed to revise. I got a phone call from him after a few days saying he was trying to contact the previous owners of the flat. The estate agents wouldn't let him contact them without themselves acting as go-between, but he was sure their address was on the paperwork somewhere. He remembered being told they had emigrated back to India, so it would be a while, one way or another, before he would hear from them.

He was also going to go to the town library to see if he could find any interesting references to the building and had contacted someone at the local historical society for any interesting things that had happened on his road. Some of the buildings were noticeably newer than some of the others and he'd wondered whether they'd been bombed in the war. Was this the restless spirit of someone trapped in the wreckage? Someone who had tried to make a noise so they could be rescued, but had not been heard in time?

He was so keen to make a narrative out of it.

He called on me again after my exams were over, under the guise of asking how it went. But quickly he wanted to update me on how things were progressing with his ghost hunt. I couldn't help but be jealous that he had all this time on his hands to spend chasing his fantasies.

The latest news was that he'd written to the flat's previous owners in India, having found their address, and was looking into finding a way to trick the council into giving him the address of the owners of the empty flat downstairs.

His historical research of the area had come to nothing as of yet; no suspicious goings on to speak of. Yes, some houses had been bombed in the war – but just down the street, not close by.

The man at the historical society had been very friendly, but he didn't have anything "juicy" for him. He did, however, know someone who was researching a spiritualist guide to the area, and that he would contact him on Craig's behalf. So something good could come of that.

Then Craig stopped silent for a moment. "There it is again," he said. "The rhythm of six."

He said he'd be in touch soon and hung up. Later that night he texted me asking if I wanted to come over the evening after. I suggested an earlier time – somehow I didn't want to go over there again and be around when night fell.

I called around at about two in the afternoon. He invited me up and almost as soon as I had reached the top of the stairs there it was:

Tap-t-t-t-tap tap.

"I knew it," he said with relish.

"Knew what?"

"It doesn't like you."

"What?"

He walked me into the living room. "I think it reacts when you're here."

"What on earth are you talking about?"

"I'm here all the time. It never bothers me. I hear it hanging around, making its noise, but it's always in the background. You show up and suddenly it gets all agitated. Starts doing its tapping loud – did you hear how sharp and clear that was?"

"Oh come on Craig – you're letting your mind run away with you."

"And it does it when I'm on the phone to you. It's like, when I'm on the sofa, just watching TV and it makes its noise, does the tapping, it's like it's just reminding me it's there. You know, like it doesn't want me to forget about it. But I start talking to you and suddenly it's banging its fingers down in a mood."

"Just stop it Craig. Seriously, just stop it! You're starting to freak me out."

"But get this: haven't you noticed how cold it is?"

"What?"

"When you came in the flat; it's suddenly gone cold".

"It was cold when I came in."

"It's June – it's 24 degrees outside. Why would it be cold in here?"

"It's not that cold in here," I lied – it was chilly. "Look, I don't want to talk about this. Can't we go out somewhere, get a coffee or something?"

"Not yet, I brought you here to help me with something."

"With what?" I hissed.

"I want to take a look downstairs."

"And how are you going to do that?"

"The backdoor isn't locked properly. The bolt is unlocked; I think I can wriggle the other lock with a credit card or a scraper."

"You want to break in!"

"I climbed out the bedroom window last night and got down there – look."

He took me into his bedroom. Directly under the window was the roof of part of the flat below.

He opened the window: "I just climbed out and dropped down; it's easy."

"You just walked out onto the roof? Are you crazy?"

"It's perfectly safe. I remember the estate agent telling me that the old owners wanted to build a balcony up here, but they weren't given planning permission."

"That doesn't mean the roof is already strong enough!"

"It supported my weight yesterday."

"You're so irresponsible."

"I need you to keep a lookout for me while I try to get the door open."

"Absolutely not, I'm not having anything to do with this."

"Come on, where's your spirit of adventure?"

"This isn't a game Craig. You're breaking into someone's house."

"It's empty."

"It's still a crime. What if someone catches you?"

"We'll just say we thought we smelt gas. Better yet, we could tell them that we'd left a tap on and were concerned there might be water damage downstairs."

"I can't believe you're trying to do this."

"I'd rather you help me, but I'm doing this without you if I have to. I'd rather you were there, that way I can know if the neighbours are coming."

"What do you even expect to find?"

"I don't know. When you investigate you have to rule out the dead-ends first."

"You've read too many detective books."

"Are you coming?"

I thought it was stupid and crazy, but part of me did want to give it a go because I was curious about what was going on. And it was sort of daring breaking into someone's home – stupid though it was. Besides, I was afraid he would get into more trouble, or that something bad would happen to him. It was cold in his flat; something was not right here.

I let him walk out on the roof first – I wasn't going to let both our weights risk making it break. He got to the end and carefully lowered himself down to ground level.

"There's a bench here you can drop yourself on to; it's really easy."

With reluctance I climbed out onto the roof, which thankfully did not groan or creak. I walked to the edge as he suggested and lowered myself down onto a rusty cast-iron bench. The garden was overgrown with thick grass and weeds – no one had been here in quite some time.

It was left, around the side of the house, to the back door. Craig was already there, trying to force the door with a credit card. I didn't like that the old wooden fence panels behind him were coming loose and that there were gaps between them where we could easily be seen.

"This is going to break my card," Craig said.

I looked through the gaps into the garden next door. It was paved over, a depressing grey and tired looking place, with a rusty bike and broken garden furniture – but at least there was no one there.

"Hurry up," I said.

He was trying the paint scraper now, forcing it into the gap between the door and frame. He wiggled it a little, then made a fist with his other hand and struck the top of the scraper's handle. The door opened with a loud creak. "Get in quick," I gasped.

I virtually pushed him inside, slamming the door closed behind us.

What we found was a disappointment. The kitchen and living room had an open corridor between them, with the bathroom sitting in the middle. Then down the hallway were two bedrooms – Craig's place had a much better layout.

But there was nothing remarkable about the place at all. It was empty, nothing on the walls or floor, no left-behind furniture or waste. Just a clean, empty home.

"Well, was this what you were expecting?" I said sharply.

"There's nothing..."

"In an unoccupied house? No kidding."

"No, but there's literally nothing. This place is spotless. There's not a mark or... a scrape or scuff. It all looks brand new. Look at the floor... And walls, no marks, no wear, no dirt..."

I took a step into the kitchen – it all looked pretty sparkling now that he mentioned it. I ran my finger across one of the countertops. There wasn't even any dust.

"It's brand new, completely re-decorated". It was quite warm too; not chilly like upstairs.

He waved his finger in the air. "Something happened here."

"Yeah, they did the place up to sell it."

"But it's not on the market."

"How do you know? Just cos there's no sign outside."

"I checked online, it's not listed anywhere."

"That doesn't mean anything."

"I think something happened. Something bad; something bad enough for whoever owns the place to want to do it over completely. To wipe the slate clean. But even now, they're too afraid to put it on the market. Because of what happened."

"You're just making it up. You don't know any of that. Stop writing a story out of this. You don't know any of this–"

"Hey, hey, ghosts and stuff – that's my specialist field. Trust me; I know what I'm talking about."

"It's all rubbish. You're talking rubbish. All this crap about it going cold and it getting aggravated – you don't know any of that. You're just guessing and making it up as you go along. You don't know anything Craig, you don't know a damn thing!"

He was about to answer back angrily – his mouth opened wide – but then we heard a loud creak.

We both looked up to the ceiling – there were footsteps. Short, gentle, creaking footsteps above, in Craig's flat.

We both looked at each other – then we dashed to the doorway. Craig threw it open and slammed it shut behind me. He was up on the roof at an incredible speed, more athletic than I'd ever seen him. It took me longer to pull myself up from the bench and scramble through the window.

He was stood in the hallway looking around. "Nothing," he said. "There's no one here."

I didn't know what to say, I just stood there, in his bedroom doorway, out of breath.

We listened quietly for a moment, looking up and down the hall and across the landing.

"There has to be some logic behind it," he said pointing at me. "Whatever's going on, there has to be some logic behind it."

Tap-t-t-t-tap tap.

It was quite loud. I couldn't tell where it had come from.

Tap-t-t-t-tap tap.

"Who's there?" I said carefully. Craig looked at me with surprise.

Tap-t-t-t-tap tap – louder.

Tap-t-t-t-tap tap – louder still.

I walked towards him. "Where's it coming from?" I hissed.

"I don't know," he said quietly.

Tap-t-t-t-tap tap – becoming a thundering drumbeat.

I was trembling: "Let's get out of here".

Tap-t-t-t-tap tap.

Tap-t-t-t-tap-TAP – the bathroom mirror leapt from the wall. It bounced off the edge of the sink and crashed onto the bathroom tiles, smashing into pieces.

The noise stopped. Glass was all over the floor – it hadn't just broken, it had exploded into fragments. Even the frame looked like it was torn apart.

Craig stepped over it, and picked up two of the frame's pieces – they were joined by the picture wire used to hang it. It hadn't snapped, and the hook was still in the wall.

It had literally flown off its own hook.

"We need to get out of here."

"It's all right," he whispered. "I think it's ok now."

"I don't care what you think!" I cried. "I want to get out of here now!"

He paused for breath. "Yes, all right" he said. He went for his keys and we made a hasty exit.

We went to a café a few streets away, wanting to put a fair bit of distance between ourselves and the flat. It was a Greek place that was pretending to be Italian; we just ordered coffee, neither of us felt like eating.

"That settles it then," he said.

"Settles what?"

"It's a poltergeist, not a ghost. Ghosts are benign, this thing reacts. It can be angry and destructive."

He took a sip of coffee. "You're not on your period are you?"

"Excuse me?"

"Well, they can react to changes in the body, especially sexual ones."

"I'm 31, Craig, I'm not going through fucking puberty."

With a line like that, it wasn't surprising that people started to look at us. We should've gone somewhere quieter.

"What are you going to do?" I asked him.

"I don't know." He was scared now. This thing was no longer fun or extraordinary; it was a problem. A problem he really couldn't explain, not with all his books and horror movie trivia.

"I think it's best you don't come over any more," he said with a slight tremble in his voice.

"I think so too. But I'll have to go back over with you now because I've left my bloody handbag there."

We sat drinking for a moment or two in silence.

"Exorcism's probably the best thing."

"Moving is probably the best thing."

"I can't just move. You can't just pull out of a mortgage."

"You could say that the owner concealed information about the place from you."

"And what? Sue them for not saying there's a ghost living there? We've got to get rid of it somehow."

He finished his coffee. "At least we've both seen it. No one can just tell me I'm crazy."

I walked with him back to the flat. He said he'd bring my handbag out to me, but, and I don't know why, I suddenly felt defiant – I would come in and get my handbag. Whatever this thing was, I wanted to show it I was not afraid. Though my fearlessness didn't take me beyond the landing at the top of stairs.

"Where'd you leave it?" he asked.

"On the sofa I think."

He walked into the living room. I stood nervously waiting.

"Are you sure? I can't see it."

"Definitely," I was about to go in there and get it myself, but I heard the floor creak behind me.

I turned and saw it – an old man, grey-skinned and bony, walking into the library. He was stick-thin, bald, with liver spots and totally naked. But not just naked, clammy, almost sticky looking – he had almost no colour at all. Just faded, slimy and grey.

"Craig!" I screamed. Terrified and repulsed, I still ran towards the library after it. But as you might guess, when I got there,

there was nothing. Craig thundered across the floor after me, arriving in the library as I went around the bookcases trying to see it.

"What was it?"

"It's here, I saw it. It's an old man. A disgusting old man!"

I didn't stay long after that. I made him promise that he'd call someone, anyone who could help, first thing in the morning, Monday. But I should've known that that was far too sensible a thing for him to do. When I called that evening, he excitedly told me that he'd visited his local electronic store and bought himself a whole bunch of recording equipment.

"Are you crazy?" I yelled.

"Look, I need proof. No one is going to believe me if I go and tell them I've heard bumps in the night and that my mirror has jumped off the wall. But if I record something, then I can be taken seriously and, I dunno, maybe get some proper researchers around."

I almost slammed down the phone.

But then I wondered if I'd been watching too many movies too. It hadn't really done much before, why should it suddenly mind or care if cameras were put up in the house? Life isn't like Paranormal Activity – he could just leave the house if things got bad, couldn't he?

It was all just guesswork; nobody really knew anything.

There seemed to be only one thing that was certain – it didn't like me. All the worst things had happened when I was there. Perhaps if I just stayed away, nothing would happen. I shuddered at the thought of it. To be desired by a disgusting old man from beyond the grave. It made me want to have a shower.

I didn't feel like being in the house alone that night. Milly, my housemate, was out touring Faust with her opera company, so it felt uncomfortably quiet. I put on a series of the Sopranos and started on some red wine to help myself relax.

I fell asleep at some point; I don't know what time. I woke up with a start at around 3:30 am; the TV had turned itself off, but my mobile was still on and it was vibrating its way towards the edge of the coffee table. I picked it up – it was Craig.

"Hello," I groaned.

"I'm coming over!"

"What?"

"It's gone fucking mental!" He was out of breath.

"What?"

"It's gone mental; I think it's going to kill me!"

"Craig, are you running?"

"I'll be there in a minute... I need somewhere to stay. I can't go back there."

He was on my doorstep dripping wet with rain and sweat just minutes later. He could barely talk; he was struggling so hard to catch his breath. I took his coat, but had no dry clothes to give him. He was wearing slippers; he must've just thrown on whatever came to hand. I put his slippers and coat in the dryer. I gave him a towel for his face and hair and sat him next to a fan heater in the kitchen while I put on the kettle.

"It went beserk!" he said, shivering.

"What do you mean, beserk?" I asked with a lump in my throat.

"I set up three cameras; one in the hall, one in my bedroom and one in the living room. Just cameras on tripods, nothing special, set to record for as long as they could."

"You wanted it on video – for fame and glory purposes?"

"I wanted proof! You don't understand; I went online, I looked around. People, nutters, they say stuff like this all the time. No one takes you seriously unless you've got video or the word of an expert; and any expert requires that you get cleared by a psychiatrist first before they'll even consider anything you say to be true. Catching it on tape would've shown anyone that I wasn't lying!"

His eyes were red and his face pale – he looked desperate and terrified.

"I went to sleep. Nothing was happening, I just dozed off. Slept for a couple of hours and then BANG! I don't know what it was, but it was loud, like someone hitting a steel container with a hammer. I jumped out of bed and then it started. Rhythm of six: Tap-t-t-t-tap tap, faster and faster, louder and louder until the floor started to shake. The doors rattled on their hinges. The pictures began to fall to the floor."

"It was insane; I couldn't take it, so I screamed: Stop it! Stop it! Please stop it! And it did. Just for a moment there was no sound. Nothing at all. I walked out into the hall. All the lights were on – you know what I'm like; I never forget stuff like that."

"So I'm seriously freaked out. I'm thinking, what the hell's going on? I looked at the camera, set up on the landing and suddenly it leaps three feet in the air, like someone just kicked it. And then it happens behind me to the one in the bedroom. And then the lights go out – they blow out one by one."

"I run back into my bedroom. God knows why, I swear to you, like a child, I tried to hide under the bed. I don't know why there; I just wanted to take cover. But then everything was quiet again for a moment. Just a moment, before it started up again: tap-t-t-t-tap tap, tap-t-t-t-tap tap."

"It was hurting my head. The sound of it! But then after a moment, I realised something. That it hurt my head because it was in my head. The rhythm of six was in my head, beating away like a headache, throbbing in my mind. It wasn't in the flat any more, it was in my brain. I swear to God it was in my head."

"I believe you..."

"I couldn't tell where it was coming from – because it was in my mind."

"Craig, I believe you – you're doing it now!"

His left hand was on the kitchen table; while he was speaking he'd started to tap against it. Without even thinking, his hand had been tapping away: tap-t-t-t-tap tap.

He lifted his left hand straight away and put it in his right hand to examine it, almost as if it was something foreign.

"I was, wasn't I?" He put both hands over his mouth. "Jesus Christ, it's in me. It's inside of me!"

I went to him and put my hands on his shoulders. "It's all right, it's all right. You can't hear it now can you?"

"No, my head's clear," he was almost in tears.

The kettle had boiled. I walked over to it and tried to think rationally.

"What am I going to do? What am I going to do?"

"You can't go back there. You just can't." I made his tea and brought it over to him. He took it with his hands shivering, like he'd been out in the cold for hours.

"We need to get you a doctor."

"I'm not mad!"

"You're hearing things in your head, never mind the state this has got you in. See a doctor; I don't think you're crazy, but you're not well are you?"

After a moment's silence, he said: "Fine". I don't think he had the will to argue.

I sat with him for half an hour but I was keen to get him to sleep. He needed it and we needed to calm down and think more sensibly about the problem. You have a home you can't go back to, what would you do? Assuming it was a normal problem and not a fucking ghost.

I put him to bed on the sofa, next to a hot chocolate. I took the duvet from Milly's room; she wouldn't like him sleeping in there, but probably wouldn't mind him using the duvet. Despite the stress he seemed to fall asleep quite quickly – far quicker than I did. I remembered going to see him part way through the night, just as the dark was starting to brighten. He was sleeping but not soundly; he was wriggling and shuffling.

As I went to the bathroom I even heard him mutter something, something unintelligible. I wondered if it really was in there with him? Something supernatural, something rotten and cruel.

I watched him for a little while after. He was unsettled, but he didn't seem to be distressed or having a nightmare, at least not that I could tell.

I fell asleep not that long after climbing back into bed. I slept soundly till about ten-thirty, when I shuffled myself out from under the sheets and went to check on Craig.

To my horror, he was gone. The duvet was lying on the floor; his coat and slippers were gone too. I shouted for him, but there was no answer. I tried his mobile – again, no answer.

I suddenly felt an overwhelming feeling of dread – he'd gone back, hadn't he? Why? For some of his things, or worse? If this thing was in his head, had it made him go back? Forced him?

I didn't know, but I knew I had to get over there. I threw on some clothes, grabbed my keys and phone, and made a run for it. The air outside was damp and muggy; I was dripping sweat by the time I reached the end of the road. The distance to his had never seemed so long before, and every part of the journey conspired to make it take longer: roadworks, traffic lights, old people, no one stopping at the zebra crossing – I just ran out and took my chances. I had to get to Craig's.

As I reached his street, I knew something had gone badly wrong. As I ran towards his doorway, I could see it hanging open. I ran into the inside hallway, where I found Craig slumped against the door frame at the bottom of the stairs.

"Craig!" I screamed.

To my relief he heard me; his eyes arose slowly and he tried to shuffle into a seated position.

"What happened?"

"I tried to leave," he said weakly. "I tried to leave and it wouldn't let me!" A tear fell across his cheek. "It's in my heart!"

"We've got to get you out of here."

"No, don't, don't!" he cried. "It's in my heart Laura. I tried to leave and it stopped my heart. And then all I could feel in my chest was the rhythm of six; I couldn't walk, I couldn't breathe!"

"I'm calling an ambulance."

"No, I'll be fine. I just have to get back inside."

"Stay there!"

"He won't hurt me if I go back inside."

I dialled 999 hurriedly, walking outside to get out of the cramped hallway.

"Hello, this is emergency services. What service do you require?"

"Ambulance, now please."

"And what is the nature of the emergency?"

"My friend, his heart's failed or something. He collapsed, and now he can barely breathe, says it's his heart."

"Ok, I'm going to need your name and address?"

"My name is Laura _____. I'm at..." I had to look at the door. "45 _____, Clapham South."

"Ok Laura, and what's the name of your friend?"

"It's Craig, Craig _____. Please hurry, he's – Craig!"

He'd moved. He wasn't at the bottom of the stairs, but had started to crawl his way up again.

"Craig, come back!"

"It's all right," he said, while pulling himself to his feet by gripping the bannister. "I'm going to be ok."

"Get back down here right now." I ran into his flat and up the stairs without thinking – without seeing.

When I reached the top, I threw out my arms to grab him. But something swept me aside; a great arm came from nowhere. I'm not even sure I even really saw it, or whether I just imagined I had.

It struck me in the chest and sent my head back and my feet forward. I went head over heels down the stairs, tumbled all the way down.

My world went spinning; I hit the door as I smacked against the floor at the bottom, pushing it closed. I landed leaning against it, my head just about propped up.

I tried to lift myself up, but I was too dizzy; I felt part of me was still turning.

My vision was distorted, blurred, but I could see Craig; he was on his knees.

"Please!" he wailed. A figure was stood before him, grey and long, arch-backed. Its long-fingered hand grabbed him by the shirt collar and forced him flat on the ground as it bent down over him. With the other hand, it stroked its fingers across his cheek.

I can still remember the shape of its face, grinning, stretched and narrow; its broken and brittle teeth like shards of glass. It wrapped its arms around him in a disgusting embrace and lay down on top of him.

That's when I passed out.

A broken wrist and a sprained ankle – all things considered, I got off lucky. I woke up probably just a few minutes later, as they were pushing me on a gurney into an ambulance. I cried out for Craig, but they didn't want to tell me anything at the time. It was an hour or so later when I learned that he was dead.

I didn't know what to tell the police. Of course they were called; his flat smashed up, all the bulbs broken. I couldn't tell them the truth, the truth was ridiculous. I edited it down to say that last night he had come to mine complaining of words in his head. And that then I had found him at his home in a state. They didn't believe me, but it didn't matter since heart failure is considered a natural death; it's only suspicious in men of his age. Apparently his heart just stopped.

I felt terrible about not telling the truth, especially to his parents. But what good would this story do them? That's why I've put it all down in writing, so that I can tell the truth, just once. Tell it just how it was, without a single lie.

But now I think this will have to be my epitaph too. I can hear him. Hear him in the walls tapping away, playing his little game. You see, I know what he is now – he's a hunter. A man who likes to stalk and torment his prey, before making his move, springing his trap.

It started straight after the funeral, just a little tapping in the distance. Barely noticeable, but noticed. He likes to play games. I'm going to have to try and out-run him. He's not in my head yet. I'm going to leave here and see how fast he can travel, how far he can go.

I feel bad for Milly. Maybe he'll wait here for her. But I don't think so. I think once he's found his mark, I don't think he lets go.

Then I'll be number eight. You see, I know exactly how many he's killed. Because now he makes a rhythm of seven, instead of six.

KNOCK DOWN GINGER

Nan was a difficult person; always complaining, always moaning. I'll be honest and say that I never really liked her very much. That might sound harsh, and I wouldn't want to speak ill of the dead, but Dad would probably agree. He was upset when she died, but he was relieved too. I remember her being awkward and uptight growing up, but since Grandpa died, she'd gotten worse.

On the night before her funeral, Dad was telling me how he thought she had gone mad. She hadn't changed her life at all after Grandpa died. She did all the things that she'd done when he was alive, she didn't make any changes. Sometimes she'd even wait or call for him, forgetting that he was gone. But if you asked her about it, she'd deny having done it.

She just got more difficult; becoming more obsessive about her routines and insisting everything be done just right or else she'd complain, shout, grumble, get angry... Nothing was allowed to disrupt her routines.

That was why I hardly ever saw her in those last few years. It was difficult to talk to her; she never had the time. If you called her, you were always interrupting her. She couldn't cope with spontaneity. If you phoned her, out of the blue... She couldn't understand that impulse. She'd always ask "What have you called for?"; you couldn't just feel like it, there had to be a reason why you were interrupting her precious routine. She wouldn't talk to you then, she'd tell you that she was too busy to talk and get all agitated, tell you to call back later but she wouldn't be any more welcoming then either. She just didn't have time for anyone else; you were always in the way.

Once I wanted to stay over, I had an interview at Falmouth College in Cornwall, and she lived close by in Penryn. I asked her and it left her all of a fluster, almost in a panic. She was busy, this wasn't a good time, why hadn't I called earlier? I called a whole month ahead but she was already fretting about not having enough food in the house or it being the same day as she was supposed to go shopping or something. I just didn't go in the end; it was too much of a headache.

I didn't go to college that year anyway; I took a gap year and went travelling. It was on my travels that me and Alan met. Our groups started travelling together and one thing led to another, and well, we're settled down now, married. Nan didn't make it to the wedding; I remember Dad being quite upset about that. More than I was; Alan's parents were enough of a challenge and I hadn't spoken to Nan in years at that point.

She made it to the christening at least, although she didn't seem happy to be there. I think Dad might have literally dragged her. She muttered a lot, kept saying what a distance it was and how much she'd been put out. She didn't stay long after the lunch. That was the last I saw of her, or heard from her. She died four of five years later, in her sleep. The cleaner found her – Dad was upset, but hardly devastated.

There was no will. All her belongings went straight to Dad, including her house, a beautiful Penryn town house. Dad dealt with all the funeral and estate arrangements himself; he was never good at accepting help. He'd inherited some of her stubbornness.

He got quite a bit of help from Nan's cleaner at least. She was the only one who saw her day-to-day; she'd been with her a couple of years – a record by Nan's standards. She couldn't get on with cleaners; everything had to be just perfect, everything had to be in its right place. They couldn't take her fussiness; there was a period when every time I spoke to Dad he seemed to be complaining that another cleaner had come and gone. She kept accusing them of stealing and deliberately moving things around. But the thing was, Nan was fussy and didn't like change, but she couldn't remember things either. She'd move stuff and then forget about it.

But this last cleaner was a retired hospital nurse, so she'd dealt with worse and knew how to handle difficult folk like Nan.

Anyway, it was about six months after she died that Dad offered us her house. I was flabbergasted; he was offering it to us for free, as a gift. He said he wanted to give something to us, and he knew we had struggled to get a mortgage – we were still renting in London at the time.

He thought it would be good for Jessica too; he didn't think we should bring her up in the city, and frankly neither did we. We hadn't planned it that way, but money kept getting in the way; we couldn't get enough together for a mortgage and Alan was afraid about getting work away from his contacts in London. By the time Nan died, Jess had already started school and we had started to think about moving away again.

Well, Alan mostly – I knew I'd miss living in the city. I'd been living in London since I was a kid and I just couldn't imagine living out in the country. I mean, what do people do out there? I know that sounds stupid, but you just get to thinking like that when you're in London, like everything in the world revolves around it.

I agreed that Jess would be better off going to school somewhere else. You hear bad things about city schools, and there's all that bad stuff about gangs and hoodies as they get older. But I'd already given up so much to be a mum; I hardly saw my friends anymore, hardly got a chance to go out. Don't get me wrong; I never regretted being a parent, but I missed the excitement and freedom, you know? Everything had moved so quickly with Alan, I sort of felt I'd missed out a bit on my twenties and then moving away from London seemed liked I was finally settling down once and for all into my middle age. I'd only just started working again too, and it seemed like such a shame to give all that up already.

Dad said we should go down there for a week and see what we thought. He was convinced that we'd love it there, and that kind of close-knit community would be perfect for Jessica. And the schools were good too, so we'd heard. And Cornwall is beautiful, so it did sound appealing. And a free house? That was too good an offer to just pass up on.

It was a good excuse for a holiday too. But Alan couldn't get the time off work because of project deadlines. We tried to work it out; I was determined to make it a short break down there, really get to know the place if I was going to move there. But we couldn't make it work with his schedule, not for months anyway. In the end, I decided to go down for the week, and he would come down for a long weekend.

So I packed our things and set off. It's a long drive down there; if you've never done it, you have no idea. You almost can't believe the country goes on that far. You take the motorway for ages and ages and then you end up on long country carriageways that wind round through town after town, each one with Pen or Tre in the name.

Beautiful though, all very healthy clean and healthy green. Stunning views too, but only I got to enjoy it though; Jessica slept the whole journey!

We'd never really been on a proper holiday since she was born, just a few short breaks. I knew she'd enjoy seeing the beach again, and proper sandy beaches too, not like the rocky one down at Brighton.

I'd almost completely forgotten what Penryn was like. Picturesque, if a bit odd. It's all up the side of a hill, one small high-street with a small scattering of shops – bakery, pharmacist, unusual number of hair salons… oh and a combined tattooist and sex toy shop – just what every town needs!

I remember as a child seeing druids in robes walking down the high-street. That sort of thing probably still happened; you get a wide range of "alternative" types in places like Penryn.

Yes, a peculiar place. Lots of winding alleys and odd-shaped houses. Very improvised as towns go, it looked like it had all been built in blocks. Small bursts of construction – three or four buildings that looked the same, followed by another small burst of construction, three or four more houses but they'd look a bit different from the ones before. A town like a patchwork quilt, but a pretty one; a bit odd, but quite pretty in its way.

It feels like a small place at first because the high street is quite small. But actually it's not so small after all. There's this whole more modern estate hidden in a sort of valley behind the high-street. Now there's also a development down by the harbour. Expensive flats and other things being built down there. Probably finished by now, but still being built when we were there.

Nan's old place was down one of the roads that dipped down from the high-street. Sort-of newer houses, but still in the old style, fairly even in the way they looked. Nan's was the one with the red door, I always remembered that. It was always bright and polished – I suppose good impressions start at your door step.

I didn't like the smell when we arrived. Stale musty air, but the place was very clean. It was only when you opened a cupboard or drawer that you realised the place was full of junk. She was one of those people who never threw anything away. I bet she knew where everything was though. She probably knew where each piece of junk belonged; she just wouldn't have been able to get at it because of all the other junk on top.

It was part of my agreement with Dad that I'd start to clear the place out. I don't think he cared really what we did with the stuff: give it away, sell it or bin it. I don't think he wanted to go back there. Too full of bad memories for him.

It is amazing how things flood back to you. One of the things that my Nan always used to complain about was knock down ginger – the old kids' game. Run up to a door, give it a knock and then run off. She made out that it used to happen all the time. Dad used to tell me about it, and even I remember hearing her complaining about it too.

She was always going on about the neighbourhood kids anyway, too noisy, too rude, too badly behaved, etcetera. But knock down ginger; that was the thing she complained about the most. It made me smile: a grumpy, strange old lady like her; she was a born target for young boys I suppose. Bad tempered, but harmless. Like poking a toothless old dog with a stick; it barks but doesn't bite.

The reason I remembered so quickly after I arrived, was that I had been there for no more than maybe 15 to 20 minutes before it happened to me. I was going through the cupboards, seeing if any of the tinned food was worth keeping, when we got a knock on the door. I thought it must be a curious neighbour, but there was no one there. No one at all. I looked up and down the street, no sign of anyone. I thought to myself, the kids in this part of town must be pretty quick off the mark to pick up on me arriving so quickly.

The house was as nice as I'd remembered: three bedrooms upstairs, large living room, dining room with porch and a small garden. Jessica liked that, obviously we didn't have a garden in London; we had a minimal-maintenance concrete yard with no sunlight. She particularly liked the pond, although I instantly had nightmares about her falling in and tried to keep her away from it.

I had packed a Fireman Sam DVD to keep her busy, so I stuck it on while I explored the place and sorted out the bedrooms. Although the sheets would've been changed after she died, I still felt like I had to change them again, just to be sure. I brought all my own sheets too. Nan had about a dozen I could've used but they didn't seem to bend as much as I usually like my fabrics to. Practically starched rigid!

We were both pretty tired after the journey down and I really didn't fancy cooking. There were a couple of fish and chip shops in the area, so we made do with that. Jess fell asleep watching Eastenders with me, and, after putting her to bed, I felt like going down myself too.

It was only ten o'clock when I turned the TV and the lights off – not that late, but late enough to be spooked when there was another knock at the door. On my own and in a strange place, it made me tense very quickly. There was no peep hole in the door. And the window next to it doesn't give you much of a look around, not if the person is stood just a bit to the right of the door.

I couldn't see anyone, so I shouted "Hello?" There was no answer.

I opened it slowly and took a look outside. There was no one – again. I took a step out and looked up and down the street, but it was dead quiet, absolutely dead; not a noise or anything.

That made me feel pretty uncomfortable. I mean, sure, it's just a game, but it's a bit late for games. And I'd only just got there. Were they doing this every night? Even when the house was empty? Surely they'd have heard about my Nan dying? Or would they? I suppose today, even in small towns, people don't talk to their neighbours. But it had been six months…

They would have to have been *so quiet* though. I didn't hear anything. Not a footstep, even though they would've had to have run away, wouldn't they? Where did they go? And how fast? And how quietly…

It was weird and made me feel pretty odd. I didn't sleep that well that night, although I think that was probably something to do with the lumpy mattress I slept on. I wasn't sleeping in the main bedroom until we'd changed the bed, or at least the mattress. That was certainly where Nan had died.

I wasn't keen on doing anything too serious straight away. Instead I went shopping. Falmouth's the closest proper town to Penryn; it's walkable, but I took the bus anyway. Jess was pretty excited to see the sea, and started pestering me to get her a bucket and spade. Nice town; busy, but quaint. Lots of local stores, arts centre, couple of small supermarkets. Some old fashioned pubs, some bars. Not much of a club scene, as you'd expect, but we were probably a bit old for that anyway. Lot of students around, of course; it was good to see them. Made me feel like it wasn't just a place for pensioners and retirees.

The beach was quite busy, but not too busy. Jess loved playing in the sand and I bought myself a coffee and played with her and read my book while she went paddling at the edge of the water and built sand castles. We had a lovely day and she had a really good time. You forget just how good fresh air is when you're in the city. I wanted to walk back from the beach and take it all in, but Jess had tired herself out, so it was the bus back again.

It was such a lovely day, but of course, something had to happen to spoil it. I was going to make pasta for dinner (I'm not much of a cook) but had forgotten the pasta sauce. Jess was fast asleep so I thought it would be all right if I just ran up to the local shop to get some and be back before she was any the wiser. Just as I was about to leave though, I couldn't find the house keys. I was sure I'd left them in the kitchen but found them ages later on the dining room table. I wasn't sure how'd they got there; when I come to a new place I always instinctively find a place to put my keys and always put them there, every time. I didn't know how they'd ended up there; I wouldn't have put them there and I didn't think Jess would have moved them.

Jess hadn't woken up so I thought I still had time to run up to the shop. But when I got there there was this group of kids – teenagers, four of them. I heard them whispering and sniggering when I got in there, and what they said was not flattering.

One of them came up close to me, pretending to look at milk in the fridge and then he grabbed my bum. I turned around, shocked, and then another one of them came up to me and said "Sorry about them luv. Oi, leave the girl alone alright? You wanna be careful of guys like him, here let me walk you home, keep you safe from these muppets."

I told them to... Fuck off! But of course that only encouraged them: "What do you have to be like that for? Here's me trying to help, and you gotta start swearin' at me."

His mates were laughing idiotically: "Leave it mate, this lady's not for you..."

Then the shopkeeper tried to step in. He was Indian and he told them to leave me alone. They said something to him I won't repeat. After they told him to F-off he came from behind the counter, and they knocked over a postcard stand in front of him and ran out.

He apologised to me, not that it was his fault. As I left the shop, they were outside, just across the road. They shouted to me again; I just started to walk as fast as I could to get away from them.

When I got back to the house, pretty flustered, Jess was still asleep, thankfully. I put the kettle on straight away and broke up the spaghetti for the pan. Then, of course, there was another knock on the door. Still angry, I didn't waste time. I ran straight for it and pulled it open.

There was no one there, yet again. Not in the mood for this stupidity, I ran down the steps into the road and yelled, "Whoever's doing this, it's not funny!" I looked up and down the road. No one answered, no one made themselves known. All was quiet – again! I walked back up the steps; stupidly I shouted "Do it again, and I'll call the police," which was like giving them encouragement to do it all over again.

And sure enough, before we'd even finished dinner, there it was: another knock at the door. I just ignored it; best thing to do, just ignore it. If it was anyone important - which it shouldn't be since I'd only just got there - then they'd knock twice.

I didn't sleep well that second night. I was too rattled by the kids in the shop and by the knocks on the door. It wasn't boding well, this trip to Cornwall. The place seemed nice, but so much trouble already. I tried to tell myself it was just coincidence; that you couldn't judge a place completely just because you'd had a couple of bad experiences with kids. Everyone else seemed nice – lovely in fact.

I was pretty moody the next day; not only was I tired, but things seemed to be missing. My toothbrush wasn't there; I couldn't find my towel. I asked Jessica if she'd touched them and she said she hadn't. She did sometimes just pick things up and leave them somewhere else but I really couldn't see what fascination my toothbrush would have for her now.

It was a bad time to start feeling off as it was time to actually start doing some work. I got up and had some eggs and soldiers and sneaked a cigarette outside. I'd given them up, but once in a while, when I was feeling a bit tense, they helped me relax a little bit.

I tried to keep it hidden from Jess, but she suddenly came through the patio door. I threw it down into a plant pot in a panic as she said: "Mummy there's someone at the door again."

"Don't worry sweetie. It's no one, just ignore it."

"But what if it's Daddy?"

I smiled: "Daddy's still in London sweetie. He won't be here till the day after tomorrow."

"Oh," she said. "Well, I'm going to see who it is."

I picked up the cigarette because Alan might spot it. He hates it when I smoke.

"There's no one there Mummy."

"I know sweetheart, just ignore it if anybody knocks."

It was another nice day, shame to spend it indoors going through cupboards, but I had to make a start. Jess wanted, first though, to take a look in the pond for some fish. Dad hadn't mentioned whether there was anything living in there or not, but it was so cloudy and murky we couldn't tell one way or another. Just as I was about to go back inside, I saw Jess by the stone wall, jumping up to see if there was anyone in the opposite garden.

I asked her what she was doing and she said she was trying to see if the boy was still hiding. She said that she'd seen a boy there yesterday but he kept hiding behind the wall so she wouldn't see him. I looked into the next garden and there was no one there. There were no toys there; it didn't seem like they would have a kid, but who could tell?

I got to emptying out the cupboards, starting with the one under the stairs, separating everything into three piles: stuff to bin, stuff to give away and stuff to keep – which was the smallest pile. It was a miserable day to spend indoors; it was so lovely outside.

I'd brought Jess' art and painting things; that was usually a good way to keep her busy. That would buy me a couple of hours at least. After that, I'd brought all her cooking toys and those were her favourites so I knew they would could keep her occupied. She has to have gotten her fascination with food from Alan; she certainly hasn't got it from me!

But it turned out it was me that got bored and restless first. After a couple of hours, I decided to take a walk up to the local charity shop. I loaded up a couple of carrier bags with the ok stuff and walked up there with Jess, with a promise of a cake from the bakery. The old ladies were as lovely as you'd expect, and quickly got nosy about who I was and if I was moving into the area. They then talked my socks off for about ten minutes, while Jess got very annoyed and started to get very grumpy. I seriously considered not buying her cake after all as punishment.

I got them to give me a number for a local charity that would do house collections, so it wasn't a trip in vain. We did get some cakes, after Jess was made to say sorry, and then we went back to the house. And wouldn't you know it, not more than a few minutes after we'd arrived, there was a knock at the door. I did start to think about calling the police, this was bordering on harassment. I, of cause, decided to ignore it.

We ate the cakes together but it was soon back to work. I got back to sorting things out in the kitchen – it really was the biggest hoard of junk you ever saw. I was working into the afternoon. Jess fell asleep on her own, without me having to put her up for a nap.

But then I couldn't find my phone, and that was something Jess might've picked up and put down somewhere. I searched everywhere and couldn't find it. I started to get really wound up when there came another knock at the door.

I was in the hall way right next to it when it happened, so I grabbed the latch and opened the door fast, no time for them to run!

I swung it open and screamed in their faces: "What the hell do you think you're playing at!" But instead of a group of kids, I frightened the living wits out of this tiny old man, well-dressed and silver-haired – I think I almost shouted him off the doorstep.

I apologised quickly and told him that kids were constantly knocking on the door and that they were driving me crazy. A little unnerved, he told me that he'd spoken to the old ladies at the charity shop and they'd mentioned me. He worked for a small charity that did pick-ups and he wanted to give me some of the bags they used for collections. I could just leave them on the front step and they'd get them.

God, I felt so guilty. I said sorry about a hundred times but I could still see that I'd shaken the poor man up. I took the bags and went back inside. What was wrong with this place? I found my phone outside on the patio, how on earth had it gotten there? Even if I'd taken it out, which I was sure I hadn't, I wouldn't leave it on the floor. Jess could've done it, but surely I'd have heard her if she'd gone outside.

And the knocking... I asked the old man if he'd seen kids around and he said he hadn't seen any. He said it might be the students, but they seemed a bit above knock down ginger to me. They had more exciting ways to create trouble – at the tattoo and sex toy store for starters.

I had a missed call from Alan. I thought about telling him about all the stuff that had gone on, but he was so stressed with work. He didn't really have time to talk, he was just checking in. He asked me how I was liking the place. I was a bit cagey, said it felt weird there, but struggled to explain it. It didn't seem like much – kids playing tricks, things going missing – not when you spoke about it. Besides, I knew how keen he was and I didn't want to upset him. But I was starting to freak out and was really not seriously considering moving in for the long term.

We didn't talk for very long. It was late and Jessica had woken up. I turned on the oven to heat a pizza I'd bought when, again, there was a knock at the door.

Was there really nothing else for kids to do in this town! It wouldn't be the old man again, I'd well and truly scared him off.

"I'm not answering," I said to myself quietly. I'm going to ignore it, properly ignore it, not let it get me all hot and bothered. The evening went slowly; I cooked the pizzas and watched a Disney film with Jess before putting her to bed properly. She swore blind that she hadn't touched my phone and I couldn't bring myself to blame her, but who else could've moved it?

I stayed up a little late, but I was still on edge. I thought I heard another knock on the door, but I wasn't sure. I was getting all wound up about nothing. They'd soon get tired of it. They'd soon leave me alone.

The next morning I planned to drive over to Truro; I was desperate to get out of the house and used it as an excuse to take away a few more bags of rubbish to the charity shops. But it was a disastrous trip from the start; it was a wet miserable day and traffic into town was terrible. I don't know why, some kind of accident was mentioned on the radio.

And Jess was a nuisance all day. I found the car keys amongst her toys that morning after a long search, so I knew she was the one who was picking up things and moving them about. She denied it and we had an argument so she was grumpy and moody all day and because I wasn't expecting rain when I packed neither of us had any proper wet-weather clothes.

We gave up on the trip and came back just after lunch. As I was putting our clothes in the dryer, there was another knock at the door.

"I'm not answering it!" I said out aloud, and went back to drying my hair. Jess was getting changed in her bedroom upstairs and I'd started to make us some sandwiches.

There was a knock at the door again. "Still not going to answer," I said quietly. But this time it doesn't stop. They knocked again and again. And they didn't stop knocking; it went on and on and on. And it started to get louder, and louder, and louder. They were pounding on the door – banging their fists against it.

I screamed; I was so angry – I wasn't going to put up with this. I ran to the door; the pounding still getting louder; I threw it open and yelled: "What the hell is wrong with you!!!"

The second the door opened, the knocking stopped. I was yelling at an empty street – there was nobody there, nobody anywhere near!

I was breathing heavily. Something was wrong, very wrong. How could they have gotten away so quickly? The knocking had just stopped, in an instant – it wasn't possible.

I descended the steps and walked into the street, looking up and down just to see if there was anyone. But there was no one. How could they be doing this?

I suddenly felt very cold – I was totally freaked out. The sky was grey and dark; it was gloomy and deathly silent, not even a car on the road in the distance. It was unbearably quiet, it was as if I was the only person within a mile; it was like a ghost town.

I heard the door creak behind me. I spun around and saw it suddenly slam shut. I almost jumped out of my shoes in shock – I raced up the steps and tried to pull it open. But the bolt had sprung and locked it from the inside.

"Hey," I shouted, pounding on the door, giving it a kick. It was locked firm and didn't budge.

Helpless, I started to shout to Jess: "Jess! Jess, honey. Mummy's outside." I pounded on the door with both hands: "Jessica, open the door".

Then I heard screaming…

Terrifying shrieking, coming from inside the house. It was Jess screaming – I would've known that sound anywhere. She was frightened, petrified; screaming for her life.

"Jessica," I cried. I hit, pushed and kicked the door. Tried to ram it with my shoulder, but it didn't budge an inch and caused me to slip and fall down the steps. I landed on my side, grazing my leg and twisting my ankle.

She was still screaming; I'd never heard her make such a noise, not even when she was a baby. I ran as best I could around the side of the house to get to the garden. The gate door was on the latch and I couldn't open it from this side. Without thinking, I charged at it; ran right at it with my shoulder, giving it everything I could.

The latch broke off as I hit it. I tripped and fell, crashing to the ground in a shower of splinters.

I'd hurt my shoulder and scraped my palms, but I couldn't stop – she was still going, still screeching, shrieking, crying for help. I couldn't stop; I got right back on my feet and dashed around to the patio doors.

They were locked. I tried to yank them open, but when I couldn't I went straight to the rockery and picked up the first heavy stone I could get my hands on. I threw it through the door window. It shattered and I jumped through, cutting my arm and shoulder on glass still hanging in the frame.

The screaming had stopped. I ran into the living room: "JESSICA!!!!" I shrieked. And then I heard the sound of a toilet flushing. I rushed to the bottom of the stairs, and she was there – up on the landing. She was rubbing her tired eyes. I stood watching in shock – she was... fine.

"What was the noise, mummy?" she said.

I ran up the stairs, hoisted her up and held her so tight. God, I held her so tight. She was oblivious; she had no idea what had happened. I held her tightly for so long – the relief, I can't even describe it. I thought I was going to come in and find her dead, beaten, throttled or worse. But she was ok, after all that, she was ok.

"Mummy, you're bleeding."

I had blood on my clothes; cuts on my legs... I started to cry: "It's ok sweetie, it's ok."

As I stood there, holding her, my eyes caught sight of the front door. It was now wide open – thrown open, and all the way back on its hinges.

I walked down the stairs slowly, with Jessica in my arms. I put her down and then slammed the door shut. I leant back against it, breathing heavily. Whatever it was, whatever had been in the house, it was gone now and it wasn't going to get back in.

Then I remembered the patio door. I had nothing to cover the smashed window, nothing to put over it. I panicked; I got all my things together, told Jessica to get all her things together too. I left stuff behind, and I never went back for it. We went straight to the car and drove straight back to London that night. We just plain bolted for it.

Alan and Dad didn't know what to make of the story, but I was too distressed for them not to take me seriously and I was in some serious pain and cut and bruised all over. Dad went back to the house himself to sort out the patio door. As you might've guessed, we decided not to take the house.

Then, a few days later, Jessica, who was confused and didn't really know or understand what had happened, she was drawing and painting again. I watched her paint and then I noticed in one of her pictures she'd painted a garden and was colouring in a rock wall she'd already sketched. There was a head peering over the wall, the head of small boy – I suddenly realised what it was and I asked her "Is that the house in Cornwall?" She nodded and then I pointed to the head and asked, "Who's that?"

She said that's the boy that kept hiding. And that he's sad now, because he has no one left to play with.

Case no. 52
THE BLACK CLOCK

It was a very long time ago, and I was very young; maybe ten or eleven. I spent most of my time growing up in boarding schools; my parents were civil servants, diplomats really, and they seemed never to be in the country. You know, I think that during some of my formative years I may have only actually seen them two or three times a year. Although, as I was born in 1914, I suppose I should be grateful that I had a father at all.

He spoke French, German and Spanish, so they took better care of him and didn't just throw him into no man's land to get shot. Ironically, the result of his and my mother's international travels meant that I grew up hating foreigners and resolutely refused to achieve in any of my language studies. English excepting of course.

I grew up a very lonely child, introverted and more prone to quiet activities and hobbies than sports or 'performing'. When holidays would come around, and my parents weren't at home to accept me, I would stay with my Uncle Guillam, who ran a shop in Egham. This gave many of my school friends great amusement; we were all snobs from the upper crust and the thought of me spending summer in a little shop was funny to them.

It wasn't funny for me; not because I was embarrassed that my uncle wasn't a minister or a land-owner or a deacon, but because he was an exceptionally odd chap. He didn't run a normal sort of shop; his was a clockmaker's shop. In fact, he preferred to think of it as a clockmakers' museum, because he had ambitions to turn his collection into a kind of exhibition. But he never quite got around to doing it because he was too busy with his tinkering to actually get around to doing anything definitive. He was so very easily distracted.

This particular summer – the last summer that I went to stay with him – he was so preoccupied with his work that he forgot to get a room ready for me. He was incredibly untidy. You wouldn't believe it; he had a respectable town house and shop front, but it was full of rubbish. His whole home was his workshop; there were bits and pieces of clocks and cogs and mechanics everywhere.

The worst thing was that every so often he would get the idea to expand his knowledge beyond clock works and bring in a motor or a sewing machine or some other mechanical thing. And then he'd get bored with them and they'd just get left in whatever room he'd put them in; doomed to remain in the 'must get around to doing that' pile. One year I went there and he had a motorcycle in his dining room. He had the dining table stood on its end, leaning up against the wall to make room. At least he finished that by the next time I visited; even he realised that he needed somewhere to eat.

There were no bedrooms empty though, either that or he just didn't want me in his hair. So I stayed at the pub across the road. Besides the initial sorrow of being neglected by my family again, I actually came to like it there. The food was good, not special, but filling and wholesome. And I was getting to the age when I was starting to feel for women, and there was this charming young barmaid working there. I wish I could remember her name, but she was probably my first love. She was very sweet to me and I absolutely adored her.

Uncle Guillam for all his eccentricities was an expert in his field, and people would travel quite a distance for his skill and to hear his expertise. And Guillam loved visitors, because he would cajole them into seeing his museum, such as it was. I wasn't particularly interested in clocks and watches, but I was lonely and I was keen to feel the affection of a parent, even a neglectful one. So I would often watch him work and spend time in his shop.

Now this particular visit, Guillam was working on something special; it was a 16th century German clock. It was black, a sort of gothic design, with covers on the front and back, but with the cogs exposed on the sides. It had two bells on the top, one on top of the other, and, I'm not certain how to describe it, these little embellishments on the arches; the ones that went from the body up to the top where they held the bells. There were these... nobbly things; I suppose they were supposed to be leaves or maybe just simple decorative twists, but they looked to me look like gargoyles or cruel birds, like crows or ravens, perched threateningly. Along with the spiked feet and points at each of the top corners, it looked rather... unpleasant. I didn't like the look of it, and I told my uncle so, and this made him rather upset.

"Don't you know who this clock belonged to?" he asked, as if I could possibly know. He said it belonged to, and I think I've got this right, Count Emilio Martinez, a Spanish nobleman who was known to have a love of timepieces and clocks. By all accounts he was not a pleasant figure and his love of clocks came from a ruthless need for efficiency from his staff and business associates. We'd probably call him a compulsive these days. Anyway, the clock had carved on a small plate on its front the Count's name and icon. And if the clock was owned by the Count it must be a quality piece, one made by a clockmaker of some renown.

Guillam was quite puzzled by it though. He was sure that the design and mechanism were German, but he could not determine who had made the clock, because the maker's mark or stamp was missing. But also because the gothic design wasn't one that would appeal to a noble family, at least not to more florid Spanish tastes. It was a fine specimen of its type, in good condition, but not very ornate. More of a clock for an official or a judge than a wealthy nobleman of some standing.

The clock was a mystery, which was why my uncle was distracted by it. It was something he was determined to get to the bottom of. But the clock needed repairing too. Although outwardly, it had been well looked after, it hadn't told the time in many years. Guillam spent all afternoon making measurements and making sketches. He recognised the mechanism, but felt that somehow the pieces were out of proportion, not the sizes he'd expected, and certainly not the work of a master craftsman. He garnered the opinion that it was a botch job; that some amateur had attempted to mend the clock after its original workings had worn through.

The clock presented a challenge, if a frustrating one. The clock's owner, who knew something of the clock's strangeness and obscurity, had promised that if Guillam could make it tick, and solve the mystery of its origin, he would allow him to display it in his museum for six months, along with full payment for his services. As if the fulfilment of this bargain was a certainty, Guillam had already made a place for it in his hallowed museum; a high shelf on the right-hand wall.

Uncle Guillam, though a man of considerable skill, had no sense of aesthetics. His museum was a mess. His clocks and watches badly organised on these unattractive metal shelving stacks, all too crowded together and over-stocked.

His other mistake, which I suppose was more understandable, was to have all his clocks working in his museum. You can understand why, after all, that was his job, to make his clocks tick. But the noise! It was like a field of crickets going bananas – *tick, tick, tick, tick, tick, tick, tick*. It was an incredible sound, quite something to experience, but not something you could stand for very long.

Uncle Guillam liked to say that he could listen to the sounds of the clocks ticking and tell instantly if any of them had lost time. Of course this was absolute nonsense; when it was the turn of the hour, clocks would start to ring their bells and chimes five minutes before and some ten minutes afterwards.

It really was quite a collection tough; there were extraordinary items in there: Grandfather clocks, pocket watches, wall clocks, astrolabes… The cuckoo clocks were my favourite growing up; sometimes they were very imaginative and playful. Little wood cutters would pop out and chop the wood, or little canaries would come out and sing just for a little moment.

Amongst them the black clock looked positively miserable. Yet it got pride of place on a high shelf above the wall clocks with the hanging chimes. The hands, although one of them was broken at the end, pointed to just after four-thirty. I swear to you, to this day, if I ever look at a clock and it's four-thirty-two or four-thirty-three, it sends a shiver right down my spine.

Now, I'll tell you what happened: Although my main love was the inn's barmaid – I wish I could remember what the pub was called, although I think it's gone now – I had struck up a relationship with the grocer's daughter. Entirely through self-interest of course, because she had daily access to boiled sweets and was good at stealing them without her father noticing.

We'd become friends in the Easter holiday before. Her father wasn't sure what to think of me, probably because of my family, but her mother absolutely encouraged our games. I think she hoped that we might be married one day and that her daughter might be moved up the social ladder. Seems silly, doesn't it, that we really thought like that back then.

But we did get on famously… Iris was her name. I wonder what happened to her. She was a loner like myself; a dreamer with her head in the clouds and not good at paying attention at school. We both liked to draw and to walk in the country. We weren't so far from the edge of Windsor Park, where we could watch young couples punting along the river or the lake. Happy days. Well, happy mostly.

To my slight embarrassment, I didn't know how to fish, and it seemed to me that everyone knew how to fish in the village. It was something that seemed to bridge divisions; I remember the young men at my school speaking fondly of it too. And Iris could fish, and I felt a bit silly getting lessons from a girl. But she was very keen to teach me and I couldn't help but feel obliged to accept her offer.

So plans were set for us to go fishing. I was able to find a fishing rod in Guillam's attic and he was able, after a full day's pestering, to get it in working order for me. We were all set to go when I found, much to my surprise, her father's shop closed. Not to be discouraged, I went to her family home, which was not so far away. There was quite a commotion, raised voices, screaming – tearful screaming – from the house. I was pretty wary, as you can imagine, but I was still keen to keep my appointment with Iris, so I still went to the door. And I was about to knock, I remember, when there was this terrific smash. Something thrown and then breaking – crockery, a glass – something like that. That made me scared so I was about to leave, but just as I was about to go I heard my name called.

I looked up and saw Iris in her bedroom. She had the window open and shouted me to meet her around the back. I quickly obeyed and she appeared a few moments later in the alley, with her fishing rod and all her bits and pieces. She was never one to let anyone tell her what to do. That was something I liked very much; I was a much meeker child.

We went to the lake and I tried hard to find out what was going on at her home. She said that her brother Billy was home and this was news to me because she'd never once mentioned a brother. She said he was a wrong-en and always in trouble. And that her parents preferred him to stay away, but now he was home again and was insisting on staying.

She didn't seem to know much more than that, either that or she wasn't telling. I didn't enquire too much I don't think.

So we went fishing; we had fun I seem to remember, although I didn't really understand what the fuss was about. Dangling your rod into the water and then just sitting around waiting. You know, I don't think I've ever been again. I wasn't very keen on the wriggly things – worms on the hook, that sort of thing. She didn't seem to give it a moment's thought. Then when we caught a fish, and it was there in my hands, its big eye looking up at me, with the hook through its mouth – I was so shocked I dropped the poor thing. Iris was quick to save the day, and got it into the net in the water. She teased me about being a posh nob – I remember being a bit upset about that. But it was a nice afternoon ultimately; we caught four or five fish, all tiddlers.

It was only on the way home that we got into trouble. I should've left her and let her go home alone, but I followed her all the way back, completely oblivious to the fact I was walking into trouble. The second she got home, she received a very severe telling off and a threat of physical harm from her father – the belt was not uncommon in those days. I was told to go off home straight away or else they'd speak to my uncle.

Now, I didn't think I'd done anything wrong, but I thought it probably best Guillam didn't know, not that I could imagine him doing anything as crude as smacking me. But as I was walking away, their front door opened up again and I was shouted at: "Oi, you!"

I turned and found striding towards me the man I immediately guessed was brother Billy. Huge hulking brute, broad shouldered with a granite jaw and chin you could chop wood on – he was a frightening figure to behold. And he was marching towards me and he reached out and he picked me clean up off my feet.

"You been playing about with my sister have you?"

I think he assumed I had more knowledge and feelings about women at that age than I really had. "We went fishing," I told him, scared out of my wits.

"Oh yeah," he said. "That's all is it? Just fishing?"

"Yes please, let me go." I was almost in tears; I was so frightened.

"Now you listen to me, your lordship. I don't want any of your type near my family. You make me sick, you hear? No rich toffs near my sister. I hate bloody rich ponces; you stay away from her or I'm gonna 'ave you. You getting me?"

I nodded furiously, and he let me go. I landed hard on my behind as he lumbered back to his house. "Don't let me catch you anywhere near this house again!"

Upset, I went very quickly back to my uncle's. What he was supposed to do about it, I don't know. He probably didn't even know what a punch was. But I went back to his shop for comfort, or support, or merely for someone to talk too. Iris was my friend and the thought of not seeing her again... I was unhappy about it. And I wasn't too keen on getting my ears boxed in by brother Billy either.

Guillam's shop door was open, even though it was past his closing time. I shouted for him when I got in, but he didn't answer. I walked up to the counter and shouted for him again; still there was no answer. I went through the door to the left of the counter, into his museum. Amongst all the noise it was as likely as not he wouldn't be able to hear me if he was in there.

It was as intensely loud with tickings and clickings as always, but there was no sign of him. I shouted again, as if he could hear anything coming from amongst such a din. As I walked slowly through the aisles, feeling sorry for myself, the clocks started to ring for half-past the hour: half-past four. I sighed, because Iris had always said she'd wanted to see the museum, but I had never taken her. For Uncle Guillam there was never a good time for it.

As the bells and chimes rang, I became aware of one ring above all the others. A sharp, shriller ring that somehow I was able to make out over all the other chimes – like the ringing in one's ear you get when exposed to a loud noise, or when your ears pop. I identified its origin almost instantly; I don't know how or why, but I looked right up at the high shelf, to the black clock – it was ringing.

I had no idea that Guillam had got around to fixing it. It was an odd sound, very clear, very high. And it seemed to be echoing, even in that small space. The high-pitched sound seemed to be bouncing off the walls.

I thought it was peculiar that I had been able to single out that sound amongst all the other sounds in the room. And that's when I discovered, much to my total astoundment, that it was the only clock ringing... or ticking for that matter

The room of clocks, the ever incessantly ticking clocks – was silent! There was no sound at all. I looked around me – all the clocks had stopped; the hands weren't moving, the pendulums were caught mid-air. Nothing moved, stirred, ticked or clicked a sound.

I couldn't believe it. It was as if the whole world had come to a stop. And I was caught in the middle, in a little pocket of... dead time. Literally stuck in a moment. It was an extraordinary, unsettling feeling.

Then I looked again to the black clock. The bells rang again; I could see them shake – their sharp hum was the only sound in the air, everything else was still. And then when they stopped, it was deadly silent.

There was no sound, no noise at all.

And then there was a footstep...

My skin fell cold. I was breathing heavily – I was not alone, there was someone behind me. Their shadow fell over me, the floor creaked underneath them; I could hear their breath above mine.

I spun around in terror. The figure I saw there, the face – I've never forgotten *that* face. It was scorched, all down one side, from the right eyelid all the way down past the mouth. Half-blind – the burn had sealed up his right eye; only one dark eye looked out at me. He was bald, but with black eyebrows, standing out against the white of his face. Half his teeth were missing; his jaw hung lazily open, but his lips were curled up in a wicked grin and he was staring right down at me.

My God, I was scared so witless I fell backwards screaming, screeching out all the air in my chest. I started to crawl, terrified, on my backside towards the wall.

But as I looked up again he was suddenly gone, no longer in front of me.

Then I heard the floor creak, and I saw him again. Just the barest of glimpses; the back of his shoe heels as he passed behind the end of the aisle and away. He had been dressed all in black, old clothes, the type I'd only seen in history books. A sort of cloak and robe type arrangement. Kind of like a monk, but a touch more flamboyant, if you could call it that. Maybe elaborate is the word...

It was then, within a beat of him disappearing, that suddenly the museum came back to life. Pendulums started to swing, cogs began to turn, gears began to move...

The place was alive again. The clocks were ticking in their constant synchronism, time was moving forward like it should. The slow clocks finally began to ring in the passing of the half-hour too.

I ran around the shelves, looking for the frightening figure. But there was no sign. There was no way out of the museum, but for the shop entrance, or the back door, neither of which he could have reached without me seeing him. As I ran into the shop entrance, Guillam appeared, wondering what on earth all the noise was about. So I told him, and understandably he didn't believe me. Well, why would you?

He was angry that I had caused such a hullabaloo and called me a little liar. I can understand that he would find it difficult to believe me, but why would I make up such a story? And I was so clearly very distressed. He was emphatic in saying that there had been no one in the museum with me and that he hadn't mended or fixed the black clock, so how could it have rung?

He sent me back to the inn insisting that I go to my room and stay there or he would get his cane and thrash me. My uncle had never been one for physical discipline, but he seemed more determined now than ever to hand it out. I never even told him about Iris and her bullying brother.

So I went back to the inn and there I stayed. I found it difficult to sleep that night, every creak on the stairs and I suddenly imagined him there, the man with the burnt-face, waiting for me, coming for me. I've seen some terrible things in my life – I lived through the Second World War; I've seen a man take a bullet through his cheek and seen a boy's face swell-up from mustard gas – but his face; his is the one that's always stuck with me most.

I remember being thoroughly miserable the next day. Without Iris, I didn't have a lot to do and I didn't fancy too much going back to Guillam's shop. I moped around and tailed my beloved barmaid until she was sick of the sight of me.

Eventually she barked at me to make myself useful. She commanded me to go to the post office to send some letters from a few of the guests. I was keen to go because the post office was close to Iris' Grocer's shop. And once the letters were delivered, I paced carefully down the opposite pavement, trying my best to look into the window. I remember thinking that I could see her through the window, helping her father behind the counter.

I began to cross the road very slowly – not so much traffic back then. And I saw her father cross to the door, to open it for a customer. Or at least I thought it was her father. When the door opened, I saw it was Billy, playing at being the good son and helping in the shop. As soon as I saw him I turned and went back to the opposite pavement.

He didn't spot me at first; he was too busy making conversation with one of the old town spinsters. But I looked back and I caught his eye. His eyes – he had these big menacing eyes – opened wide and he pulled up his hand from his side and pointed out two fingers to make a gun gesture. And he pointed it at me with all the conviction of a man holding a real fire arm. I ran away quickly.

I continued my sulk into the night time, and languished in my room with an old book. Then suddenly I got a knock at the door and was told my uncle was here for me. This was an odd occurrence; Guillam would very occasionally come to the inn to play cards, but even then there was little likelihood of him calling for me. I walked through the busy bar; at that time of night it was very busy.

Guillam was there drinking a half-pint fussily as though he'd never wanted it in the first place. I walked slowly towards him, but unfortunately there was no way to get to him without passing my enemy, Billy, who was in the pub as well, making a terrible noise; the kind that bullies make to see if anyone dare tell them to stop. He watched me cross by and I couldn't help but look into his eyes as I passed.

He barked at me, barked at me like a dog. It made me jump and he and his friends laughed, although I doubt they really found it that funny.

Guillam seemed more preoccupied than normal. He looked tired and weary. He told me that he'd been researching the clock but he had come to a dead end and would need to go into London to visit the guild library and that he'd be gone for a few days.

This didn't bother me much. What bothered me was that he wanted me to stay in the shop while he was gone to look after the place. Now you can imagine, after what had happened the day before, just how I felt about this, but he would have none of it. In fact he snapped at me quite sharply; he was clearly out of sorts and somewhat keen to get away. In retrospect, of course, I have an idea why.

I was to meet him there, seven-thirty sharp in the morning, to take the keys. He gave me little chance to protest, only telling me to do as I was told. He finished his drink quite quickly and told me it was time to make myself useful. I returned to my room solemnly, dodging an attempt by Billy to trip me up on the way. He'd been listening to the conversation; quite closely I'd come to discover.

So the next morning I did as I was told and met Guillam at the shop. He was in a rush – I was a little late – and he was keen not to miss his train. He gave me the keys, but I was to keep the shop closed, which was a relief.

However, I was to deal with one customer; Mr Towney was to pop-by sometime in the afternoon to collect his wife's watch, which he had had repaired. I was to stay in the shop until he visited. I could do whatever else I wanted – I just wasn't to touch anything in the shop and I was to stay out of the museum all together. And that was fine by me!

Well, it was an uncomfortable day. I didn't know much about how to cook, but I was able to manage on the stove to cook some bacon, which, at that age, I couldn't get enough of. After that, there was little else for me to do. His home was as full of junk as it always was. But if I were to touch anything, he'd know. Guillam was one of those people who appeared to live in chaos, but who knew every inch of it, and didn't like you inferring with his sprawling madness.

I found an old jigsaw and began to get to work on it on the shop counter. I wasn't very interested in it, but it helped to stave-off boredom, and the fear that something in that shop was out to get me.

I kept the connecting door to the museum closed, although you could still hear it ticking away, like the rumbling of the tides of the sea. The shop itself was actually mostly quiet; most of the timepieces in there, those on sale, where kept quiet to keep them in mint condition. A few still ticked away, reminding me of the time. I was of course terrified at what might happen at four-thirty, if I was still there. I prayed Mr Towney would show up before then. He was a miserable old swine; a fat banker with no patience.

I waited impatiently, tensely, as time ticked on. I finished the jigsaw, paced up and down, played marbles on the carpet... I kept looking over at the museum door, half expecting it to open and for the one-eyed man to step through at any time. By the time Towney turned up I was virtually climbing up the walls, I was so wound-up. I remember that he complained that the watch wasn't wrapped up, like a gift, but people like him always had to complain about something. He gave me the money, I dropped it in the till, which was empty, and then locked up the shop and got out of there. It was ten to four – I'd already decided that if he'd been longer, I'd have locked-up and gone before the dreaded half-hour.

I didn't stray far though. I wanted to see what happened at four-thirty, so I went around the alley, behind the shop and climbed the wall into the back yard. There were windows into the museum, but they had been painted over, leaving only the top windows, the narrow panes that opened, clear. It wasn't easy to see in, but I tried my best. I climbed onto the roof of the outhouse and tried to peer in. But I'd made an elementary mistake; I'd forgotten to take a watch with me! I lay up on that outhouse roof for more than half-an-hour, I must've done, and it started to rain, a real downpour. I only knew the time from the church clock, which was hard to hear in the rain.

The rain made it even harder to see anything, or hear anything for that matter. Although the ticking clocks could still just about be heard outside. If the clocks stopped or the black-clothed figure returned, I could not tell.

I sheltered in the outhouse for a little while and then went back inside to dry off in front of the best fire I could make. There wasn't much more to do there in the evening than there was in the day time. At least my meals were still paid for at the inn and I ate there handsomely, but was not encouraged to hang around in the evening, as in those days drinking houses were not open to children. I think I persuaded one of the regulars to play darts with me, but I was chased off by the landlord soon after.

I skulked back to the shop and passed the evening with a book. The place was cold; I couldn't get it warm. The rain had stopped, leaving the whole place quiet. Well, quiet except for the ticking. Even in the upstairs you could hear it through the floorboards. I began to think of it as being like woodworm, like creepy-crawlies munching their way through the walls. I would forget it was there for short periods, but then I'd notice it again. I really grew to despise the sound. You won't find a ticking clock in my home, not even today. Never been able to stand them since.

I slept in Guillam's bed; it was the only one in the house. It was awful, he had these two great big curtains, too long for the window, which dragged on the floor. And, of course, in the dark of night, with the moonlight shining through, what did they look like?

It was a terrible night; every time I woke up I thought there was someone there. Some great cloaked figure, standing at the end of my bed. I'd jump up from the under the sheets – but of course it was nothing.

I barely slept a wink. And you know what it's like when you're unsettled. Every creak of the floorboards, every clank of the pipes, every... bird on the roof; the slightest of sounds makes you startled.

But the most frightening thing, the thing that really shook me up, was that at one point everything was calm; calm, quiet and silent – no sound at all. There was no ticking under the floorboards, no creepy-crawly sounds in the walls. The clocks had stopped again.

I leapt out of bed, I rushed to the door; I swung it open...

...And everything was fine. The rustling rumble of the incessant timepieces was going again, just as usual. Had I imagined it? I don't know. I didn't know what time it was, because I couldn't see in the dark.

The next day I resolved to keep myself away from the shop as much as possible. I journeyed up to Windsor Park, to see the Red Indian Totem Pole up there; Iris was supposed to have taken me to see it. I deliberately travelled near places I thought she might be, in the hope that I would catch her. I wasn't so lucky. I took a packed lunch, bought with the remainder of the money Guillam left me; he hadn't given me much, probably hadn't thought that far ahead. I didn't know when he was returning. The only money in the shop was the money from Mr Towney in the till, which I didn't dare touch; everything else was in the safe.

I climbed some trees, explored some rocks – I passed the time as best as a young boy with an imagination and a want to forget his troubles could do. Importantly, I brought a watch with me this time; I was not going to risk being there at the dreaded half-hour. My only target was to be back at the inn for six, for the serving hour.

It was pie and mash that night – still very much a favourite. Once again, though, I was not allowed to loiter. The landlord specifically said to me when I started eating that I was to go when I was finished. And he waited for me. I gave him a bit of lip about how I was a good customer and he should treat me better. He responded by grabbing me by the ear and throwing me out.

So off I went back to the shop, to do nothing all evening. Guillam had a few old copies of The Strand; I read those and then, well, then I decided I would try a few things from his drinks cabinet. I had a sudden keenness to be ill-behaved. But Guillam being Guillam, it was practically empty – full of dried up decanters and almost-empty bottles. Only the port was full enough for me to be able to thieve a little without my uncle noticing. I had only a little, but it was enough to relax me and help me to settle down to rest. I fell asleep in the chair in the lounge, fire still burning.

At some point I drifted into a dream. It's difficult to remember how it started, but I know that I was in the dark; there was light, but very little, and I felt heavy, very heavy. I was lying on stone, it was cold and hard but someone forced me onto my feet. I was being weighed down and realised that I was in chains; I was a prisoner. I was exhausted and unwell, but I was poked and prodded on down this corridor. I wasn't afraid, but I don't remember feeling very much of anything, except that I was tired and... resigned, I suppose, empty.

I was barefoot, because I could feel cold stone under my feet. And I was forced down this dark corridor, with stone walls into this dim chamber, and there were voices in the background, screams and wails, and these made me anxious and afraid. But I was just too exhausted to feel much of anything. This stone chamber was lit up by oil lamps, but was very gloomy. Then this figure approached me. I was looking down at the floor; lifting my head was too difficult.

And this figure, he stood looking at me for a moment, and then he said something, something I couldn't understand – it was in a different language. And then I was pulled away, marched away, not the way I came. But I wasn't scared, I felt relieved. I was being dragged towards light, but before I was pulled away, I found enough strength to lift my head and look at the figure. And just before I awoke, I saw that face, the horrible burnt face again, and once again it smiled at me, grinned at me wickedly.

Then I woke up. I woke with a start, not because of the dream, but because I had heard something. A sound from the shop – a crash; the sound of something breaking. The fire was out, it was dark. I was frozen in the chair. I listened carefully for anything, any noise or sound. The damn clocks made it hard to know, but then I heard the creak of a floorboard, and I knew, I knew that someone was in the shop, that someone was with me.

I was frightened, but I didn't fear the one-eyed man; the clocks were still ticking.

I lifted myself slowly out of the chair and walked gently into the hall. Just a curtain separated the hall from the shop, but as I crept towards it, I could tell that I had not been mistaken. Someone was in there and they were trying to force open one of the display cabinets.

Carefully I pulled the curtain to one side and slipped my head around. A figure was using a knife to try and force the lock on a tall cabinet near the window. I still couldn't quite see them and slid behind the counter, taking each step cautiously. The man swore under his breath; I should've known straight away – it was Billy. Knowing my uncle was away, he'd come to help himself to some of his stock. He'd already been in the till and taken the money Mr Towney had left.

I was angry, but I didn't know what to do. He'd broken the glass on the front door and let himself in; I couldn't get past him that way. I needed to get to the police station, or just somewhere to find help – I didn't stand a chance against Billy. The back door – I'd go out the back. But as I turned on my heels, the floor creaked under me and I knew instantly that Billy had heard me.

He was extraordinarily quick. As I looked around to see if he had noticed me, he was already lunging towards the counter. He tried to throw himself over it to grab me. I hesitated in fear and only just managed to get away. But in avoiding Billy's grasp, I leapt towards the door to the museum and away from my obvious route of escape!

Surrounded again by the ticking clocks, I went instantly to hide. There were four shelf stacks standing parallel in the centre of the museum; if I could give Billy the runaround, get past behind him and into the shop, there was a chance I could escape through the front door – he wouldn't follow me into the street for all to see. The back door would be locked and I didn't have the key to hand; the front door was my only chance. I crouched behind the very last stack, behind some thick box-like clocks.

Billy came in slowly; he must've been taken aback a little by what he'd found. Amongst the ticking din I heard him say "Where are you?"

I should've been ready to make a run for it, but I was paralysed with fear. I tried to peer over the tops of the clocks and through the shelves. I could just about see Billy moving; his shape was just behind the second stack. He was moving slowly – he knew I was there, somewhere, but at that moment he was probably admiring the things he might steal.

But just when I thought things couldn't become more terrifying, the clocks began to ring in the half-hour. I looked at the heavy box-shaped clocks in front of me and they were showing the time – four-thirty – and ringing it in. And sure enough, ringing shrilly above all other sounds was the black clock.

"Where are you?" Billy hissed again, he'd moved from around the front of the second stack to between the second and third, not so far from me. I wondered if he could see me. My eyes were fixed on him; could I make it past him to safety?

And then the clocks stopped – just as they had before. It was all quiet – almost. Only the black clock rang, and Billy noticed it.

Puzzled, Billy was wondering what on earth was going on. I watched him as he took a few slow steps towards the clock until suddenly my view was obscured.

He passed before the stack I was hiding behind: the figure in black with the scorched face. I saw only his clothes; I was crouched too low to see anything else. He moved swiftly, barely making a sound. He vanished for a moment. He must've passed around the end of the stack and gone to the aisle where Billy was standing.

Once again I could just about see Billy, standing at the end of the aisle, facing the black clock. He must've heard the floorboards creak, because he turned around and said in a terrified tone: "Who the hell—"

That's all he could manage – I saw something pass through the air, whoosh through it – too fast to see what it was – but it struck Billy hard with a vicious smack and he let out an almighty cry of pain.

He fell to the floor – I heard him land. I was so terrified that I turned away and buried my head between my knees, clamped my hands hard over my ears and closed my eyes as tightly shut as I could.

But I could still hear everything – the clocks did not tick, there was no other sound now. The air was cut in two again and the crack of the whip – it could be nothing else – struck Billy and he screamed in agony. Again and again. He must've been hit eight, nine times. The sound was unbearable; he cried tears of pain and begged for mercy: "Please no! Please! Don't, don't."

He was shown no mercy; he was thrashed over and over. I was weeping in terror, fixed to the spot in fear for I don't know how long. I only remember lifting my hands from my ears when the screaming stopped.

The clocks were ticking, but ticking only faintly – in the background, as if they were far away. It all felt so unreal; I looked again through the stacks and I could see no one.

I could hear Billy though; wailing, squealing in pain. Shakily, I started to move forward, very slowly. I could hear him breathing through his heavy sobbing. Carefully, I approached him; he was on all fours trying to raise himself up.

His shirt was soaked in blood, in great red streaks across his back. He noticed I was there and lifted his head. His mouth dripped with blood, the whip had caught him across the face, a great red mark stretched from one cheek to another – the corner of his lip was split open.

He reached out to me. He wanted to say something, but he couldn't; he was in too much pain.

Then I saw – well, I couldn't have seen it, I must've sensed it – the whip moving once more through the air. There was nothing there, nothing I could see, but it made its violent hiss and it smacked again against Billy's back. He screamed and I saw blood spring from his back, through his clothes, a horrible crimson arc exploding into the air.

That was too much for me – I ran and I ran and I ran. I didn't know where to, I just ran. I darted through the shop into the street, giving it all I could. I think I crashed into a policeman; it was only because I literally ran into someone that I was stopped.

The rest is something of a blur – he took me I think to the police station, because I sounded like I had gone crazy. Eventually they got enough out of me to realise that there was a man possibly bleeding to death at the clock shop. I refused to go back in, but the police constable went in there only a few moments before he came back out and demanded that an ambulance be sent for.

Billy was brought out on a stretcher, unconscious, but still alive. Unsurprisingly they thought I'd gone mad, but they knew I couldn't have done that to him. I spent some time with a local nurse who tried to calm me down – I really don't remember much, it's all a bit of a blur. Fortunately, Guillam returned home the lunch time of that day. I remember him looking very grave, and him not quite knowing what to do with me.

When I told him the story, there was not the look of disbelief that I had faced from the police. He listened to my every word and took it in slowly. And that wasn't like him; I was used to him being distracted and preoccupied, mumbling, muttering and talking to himself. But he listened intently and carefully. And when I finished the story, he made no comment, asked no questions. He simply nodded and said I had better get some rest. The more I think back to that day, the more I think he believed me. That he found something out when he was doing his research, and knew something strange about that clock. But he never said, so I can only guess and assume.

The only thing he said was that he thought it best that I was sent back to school early. I was only in town one more night, which I spent at the inn because I refused absolutely to go back into the shop. Guillam saw me again in the morning; he was tired and worried-looking and gave me the money for my train ticket.

That was the last I ever saw of him. The next time a holiday came around and my parents were away, I spent it with a wealthy family my father had befriended. When I asked about Uncle Guillam, I was simply told that he was unwell. It was years before they admitted to me that he had died; I didn't know when.

I tried to forget everything about that day, and my parents never asked about it or discussed it with me. But they knew; they knew something. If I ever mentioned Guillam, the subject was swiftly changed.

Years later I went back to Egham. I was working nearby, so I thought I should have a look. The shop was no longer there, the buildings were all new. I had thought them bombed in the war, and rebuilt – but I revisited the inn where I recognised a few faces, though much older of course. I asked them about the old clock shop, without revealing who I was. They all knew – it had burnt down. A great fire had broken out and spread to several other shops, destroying them all.

The owner had died, apparently the only casualty. They described him as a queer, odd little fellow who had always been a bit strange. Apparently there had been a dreadful accident in there just a few days before – a man was flogged to within an inch of his life and no one knew how it had happened.

So the legend goes. I can only testify to what I saw. And of course that was many, many years ago.

WHEN IT RAINS...

Those were the best days – I was at the top of my game. I had everything a guy could want: money, girls, a new fucking Jag XF. I was living it up. Man, the money was good. 32 and I'd already earned more than my dad had made in his whole lifetime.

It was time to move out of the backwater and get a place in central. I was a team leader now, and the pressure was on; I'd need to be able to get in and out of the city fast as. Work hard, play hard. Got myself a penthouse suite, half-mile from Angel tube. Beautiful – two bedrooms, both ensuite, one with a skylight and a door to the balcony. It had a huge balcony, went all the way around; had them big patio doors – one big window from the living room all the way around to the kitchen. Had this stone table, with little leather stools next to a barbecue – I was going to have amazing parties there, awesome parties.

It was open plan: hall, living room, kitchen. Could've been bigger, but you pay for the location, and the location could not have been better. Service on the front door, basement parking for the Jag. And Islington, that was the place to be! Got all my shit moved in; it was all perfect, just perfect.

But there was this one thing. Yeah, this thing: I kept hearing the taps dripping, like, all the time. I'd be asleep, lying in bed – I chose the room with the skylight, obviously – and I'd hear it from the bathroom, this drip, drip, drip.

So I'd go into the bathroom and turn the taps off. Nothing to it. But they didn't stop. I woke up in the morning and they were still dripping. I went back to the bathroom, turned them extra tight. They stopped.

But then I was in bed the next night and they were dripping again. So I went and turned them taps tight, tight as I could. But after a few more hours, I woke up and I could hear them again. I went back into the bathroom, and the sink was dry. So I went into the kitchen and those taps were dripping now. So I turned them off tight, even though I was sure, dead sure, they weren't dripping before I went bed.

The next night was Friday I think. Yeah, Friday. The guys at work bailed on me, left for home early. So I was enjoying a few cans at home, still tidying things up and unpacking my shit, when I heard the taps dripping again. Drip, drip, drip. It was getting on my nerves. I turned them taps so tight – I am telling you – I turned them so tight. And I checked the ones in both bathrooms too, because this was starting to piss me off.

So I went to bed and I lay awake; couldn't get to sleep because all I could hear was this dripping. It was like a headache, in my head: the sound of drip, drip, drip driving me up the walls. I got up and I checked the bathroom, the kitchen – those taps were not dripping and the sinks were dry. I went into the other bedroom to check the taps in the bathroom there. The sink in there was bone dry. Dry in the shower, dry in the bath. I checked the shower and the bath in my bathroom too – there was no dripping.

I could not find where it was coming from. I went out to the balcony. I looked at all the drains and pipes; couldn't see any dripping, and it hadn't rained for days, honestly. I didn't like this; if it wasn't dripping from the taps it might be dripping from somewhere in the walls or in the roof. So I went down next day and talked to the man on the door and he said he could call me in a plumber.

So they got this guy in. I was at work; I came home and found a note saying there was nothing wrong, that there was no leak. I thought, what the fuck? I called them up and I told them I could hear dripping; I could hear dripping all the time. They said they'd checked the whole place and had found nothing. He'd the fucking nerve to say that I was making it up, that it was all in my head. I said: "Fuck you, fuck you ass-hole!"

But I admit it, yeah, I did start to doubt myself. There wasn't any sound of dripping, not for a couple of days. I relaxed the whole thing. Finished my unpacking, decorated the place. Got it looking spic and span.

Thought it was time to flaunt my pad. We had this new girl at the office; new temp, Polish, name was Agatha, or Anouska, or something. And I got to her first. She was fit as...

We got her out after work; the other guys had their try, but in the end, there was no contest. After a few drinks, she was putty in my hand.

Got her back to mine, showed her my pad, got her on the sofa. And we're going at it, full-throttle, when I start to hear it again. In my ear; I can't get it out of my head. Drip, drip, drip, drip, drip. Nagging at me, distracting me.

I say to her "Can you hear that?" She says, "What?" I say "The dripping, the fucking dripping". She still can't hear it. I tell her to shut up and listen, but she still can't hear it. I tell her, I tell her about how it doesn't come from any of the taps, but it's always there. I show her the taps in the kitchen and my bathroom. But she still can't hear it.

I ask her, "Are you fucking deaf?" Then she starts getting all mouthy with me, calling me crazy. I try to say sorry, calm her down, but she insists on leaving.

Fuck her, you know?

I was still fuming when I went to bed. I can still hear the dripping, but I'm ignoring it. I don't know where it's coming from, but I'm just going to ignore it.

I get to sleep but I'm tossing and turning. Drifting in and out; waking up, going back to sleep.

I wake sometime early morning and it's light outside and I'm lying on top of the sheets. I'm looking up at the ceiling and I can see this spot, this dark spot; about the size of a tennis ball. I'm staring at it and it starts to get bigger. And bigger and bigger. It grows to the size of a football, a beachball, and it keeps going.

Within seconds the spot's as big as the bed and the ceiling's starting to bulge and the surface starts to ripple. Then the whole patch explodes, bursts – and this wall of water comes down, raining, pouring down on me.

I wake up again, suddenly; big jolt. I've been dreaming, but I'm soaked with sweat. It's four-thirty am on a Saturday, but I had to get up. Couldn't sleep any more. Had to get out of that room, place is doing my head in.

I felt like shit. Rough as. But later, when I'm feeling better, I go back in there. I dragged a chair in and I felt the ceiling and it was bone dry. I thought maybe, just maybe, the water was getting trapped behind the skylight and getting into the ceiling somehow. But I couldn't see anything.

Wasn't myself at all that day. Couldn't chill. Spent a few hours on the PlayStation, watched the football with a few beers, but I couldn't get that image out of my head. The image of the ceiling splitting and bursting and the water raining down. Because the more I thought about it, the more I replayed it, the more I thought there was someone there. That when the water broke, someone had been up there. That there was like this figure, that they fell through the ceiling and brought the water down with them.

I couldn't see them; it was just this dark shape of a person. A shadow of a body; I didn't see their face or what they looked like. It was just a dream, but I could not get it out of my head.

I had to get out of there, I was driving myself crazy. I did my shopping, had a walk about town, but still I could not get that image out of my mind. I decided to go to the cinema; nothing wrong with going by yourself once in a while. Saw that western with Jeff Bridges and Matt Damon, they're protecting some girl. It was ok, but as soon as it was over, my mind was back on my dream.

When I got home, I couldn't sleep in my own room. It didn't feel right any more. After an hour or two of trying, I switched to the other room. Threw my pillows and duvet on the bare mattress and tried to sleep. I did manage it for a little while.

I started dreaming I was out in my car, my Jag. First day out. Ripping up the countryside. Wind running through my hair. But it starts to rain; water's running down the windscreen. I put the windows up. The wipers are going crazy, but they can't get it off. It comes running down so thick I can't see anything. The whole view of the road had gone; there was just this wall of water.

Then I open my eyes, and I sit up. For a second I forgot I was sleeping in the other bedroom. The bathroom is right opposite the bed in this bedroom, and I was looking right at the door. I could hear them, the taps. But they were not dripping, they were pouring.

The shower, the bath, the sink – it sounded like everything was running. I could hear the rush of the water.

What the fuck was going on? I didn't put them on. Was someone in there? The light was on; I could see light from the gap under the door.

The bathroom must be flooding; water was coming from under the door and running down on the carpet. The carpet was soaked with it. The damp patch was creeping towards me. Slowly coming down towards the bed.

I got up and started walking slowly. My flat was like, flooding, but I was too freaked-the-hell-out to go quick. I walked slowly to the door, my feet squelching on the soaked carpet. I put my hand on the door handle and turned it slowly.

The bathroom was full of steam. All the hot water taps were on and the shower too. The bath was overflowing, the sink as well.

As the steam started to clear I turned off the sink tap. The mirror was all fogged up. I wiped my hand across it; it cleared the view for just a second before it steamed right back up again.

I went to the bath tub, pushing the shower curtain aside. I leant down and reached for the hot tap and turned it off. But when I turned it I saw, out the corner of my eye, the bathtub wasn't empty. There was someone in the bath, hiding beneath the water. I barely saw them for a second: I only got to turn my head just slightly – but they were dressed, fully clothed.

The surface of the water broke. This arm, dripping wet, reached out and grabbed my hair. It dug its fingers in and pulled me down. My feet slipped on the floor. I was going down. I was going down and my head was going to hit the side of the bathtub – boom!

And then I woke up – it was another dream.

I was up, bolt upright in my bed, gasping for air. Just like they do in movies; full on nightmare. I was breathing so heavy; my heart beating hard.

I was facing the bathroom. The door was half open, light off. All just a dream.

I tried to calm down. Relax. But then, just as my heart starts to go and beat like normal, I hear something. I get up and walk back to the bathroom, slowly.

The carpet was dry now. So was the bathroom floor. But the hot water tap was running in the sink. The water running straight down the drain.

Slept the rest of the night on the sofa. But didn't sleep much. I thought I must've left the tap on. The rest was just a dream and dreams can't hurt you. Even if... even if there was this pain, this throbbing pain, on the side of my head. I had to be imagining it because I hadn't hit my head, not in reality.

I couldn't face staying there all day again. The place was messing with my head. But just as I was leaving. Just as I was about to go out, I noticed there was this dark patch on the wall. The wallpaper was messed up and out of shape. It was coming off the wall. Just close to the ceiling, near the bedroom I'd slept in that last night.

I knew it. I knew something was up with that place. The fucking plumber. There was water leaking in the walls. I was right, right all along.

I went to the office. I couldn't take being at home. I tried to take my mind off the place, but it wasn't working. It started to rain and I could see the water pouring down the glass windows. And out of the corners of my eyes, I kept thinking I could see something. Someone standing there, watching me. I tried to focus on my targets, getting my quarterly figures. But even going to the toilet, the sound of the water dripping in the urinals; it gave me the shivers. Made me sick in my stomach.

The thing in the bathtub. The person. The man. I didn't see him, I didn't know him. But I did know him. I mean, when I was dreaming, I knew that person. When he went at me, when he grabbed me... I was frightened because I knew who he was. But now I didn't know who the fuck he was. None of this shit was making sense to me.

But it was a dream. Dreams are weird. I was angry, furious. I called up the plumber, like 20 times. Yelled at him on his answer phone. Then I tried to call round other plumbers, but because it was Sunday no one would take the call. I emailed the estate agents, the fuckers who sold the place to me. Threatened to sue their asses for breach of contract. That place was falling to bits. They were gonna pay to get it fixed, not me.

It got late and I decided I was going to go back. I got some pizza, some beers, and headed home. As I got back I had a go at the doorman; he recommended those pricks to come and have a look at my place. I dragged him up to my flat to show him the damage. I showed it to him, but he kept coming out with this shit, said it wasn't damp.

I asked him: "What the fuck is wrong with you! It's coming off the wall because of the water." He said he couldn't feel any water. He reckoned it had been torn off. I couldn't believe what he was telling me. Said he was going to complain about me. About me! The nerve! I said I'd like to see him fucking try!

Went to sleep on the sofa. I was asleep for, I dunno, a few hours, before I started dreaming. I was out driving again. I was tearing up the lanes again, in the Jag. But I was tense this time, nervous. I was trying to get somewhere in a hurry. And when it started to rain, I didn't slow down, I started to speed. I was trying to beat it. Beat the rain by going faster.

But I couldn't; the water came down so hard the wipers did nothing. It poured down over the windscreen so thick I couldn't see a thing. Just water. There was so much water it started to come through the windscreen. Water washed down over the dashboard, over the steering wheel, onto the seats, onto my knees...

Something leapt at the windscreen. A man, arms out, smashed against the glass and the bonnet.

I woke up with another shock. I was in bed – in bed! I'd fallen asleep on the sofa, but now I was in bed!

It was the same as last night. I was in the second bedroom; I was lying on my side and I could hear the taps in the bathroom and the shower. They were running again, only louder this time. I sat up and saw this time the door was open, the light was off. But the water was still overflowing from the bathtub. I could see it trickling out the door on to the carpet again.

This time I wasn't going to go creeping in. This time I was going to go and face down this thing, whatever it was. I swung my legs out from under the duvet – but too quick. I smacked the ball of my ankle on the drawers next to the bed. As soon as I stood up I sat back down again, it hurt like fuck.

I felt the pain and I suddenly realised, had this moment of realisation: I was not dreaming this time. You know how you always know, deep-down, when you're dreaming? Well I must have thought it, when I saw the bathroom, but I knew I wasn't now, because that fucking hurt. I'd hurt myself, really fucking hurt myself.

I was awake. 100% fucking awake.

The light came on in the bathroom. I turned my head. The room was empty; there was no one in there.

And then it came up from the bath. This dripping wet arm came from under the water. It gripped the side of the tub, pulling up this body. He was fully dressed, dressed in a big brown duffle coat, the furry hood pulled down low over his head.

He stood up, water pouring from his body, pouring from his hood, sleeves and pockets. He wore jeans, soaked dark with water. He raised one foot out of the bath and slammed it down on the soaking wet floor. It was a black Doc Martin boot; water squeezed from it like a sponge as he put it down.

Jesus Christ, it was him! It couldn't be him. It couldn't be him; what the fuck was he doing here? What the fuck was he doing here!

He pulled his other leg out of the bath and stepped out. He stood still on the spot, water falling off him onto the floor.

Then after a moment his drooping head started to lift. The hood, dripping wet, started to lift up, slowly revealing his face.

I nearly shat myself. I jumped across my bed and went straight into the hall. I grabbed my wallet and phone and fucking legged it. I went right out of there; I went down to the basement to my Jag in nothing but my shirt and pants and decided to get as far away from there as fast as possible.

What the fuck? It couldn't be him. What the fuck was he doing there? I mean, he was fine. He was moving when I left him. He shouldn't have been there. What was he fucking doing walking out there in the middle of nowhere? It was pissing it down for fuck's sake. How was I supposed to see him?

I didn't know where I was going. I was just driving. It wasn't even five in the morning. The streets were clear. I hit the M25 still not knowing where I was heading.

After I was driving for like, over an hour, I thought I'd go out to my parents' place. They lived out near Oxford. I just needed to get away somewhere, clear my head of all this shit.

I had to get some clothes first. I walked into one of those big Tescos. The security guard tried to stop me; I put a twenty in his hand and told him to leave me the fuck alone.

Got some cheap jeans and a jumper and a pasty for something to eat. I got off the motorway just as the traffic was starting to come in. They had this decent place out in the country. Three bedrooms, garden. Hadn't been out there for months, that's why I forgot: they were going on holiday weren't they? Completely forgot.

They didn't want me there. Couldn't get rid of me fast enough. Here I am, going out of my mind, and they just wanted me out the way! I pretended everything was cool. I just was passing by. Thought I'd drop in on them. I couldn't tell them what was going down could I? They'd think I was fucking mental.

But they just wanted me out of their hair while they were checking they'd got everything. Lock this window, close that door. I pretended I was on my way to a conference in Manchester. That way I'd have to be on my way soon. I didn't know what the fuck I was going to do. He was out to get me. He wanted revenge. It was his fault, his own fucking fault. But he wanted revenge on me.

Yeah, I thought that's the way to approach this. To get angry. Come out fighting. I watched my dad; he told me when I was a kid that if you wanted anything you had to fight for it. He'd done alright for himself. He'd come from nothing; youngest of five. First in his family to go to college. Running his business by the time he was 25. And he'd had his fair share of shit. Been screwed by the government, the taxman; faced down his rivals. But he'd come out fighting, every time. I respected my father; I respected him proper.

I wasn't going to take this. I didn't know what the fuck this was. Whether he was ghost or a zombie or whatever the fuck. I was not taking this lying down.

I went out to the garden shed. I rummaged around and I pulled out my old cricket bat. I was going to end this! I got into my car; I was going to face this thing down. I'd come too far. This was my life; I made it, no one was going to take it from me. I was going to face this thing down; I was gonna go down fighting!

I left my parents' place driving fast. Fuck the speed limit – this could not wait.

It started to rain; of course it fucking did. It was pouring down, and I was sat in my car, just like in the dream. But the rain didn't come down so hard. I stayed on course.

I got back and marched up the stairs, bat in hand, ready to take on anything. I arrived at my front door, and reached into my pocket for the keys. I saw the floor – it was wet. I hadn't even realised it; it was wet all the way to the elevator.

I just touched the door and it came open; I must not have locked it.

I looked in and the flat was flooded. Water was dripping down the walls, dripping from the ceiling; there was an inch of water on the floor; it looked like it was raining indoors.

I walked in, bat in hand; he was here somewhere. And there he was, out on the balcony, enjoying the fucking view. Water was still dripping off every inch of him, just like before. His hood still pulled down low.

I decided now was the time. I went straight out onto the balcony. Pulled open the door and out into the pouring rain and said: "Is this the best you can fucking do, huh? This the best you can fucking do!"

He turned around slowly.

"I'm not scared. I'm still standing here. I'm not scared. I'm not scared of you or any of this shit. So bring it on. Bring it the fuck on!"

He didn't do anything. He just stood there, just fucking stood there. I picked up my bat and I went for him. I swung it hard right against his shoulder, and then back against his stomach.

He barely moved; it was like hitting a mattress; it practically fucking bounced off him.

I took a step back, lifted it up high and with everything I got I went straight for his head. I screamed; I swung right at his head and he took it, his neck bent right and he went back slightly, like all I'd done was give him a slap. But that was it; he'd still barely moved.

"What are you?" I shouted, throwing the bat down. "What the fuck are you?"

He twisted his head back. His left arm came up slow-like and grabbed the end of his hood and pulled it right back over his head.

I looked at his face: Jesus fucking Christ, it was barely hanging on his skull; like a melted rubber mask – it looked like you could just tear it off the bone. Water poured from his eye sockets, his mouth, the hole where his nose should've been. He had ginger hair, but there were huge chunks of it missing.

He looked at me; skin drooping over empty eye sockets pouring water. He looked right at me; stared at me. I was froze to the spot, I couldn't move; I almost pissed myself.

He opened his mouth slowly – then he screamed. He shrieked; I never heard anything like it. I almost had to grab my ears it hurt so bad.

He jumped at me. His hands clamped around my throat. I fell on the soaking wet concrete. His hands were like claws; hardly any flesh on them. I felt the ends of his fingers pierce the skin on the back on my neck. The water, pouring from every feature on his face, landing on my face, dripping into my mouth, on my eyes.

He kept screaming, spitting water at me. He was right on top of me, I could barely move. I felt my throat being crushed; I managed to scream. I rolled to my right and pushed him off. He slid over to the patio window. I rolled onto my front and managed just to get to my feet. But he swiped at me with his claw; caught the back of my leg, cutting my muscle.

I fell back down; cracked my knee on the concrete. I turned on my side; saw that face, the empty eyes... It was crawling after me; it was unstoppable, I couldn't stop it.

I had no choice. I pulled myself back up, standing on my other leg. I saw the patio table – the stone table next to the barbecue. I had no choice; I leapt up onto the table. I looked back. It screamed again; it came running at me. I had no choice – I jumped.

It was going to tear me to shreds. Nothing I could've done. I cleared the balcony rail. He wasn't going to get me; I wasn't going to let him take me. I jumped and I fell.

I thought this was it. I was done for. Fucked.

But I was lucky. I've always been lucky. There was another balcony below mine. Small one, but it was there. I fell through the garden table; you know, like the ones they have at pubs. It broke my fall. Most of it. I tell you the people who lived there; you should've seen their faces. Scared shitless.

They called the ambulance. Got to hand it to them boys, they was there quick. They thought I was mental. I probably sounded like I was fucking mental. But I knew I'd got away with it. I knew there was nothing he could do to me now.

As they put me in the ambulance I caught sight of him. Standing, waiting down across the road. I didn't say anything; I just stared at him and smiled. There was nothing he could do to me now.

Because I did it. I faced him down. I looked evil in the eye, and I survived. I'm a survivor; I'll take anything on.

He leaves me alone now. Sometimes I hear him – the drip, drip, drip. See him standing in the rain, waiting behind the glass. But he knows he can't scare me anymore. I risked it all. I faced death and I came out of it. He's not getting in here. He can't get me in here.

I'm a survivor. I'm going to get better and show him he can't do anything to me. I'm just resting; my people, they know that. And I'm going to walk again too; I don't care what they say. You can't keep this man down. I'm like a force of nature. You can't stop me. You can't hold me back.

THE STORM WALKER

I was out driving the first time I saw her. Sunlight was breaking through the clouds; there had been a terrible storm and parts of the road were flooded.

She was soaked through to the skin, water dripping off her. I'd never picked up a hitch-hiker in my life, but I found myself thinking that I should stop and see if I could give her a lift into the village. It was as if the city thinking was already leaving me and I was starting to think like a human being again. Or maybe I just wanted the company. She was dragging an umbrella turned inside-out; she looked so tragic.

She accepted with a nod, a slight smile and a mumble of thanks. She really was absolutely drenched. The second she sat down I started to worry about the state of the seat and mud getting all over the mat.

She was heading back to _____, same as me. I asked her if the rain had taken her by surprise, and she said:

"I always take my walk in the afternoon; I don't let the weather stop me." She meant it too. There was a look of aged formidability in her face; the type that people of a certain age get when they go militant against the weaknesses of getting older and aren't going to let anyone tell them that they can't do this or that anymore. But when she took off her hoods and glasses she was younger than she first appeared. Early-to-mid 50s rather than late 60s – she was overweight, not tall, and pale, sallow, tired-looking.

"Have you lived around here long?" I asked, hoping to build a conversation.

She was polite, but brusque: "All my life," she answered. After a pause, she followed with "You must be new; haven't seen your face before."

"Yes, I moved here about two weeks ago."

"Not from Scotland?"

"No," I smirked, everyone kept saying that.

"From London I suppose?"

"Sort of, not originally, but that's where I was living."

"We get a lot of your sort around here now." She said this in a mildly disapproving way, but less so than some folk I'd spoken to. It was true, the village was isolated but well-off, a haven for middle-class families wishing to "get away from it all". Although only a few seemed to be English.

"Not a bit quiet for you?"

"That's sort of what I wanted."

"Never saw the point of cities. Too cramped and cooped up. You get proper air out here."

The conversation continued this way for a few miles – stops and starts and awkward silences.

"You married?"

I thought for a second, and just answered "no". Later I thought I saw her looking down at my hands; if she caught sight of my ring, she must have chosen not to pry about it.

"Most folk move out here now to raise kids. Not so many years ago all the kids seemed to leave. Now the parents seem keen to drag them back again." I thought I could see a hint of a smile; I thought maybe she was starting to ease up a little, but then I asked:

"Do you work around here?"

"No," she said, becoming more hard-faced. "Can't work because of my back." She used an end-of-subject tone.

I chose not to pry either. But she'd been a good five or six miles out of the village; she obviously couldn't be that unhealthy. Although she could well have given herself pneumonia in this weather. I'd been foolish taking the car out in that downpour. As I thought about it I realised she must've been crazy to go out at all. It must've been at least a 10-mile round journey for her. What on earth was she thinking?

"You take a long walk every day?" I just had to ask.

"Not always, sometimes." She corrected herself and said "Most days. You must have a job in ____."

"Oh no. Well, not yet." I answered. "I really just wanted to get away from it for a while; I haven't decided what I'm going to do yet."

"And what did you do before?"

"I was a psychiatric nurse."

"Oh well, you should have no trouble finding work. Plenty of fools around here." There wasn't even the tiniest hint of a smile; she wasn't making a joke.

As I approached the village she gave me directions to where to drop her off, rather presumptuously assuming I was happy to take her home. It was a pleasant terraced house, well looked-after, small garden at the front, just like mine.

"I appreciate your help," she said, getting out. "Safe journey now." I watched as she walked slowly up to her front door and let herself in. Most folk around here barely bothered to lock their doors, but she spent several moments unlocking locks and unfastening bolts before going inside.

I realised suddenly that I hadn't caught her name. And she hadn't asked for mine either. I looked over at the passenger seat and scowled; I'd have to spend time cleaning it. Muddy footprints were all over the mat.

I drove home, which was about a mile or so on the other side of the village. Well, more probably it was a town; it just felt like a village, and everyone called it one.

There were no answerphone messages when I got back, which was a relief. The phone was my only point of contact now; I'd decided to give up my mobile. Not that it would probably work out in ____ anyway. I'd probably get the internet put in eventually, but I had no idea how long I was going to stay.

The old lady who owned the place seemed to know nothing about letting. I'd paid her for two months' rent and she said we'd 'see how it goes'. I think she let it normally for holidays, so she probably rarely had tenants off-season. Not that I could think why there'd be much demand for it as a holiday home, although I suppose for hikers, climbers, and outdoor types it would have quite a bit of appeal. Hills, mountains, woodlands and streams could be found in almost all directions.

It was a good job it was a holiday home, otherwise it would've been empty. I only had two suitcases, everything else I had was in storage. I was putting my past-life to one side and just thinking about me and what I wanted to do next. And there'd be no rush; there was no need for a rush. I'd just go on and see how I felt and how things unfolded.

I didn't have much to do at first. I enjoyed reading, I took a little to hiking, but the weather was generally too miserable and it was starting to turn cold. I went to the cinema, the first time in years. They had this quaint little town hall cinema; they pulled down a little screen and had their own projector. They played Casablanca and To Have and Have Not on a double-bill. All the pensioners were there; they looked at me like I was from another planet. Clearly they didn't get newcomers often.

I thought about painting, but I wasn't very good at it and gave up a bit too easily. I thought I needed to meet some people and make some friends. I volunteered at the local pet rescue charity shop. It hadn't been open long and Joyce, the manager, was pretty much doing everything herself.

They had strange ways, some of the folk around there. They wouldn't volunteer to help, but they'd sort of ask about it and if you just happened to ask them if they'd like to, then maybe they could probably just about find some time to come in once or twice a week, or more.

They used to look at Joyce like she was an alien too. She was Jamaican – she used to joke she was the only black woman for 50 miles. Although it could've been her size too. She was a good six foot tall and big-bodied. She used to tower over the little old folk. They were nice people really, just used to things being always the same.

We did have a laugh. She was irrepressible – you could hear her laugh in the pharmacy next door. And things were starting to get busy after a few slow months. _____ is a strange place, there was no high-street as such. Just odd little pockets of shops here and there, as if people kept trying to set one up, but kept giving up.

We talked a lot; she didn't know many people either, but was much better at making friends. She was just one of those people: big, open and bubbly; everyone felt like she was their friend.

I confided in her a little. Told her about my husband's death without giving away too many of the details. I just told her about the cancer and left it at that. She didn't ask too many questions. She understood that I was trying to move on with my life and we concentrated more on happy things. She kept telling me she was going to set me up with someone. I laughed and joked about it, but that was really the last thing I wanted and did my best to let her know without being nasty about it. Difficult to know who she could set me up with anyway; the only single types they seemed to have around _____ were little old men.

I'd been working there a week or two when the lady I'd picked up appeared at the shop counter. I hadn't seen her come in; I'd been talking to Horace, a sweet old man from up the road who liked to talk, and talk, and talk…

"Hello," I said with familiarity. She returned the greeting with only a hint of fondness. She placed a red umbrella on the counter.

"For your walks?" I said, attempting conversation again.

She didn't answer. "How much is that?"

"Three pounds for umbrellas".

"And those as well?" She moved the umbrella; there were two gloves on the counter, children's woolly gloves. They were pink with little yellow flowers on.

"Oh, they're a pound. Four in total."

She held out a fiver and I took it. Just when I thought she'd forgotten who I was, she said "Are you settling in all right?" She said it almost like an obligation, a chore.

"Yes, I'm settling in fine, thank you," I answered, while passing her her change.

"Good," she said, giving the smallest of smiles and a nod.

"Would you like a bag?"

"No thank you." She picked up the umbrella and stuffed the gloves into her coat pocket. "Good afternoon".

I smiled and she started to amble towards the door. Just as she was passing the women's jacket stand, the clouds seemed to burst outside and it started to rain. She stopped and stood watching it.

"Good job you bought the umbrella," I said. She didn't say anything. After a moment she just carried on. She went out the door and walked away in the rain. She didn't even open the umbrella.

She was strange, but in my profession, I'd seen a lot worse. She probably just had trouble talking to people; it doesn't necessarily get any easier when you get older. It was probably quite hard for her to even try. I felt quite touched that she was trying; it was so easy for folk getting older to just give up.

The rain killed custom for the afternoon; the street was dead after three o'clock. We closed at four. Joyce had spent the afternoon going through a large donation and not a good one. Unfortunately, the pet rescue store was much closer than the dump. There was so much rubbish it would take two rubbish collections to get it all taken away.

While she cashed up, I started to take the sacks out. They were heavy; I managed two at a time, but only just. The rain was still falling hard. I dragged them out through the side door and towards the metal skip bin. There was a girl playing in the alley, jumping joyously in the puddles. It made me smile.

I put the rubbish bags down and unlocked the bin lid. After I threw it open, I got one bag in fine. But I caught the other on the bin's side and it tore. Some items fell out – a broken bead necklace slipped out and scattered beads in all directions when it hit the ground. I swore.

"You're not throwing away toys are you?"

I looked up, slightly embarrassed, at the young girl. She was maybe six or seven, not very old. And she was dressed in a faded blue duffle coat; vintage, but worn and old. Some of the buttons were missing. She was looking at a wooden toy train that had also dropped through the tear.

I put the bag down. "It's broken dear," I said. "The wheels have all come off." She stared at me, saying nothing. I smiled at her; she didn't move. Her face was frozen in a sulking expression, eyes downcast, lips curling downward. She was white, frighteningly pale; she looked almost albino, like she was freezing.

Feeling a bit spooked, I picked up the second rubbish sack and got it in the bin. As I bent down to pick up the train, I noticed she was gone. Vanished, without a sound.

It was very strange. I tried to pick up some of the scattered beads but gave up quickly and went back inside. I didn't think much about the pale girl until later, when I started to wonder what on earth she was doing behind a charity shop in an alley leading to a row of garages? There didn't seem to be anyone else there. Who was she with? And where did she go?

One of the first things Joyce had found out from me when I started was where I lived. This was so she could discover whether I would be able to give her a lift home after work. Joyce didn't drive; she could probably walk it, but she had an amazing ability of avoiding any kind of hard work. When I was there she always managed to find some reason why it was better for me to do any lifting. I brought in the donation bags, she just did the sorting. And that way she could grab anything she liked first.

Her house, which was only supposed to be just around the corner from mine, was actually a good mile and a half away. Just past the outskirts of _____, nestled amongst some trees. She called it Grandma's House, because it looked like it had come right out of a fairy tale. It had a long winding path and a tiny rock wall fence, and a little red gate. It was a single storey bungalow, with a thatched roof; you could just imagine a big bad wolf hiding behind the door.

Anyway, we were a short distance away from there, stuck waiting to cross the bridge over the river because of a tractor, when I saw that woman again. The rain was starting to clear now, but she had her umbrella, the one she bought from me, still open. Her head was hung down, she looked positively miserable. It had been over two hours since I'd served her. Had she really been out all that time?

"It's that woman again," I said, thinking out loud.

"What's that?" said Joyce.

"That woman, I gave her a lift the other day. She was out in the middle of nowhere soaked to the skin, walking. Now she's doing it again."

"You gave her a lift? Crazy Rose?"

"You what?"

"Crazy Rose – her there with the umbrella. You gave her a lift?"

"What's crazy about her? She seemed ok." But pretty odd.

"Don't ask me. That's just what they call her. I've heard the ladies talk about her. They stay well clear."

"She didn't seem that crazy."

"Well you'd be the expert. But the women around here, they don't like to go near her."

I dropped Joyce off at her mysterious cottage. Apparently she shared it with another lady called Francesca, oft mentioned but as yet unseen by any of the volunteers. Tongues were starting to wag. Gossip spreads like wild fire in isolated places like ____. But frankly, who cares?

Yes, village life could be pretty insular. I wondered whether I could ever really get used to it. I was enjoying the slower pace, but could I ever get used to a life where the biggest news story was whether a Jamaican woman was a lesbian or whether a woman who liked to walk in the rain was a nutcase?

Honestly, if they thought she was crazy... they'd never seen crazy – real crazy. I wondered whether I could really go back to that life. So few ever seemed to get better; you knew which ones you'd see again. I felt like I'd done enough for the betterment of mankind. And that's if they'd have me back anyway.

There were still no answerphone messages. I wondered if that was a good thing, but I certainly felt that no news was better.

Nothing much happened for a few days. In between my shifts at the shop, I read some so-so chick-lit, did a bit of driving, took a long walk when the weather wasn't so bad. I think I may have even done a jigsaw; the days were so empty. So meaningless.

Then one evening – it wasn't very late – I was driving to the Co-op for my weekly shop when I saw "Crazy Rose" walking along the street, weighed down by heavy shopping bags. It was a crowded residential street. I passed her, on the opposite side of the road, and then pulled in between parked cars to let another car go by in the opposite direction.

It took a few moments for me to realise something was wrong. The car was full of kids, teenagers – they didn't look old enough to be driving. I saw them all turn towards Rose as they approached her very slowly. One was opening the sun roof.

The car passed me, but I didn't move – I watched. I saw one boy rise from the sun roof and the others lean out of the car windows. They threw eggs at Rose. They threw the eggs, then screamed, shouted and laughed at her.

After the first hit, she raised her arm to cover her face – dropping one of her shopping bags. She was hit a couple of times. With the car moving on, she screamed at them: "You bastards! You fucking bastards!" Then she stepped on the shopping bag she had dropped – tripping and falling over it. The kids cheered once more, then revved up and sped away.

I had to get involved – I couldn't just leave her. I stopped the engine and ran across the road to her.

"Are you all right?" I shouted.

"Those little bastards!" She cried. "Fucking bastards!" There were tears in her eyes. There was egg yolk on her coat – front and back – and on her neck and hair. And to add to the misery, she'd crushed her own eggs – a squashed carton lay on the street surrounded by spilled, bruising fruit and a still-intact loaf.

I tried to help her repack her bags, but one was torn. "The people around here. Bastards all of them."

"Let me help you."

"It's all right, it's all..." She broke into tears and slumped against a garden wall.

I tried to put part of my arm around her but she shook it off. She reached into her pocket for a tissue while I stood over her, awkwardly.

"I've got spare bags in the car," I said after a moment. "Let's get you home."

I remembered that she lived only around the corner. I left the car barely parked and went with her. As I walked with her there was a nagging feeling of doubt that I was walking into something bad. But this was basic human kindness – I wasn't being a Florence Nightingale again. And yet I knew I was heading towards trouble. Catch 22, but I was doing the right thing.

I understood why she had so many locks on her door. She'd become the crazy old person in the neighbourhood the kids talked about and tormented. And with a place with so few things for young people to do... well, no wonder she felt vulnerable.

It was a tired looking place and was long overdue for redecorating. The wallpaper was a nightmarish display of faded chintz; once garish, now just dowdy. It was starting to peel towards the top and at some places near the skirting. The carpet was a dulling purple, darker around the furniture and towards the walls where the sun nor feet could land upon it.

She led me into the living room with few words. It too looked unchanged from a past era, when what seemed cheap and tacky now had once borne all the hallmarks of fashionable suburban living. A television the size of a tea chest lay on top of a chipboard cabinet wrapped in a plasticky wood finish. A fold out table with a doyley and fake flowers (dusty) lay in the window concave; the crowning touch was a hideous beige sofa, the seats long since sunk in and pock-marked with cigarette burns.

She was composed again now, hard-faced once more. "I'll stick my coat in the wash and clean myself up. Then I'll make us some tea," she said. Tea – the currency of British gratitude in the north as well as the south.

The sofa didn't look very inviting. There were marks in the carpet where an armchair had once been; four deep indents and a brighter square of carpet – no other seating options. There was a coffee table in the middle with a honeycomb of cup rings making its way from the wood surface onto a pile of assorted letters, a mixture of junk mail and bills. I could see the words 'Final Demand' several times.

I'd seen worse. It was grim but mostly clean, if a bit dusty and a bit smelly. She went upstairs, presumably to the bathroom. I paced around a little – all I wanted to do was leave. I'd probably just leave as soon as she came downstairs.

The walls were largely bare. A mirror with rusted edges hung at a slight angle. There had once been a picture behind the sofa, but that was long gone. There was a small sideboard, probably bought at a later date than the other furniture – it was darker and in better condition. There was a series of four mismatched picture frames on its top. One was larger than the others – it was silver; the real deal. It was tarnished, but attempts had been made to clean it. It was a posed photograph, a school photo.

It was that girl: the one I'd seen in the alley by the shop. She looked positively luminous; a big happy grin, perfect smile, adorable blonde pigtails. Hardly at all like the sickly girl I'd seen before – but it was unmistakeably her.

I heard the door move behind me. Rose came back into the room, surprising me a little. On seeing me looking at the photograph I saw her back stiffen.

"Is this your grand-daughter?" I asked her.

"No," she said very sternly. "That's my daughter." Her nostrils flared, her lips curled in, her eyes opened wide.

How was that possible? Rose was pretty old to have a six or seven year old child. I know they can do amazing things with IVF these days, but nothing about Rose's situation made me think that any of that was likely.

"She's very beautiful," I said. All the pictures on the sideboard were of her. But the others were all faded, old photographs. I wondered if she was delusional, but I'd seen the girl, walking around hardly much older than in the pictures. Something was very wrong here...

There was a moment of silence.

"I'll get you that tea," Rose said.

I could've left it at that, I should've left it at that. But then I said – why did I say it? – I said: "I think I saw her the other day."

Rose stopped dead. She spun around; with a desperate look on her face, she said: "You seen her?"

"About a week ago, I think."

Rose launched herself at me. She grabbed me by the sides of my cardigan. "Where did you see her?" She started to shake me. "Where did you see her!"

"She was by the charity shop, in the alley – Rose, calm down!" I pushed her arms off me, but she just grabbed me higher up.

"What was she doing coming to you!" She was shaking me again. "Why'd she come to you!" She pushed me away sharply. I tumbled over the arm of the sofa, landing on the sunken seats before rolling off onto the floor. I was lucky not to smack my head on the coffee table as I landed on the carpet.

"I'm her mum, she should be coming to me. I'm her bloody mother!" She clumsily tried to kick me, but I moved my legs in time. I'd been in situations like this before, but never on my own. I was terrified.

"Rose, you need to calm down. Stop shouting, Rose."

She didn't know what to say for a moment; she backed away a little, as if she wasn't sure what had come over her. I think she knew she'd crossed a line.

"You get out," she breathed. "Get out of this house!"

She turned around and went fast into the kitchen. Petrified she might come out with a knife, I pulled myself up and made a dash for the door. Thank God she hadn't done up all the locks – I undid the latch myself as I heard her footsteps coming after me. As I ran out into the road I heard her cry out to me:

"If you see her, you come get me. You hear me! You bloody come and find me if you see her!"

I ran back to my car and locked myself in and burst into tears. I don't know how long I spent there, slumped against the steering wheel, crying. I thought I was passed all this, but obviously not. Just a prod and I was in pieces again.

I'm being too hard on myself. I was feeling pretty shaken up; that woman really was crazy. She couldn't possibly have a seven-year-old daughter. Perhaps she'd died a long time ago and she never got over it. But then how could I have seen the child in the alleyway? Maybe she was a different child? Yet she looked so much like the child in the picture, those old pictures...

My head was hurting. I wiped away the tears with a tissue. I ought to be angry at her, but losing your child was probably even more painful than losing your husband. And that hurt badly enough. Then prophetically, as if to make things worse, I got home and found a message on my answerphone. The lawyers...

It was bad news. They weren't going to say much over the phone, but they implied that it might go to court after all. That they had enough grounds to contest the will.

I felt drained and slumped against the wall. Bastards. Christ, I didn't even really want the money – I just didn't want them to have it. They'd turned their backs on him when he needed them and now they thought they had a right to what he left behind? How low could people go?

They were going to make out I'd taken advantage of him. Seduced him when he was at his most vulnerable. We didn't even start seeing each other until after he was discharged. I was careful, damn careful about it. But they weren't going to see it that way, were they? My bosses didn't see it that way. Practically forced me to leave. I risked everything because of him, and then he goes off and he bloody well kills himself.

What did he think? He was saving me heartache? Saving me pain? He could've fought it; it didn't have to end like that. And look what a mess he left. What a state he'd left me in.

I opened a bottle of wine and drank most of it in silence. I spent the evening lying on the floor and staring at the ceiling. That mad bitch had hurt my shoulder. It ached every time I lifted the glass or bottle to my lips. Christ, Adrian, couldn't you have held on that bit longer?

If only I'd been there. I never thought that he could just give up like that. They can fight these things; a prognosis is only an educated guess. He didn't even leave a note. He couldn't face me in the end. He didn't just want to save me pain – he didn't want to face me. Tell me he was throwing in the towel. It was one tragedy too many. As if being schizophrenic wasn't enough for a man to take.

I stayed indoors for two days. Cancelled an afternoon shift at the shop. Lied and said I had a migraine. I just didn't want to move. I wanted to find somewhere to hide. I spent most of one day under the bed. Hiding in the darkness. I didn't eat. I drank very little.

I ran a bath on the second day. Spent most of the day in it. Kept putting my head under the water to see how long I could hold my breath. I don't even know what I was thinking. I just felt heavy. Simple tasks were too difficult. Simple choices were too hard. Bubble bath or no bubble bath? Radio on or radio off? I chose no in both cases, but only because I never made a decision in the first place. Too much time just passed by.

Strangely enough, it was a call again from the lawyers that brought me out of my stupor. It was a reminder that I couldn't hide. And that there was still a vestige of anger in me that wanted to take on those bastards. There was still some fight left in me.

I called them back just before they closed for the day. They were going to send me some papers, which I would need to read and then go over with them point-by-point to challenge which parts I felt were incorrect, false, unfair, unjustified, etc.

Something to look forward to...

I was back in the charity shop on Wednesday. I didn't mention anything about my relapse to Joyce, but I had to tell her about Crazy Rose. I'd been outside to throw some rubbish away, just after I'd got there in the morning, and I knew someone was there in the alley. I just caught them shuffle back around the corner when they saw me. I knew it was Rose; she was searching where I said I'd seen the girl.

"I told you she was crazy".

"She needs help," I said. We don't use words like crazy in the mental health profession. "You should've seen the place; it was like it hadn't changed for twenty years. She bought kids' gloves here the other day."

"It's so sad, losing your child. But didn't you say you'd seen her outside?"

"Only thought I'd seen her. I must've been wrong, those were old photos, and you've seen how old she is." Something didn't add up. I could've been wrong, but I didn't think I was.

"Alice will know," said Joyce. "She's the librarian. And the local historian. She's got the dirt on everyone. Biggest gossip in town, and you know how they love to gossip around here. She runs the book group; I've been telling you you should go."

"When is it?"

"Tomorrow night. Still time for you to go over the material." She got up and scoured the bookshelves. After a few moments of searching she plucked out a copy of Life of Pi. "Not a bad choice this time."

"That's handy; I've read it."

As I'd guessed, the book group consisted of only ten minutes of book talk followed by a free-roaming discussion on everything from Brangelina to local teen pregnancies and who the fathers were. Alice was a woman with glasses much wider than her head. She was long-necked with a penetrating stare. She was like a woodland creature scanning its environment, in this case looking for little gossipy titbits to feast on. Her eyes roamed around the group; she dipped in and out of the conversations, entering when they got juicy, exiting when the scandals died down.

We were going to discuss Rose when all the other women had left. She gave me a wink to suggest that this was something big, beyond mere book group chitter-chatter. As soon as everyone else had left, she practically skipped past the bookshelves to get her records.

After a few moments Alice returned with a large red ring binder, A3 size, which she placed down on the table with a sense of relish.

"Nowadays I don't usually bother keeping the newspapers, not with the internet. But we used to cut out all the local stories."

The binder was a giant scrap book; thousands of stories had been diligently cut out and stuck inside. She had bookmarked the page she wanted to show me. She picked up a large clutch of papers, lifted them over and dropped them down on the desk with a thud.

What she revealed made my eyes open wide:

LIGHTNING STRIKES SCHOOLGIRL DEAD

Me and Joyce were speechless. It was one of several headlines – the story was unusual enough to have reached the nationals: Scottish girl killed by lightning; Child killed by playground lightning; Lightning strikes girl dead in playground. Only the local paper carried it as a front page story. In a rather tasteless image they had the girl's picture superimposed next to a picture of fork lightning badly pasted over a picture of a school playground. I recognised the school; it was on the other side of town; I passed it occasionally.

"_____ was in mourning yesterday after a six-year-old was struck by lightning and killed in the playground in front of her classmates. Chloe Rutter was leaving school when she was inexplicably killed as she waited for her mother to take her home."

It was her: the girl I'd seen in the alley. How was that possible? Her name was Chloe; I hadn't even known her name.

"My sister-in-law was there," said Alice. "They'd just let the wee ones go for the day. And they were just heading across the playground. Little Chloe, she sees her mum, Rose, and she goes to run to her. And Rose opens her arms open wide, ready to catch her and pick her up." Alice did the motions. "And just as she was running to her, barely a few yards away, *bang!*"

She struck the fist of her right hand into her left palm. "Lightning struck – it came right down from the sky. There was a big flash, and poor little Chloe, she fell dead just feet from her mum, all burnt-up. Smoke were coming off her. Dead, instantly. Old Nora, she said she'd never seen anything like it. No one had; it wasn't even barely raining."

I looked at the paper's date. Christ, that was 26 years ago. That meant that Chloe was older than I was! Would've been older than I was. God, I'd seen a ghost. I couldn't believe it. I'd seen a ghost. And talked to a ghost!

"That's horrible," said Joyce, scanning her way through the press cuttings.

"It's a terrible thing to lose a child," said Alice. "But to lose one like that. Right in front of your eyes. And it must be, what? A million-to-one chance, getting struck by lightning?"

"It's unbelievable," I said. But it was well documented. It was the end of the school day; all the mums and dads were there. And the other children.

"It happened in a flash," a parent was quoted as saying. "One moment she was there, running to her mam, and then she was gone. I've never seen anything like it."

"What happened to her? Rose, I mean."

"She went mad with grief, didn't she? Imagine it, losing you own daughter in front of you, killed no closer to you than you are to me now.

"She disappeared for quite a while. Institutionalised I mean. No one saw her for months. Her husband looked after the house; he started drinking. They didn't even have the funeral until she got back. And then things settled down for a bit. But they'd have these rows, these terrible rows. Then one day, he left. Never seen around these parts again. Just vanished.

"Rose, she never came to terms with it. Some people reckon she still thinks she's alive. She used to talk like she was still alive, and when you tried to tell her Chloe was gone, she'd get furious. People stopped talking to her altogether, they got afraid of her. She's mad, completely barmy."

I looked at Joyce and Joyce looked back at me. I'd seen her. I'd seen a dead girl.

"She bought kids' gloves off me the other day," I said.

"Sad really. But what can you do? She won't let you help her. Even after all this time she can't come to terms with it. Can't get over the shock."

It was tensely quiet in the car as I drove Joyce back home.

"It couldn't have been her," I said, not believing myself. I wondered if somehow, I'd seen the newspaper story before, somehow dug that picture from deep within my memory and imagined the girl behind the shop. But of course I hadn't; I was five when that happened and would hardly have been big into newspapers.

"I've heard some strange stuff in my time," said Joyce. "But I haven't heard anything like this."

"That's why she goes out in the storms," I said. "That's why she goes out walking. She's trying to find her. She thinks she's going to find Chloe out in the storm."

"But that doesn't make sense."

"None of this makes sense! But when I saw the girl, it was raining. And she, I mean Rose, she'd just bought that umbrella..."

"Look, I don't know what crazy stuff you're getting into your head, but you need to leave this woman alone. She already attacked you once. And you heard what Alice said about her husband. Never seen again. He could be under the patio for all you know."

She was right. I had to put aside my Florence Nightingale tendencies and stay well away from this. 26 years Rose had been searching for Chloe. No wonder she was angry with me. She goes rambling across hills and fields and I stumble across her in a back-alley by accident.

Why had she appeared to me? Because of my loss? No, I scattered what was left of Adrian across Richmond Park where we used to walk together. More than likely she appeared to people all the time. Who was going to remember a little girl from 26 years ago except her mother?

I dropped Joyce off and continued on back home. It had a certain gothic poetry to it. The woman who chased storms... trudged through the mud every time the rain fell. And for what? A glimpse of her child, a chance to spend time with her? Or in the vain hope that somehow, someday, the storm might return her to her, having once so cruelly taken her away?

I laughed at myself for getting so melodramatic. As I drove back to my house it started to rain, only very slightly. But as I stepped out of the car and felt the cold rain land on my face, drip slowly down my back, I was suddenly overcome with a feeling of horror. 26 years... walking alone through the cold... the rain... the mud... chasing a dream, a fantasy. Praying for rain, despairing when the sun shone. A life in darkness, grey and cold. Never ending, never changing. A life of loss and futile hope.

I went in and poured myself a large glass of wine. Christ, and I thought I had problems. I thought I could take my mind off it by watching the telly. Even the latest tensions between Israel and Palestine were starting to seem like a pleasant alternative.

But just as I thought I might be taking my mind off it, the weather came on and the girl warned that more bad weather was coming. And not just any bad weather: the tail-end of a South-American hurricane. We should expect bad storms come the weekend. And gale-force winds.

My blood ran cold. Would that make her happy? A weekend of heavy stormy weather? Would she prepare? Get her best Wellington boots ready? Her rain-mac, umbrella?

Then another unpleasant idea came into my head: what if she wanted to die too? What if she wanted the storm to take her like it had taken her child? What if every time she went into the storm, she hoped that she might die too?

I didn't sleep well. In fact, I even dreamt about it. That day in the playground...

The sky was grey, a hint of drizzle falling. The children were leaving the school building – it was small, only large enough for two classrooms. The children were all dressed in their raincoats, with scarves, wellies, gloves, bobble hats or hoods. They carried lunch boxes, rucksacks, some had little umbrellas – all small, tiny and adorable.

The parents were waiting on the periphery. Some of the children ran to them, others walked, some skipped. Friends waved each other goodbye, brothers and sisters squabbled. Teachers oversaw from the double-doored entrance, trading a few words while they did the last of their daily duties.

Chloe was still by the school doors. She scanned the hedges, then the front fence, furtively looking for her mother. There was a rumble in the sky.

I was Rose. I waved enthusiastically to her. She jumped a little off the ground and waved happily to me. She wore an expression of undiluted, untainted pure affection. Sheer joy just at seeing me. I walked a little into the playground, across a faded hopscotch game. She ran towards me, arms outstretched. I leant down to catch her and hoist her up. She giggled and laughed as she sped towards me.

A stream of white fell from the sky. There was no warning, not even a second, a moment to see or comprehend the impending terror. She crashed into the crack of light and the world was torn in two.

I gave up on sleeping after that. I washed off a layer of sweat in the shower and then took to the sofa in my duvet and watched whatever dross the television had to offer.

At some point I drifted over to the 24-hour news channel. The weather report told once more of the impending storm. Gale-force winds expected. I changed the channel; there would be no more Florence Nightingale. I had had my fill of getting involved in other people's problems. That's why I moved up here – to get away from everything.

But I hadn't, had I? The postman would be here with letters from the solicitors this morning. What a joke. The only reason I'd come out here, decided to hole myself up in this obscure nowhere in the highlands was that Adrian used to tell me about it. He'd come to _____ once with his grandparents and found the place so peaceful, so... absent, of anything. He said it was the vaguest place in the world. Towns, cities, had personality, character – _____ had nothing. It was just houses together, people walking in and out of dream. A human purgatory.

And he was right, wasn't he? I was here running away from my problems, Rose was chasing her past. Even Joyce, bright bubbly Joyce, she was living in her Grandma's cottage with her mystery woman, living their life of secrets away from prying eyes. That day in the 80s when Chloe died, that was probably the last time the world even noticed _____. One brief mention in the paper and it vanished once again.

Adrian came here to reset – to really get away from it all. To try and derail his episodes. And now I had come here too, to get away from it all. I'd come to my dead husband's purgatory, where his presence lingered around every corner.

I laughed at myself. What a stupid fool I was.

Tired and unwell, but at least avoiding a full-on depressive stupor, I pulled myself away from the house. I wasn't due in the charity shop that day, but I went anyway. Stephanie, a stick-thin, easily flustered woman was looking after things; it was Joyce's day off. I lied about Joyce asking me to come in. No it wasn't because Joyce didn't think she was up to it; it was because there was always supposed to be two people working there and now that we had enough people we should follow the rules to avoid trouble.

I just didn't want to be alone. I knew the lawyer's papers were just going to upset me. And I didn't want to get involved in that other thing either. The radio in the shop kept reminding me of the impending storm expected this weekend. I wanted to turn it off.

When I drove home, I deliberately avoided driving by Rose's house, which would've been on my usual route. My days of martyrdom were over. When I got home, I couldn't look at those papers, which were waiting ominously on the doormat. Even looking at that first page made me start to cry. I was in such a mess. How long could I carry on like this? Trapped in purgatory with nowhere to turn except the past.

Thursday turned to Friday. The weather warnings escalated in their severity. Flood warnings had now been issued, people shouldn't travel unless absolutely necessary. Joyce said she'd play it by ear, but would probably keep the shop shut.

The clouds darkened. The wind grew strong – the whole landscape felt on the brink of a full on tempest. Streets emptied; children left school early. The local news stoked the fire – "This could be the worst storm for more than a decade". I saw sandbags in driveways; surely we were too high up here to be put at risk from the river flooding? Perhaps the rain water could run down the streets as it came down through the hills?

What the hell did I know? My landlady had not thought to give me any instruction. Let the rain waters come. They were the least of my problems. Maybe I'd even enjoy some new problems.

But my new found taste for alcoholism was my first concern. If I was going to get through those papers I was going to need a stiff drink or two. And as the heavens had yet to open, there was still time to visit the Co-op for some booze.

The shelves were half empty; people had been preparing for the worst. I took the best of what was still there and started back for home.

It was on the way back that I saw her; climbing clumsily over a stile onto a public footpath. Yes, she was on her way. She had to be, didn't she?

I almost said no. I almost convinced myself that I didn't care. That I could just say "To hell with her" and just drive away. But I couldn't, could I?

And even as I got out of the car I knew I wouldn't be able to convince her. That she would just throw abuse at me and carry on, despite the risks. But not try? That's not that kind of person I could be.

"Rose, for God's sake!" I cried. "You can't go out there, you'll get yourself killed."

"Don't you worry about me," she said, barely even turning to look at me.

The wind was already strong; I could barely hear her as it roared past my ears. I didn't know what I was saying; how do you get someone chasing a ghost to see sense?

I improvised as best I could: "You can't bring her back Rose," I yelled. "She's gone."

"She's not gone," Rose turned to me in anger. "She's always with me. She's all I've got!"

"But it's not safe; she doesn't want you to get yourself killed."

"It's the only time I'm with her," tears were running down her cheeks. "It's the only time I see my little girl, the only time I can find her. I need her and she needs me. She's my baby!" She turned back to the hills, staring out into the grey wild.

There was a rumble of thunder from far away. Rose turned her head, scanning the landscape slowly. "I'm coming my love," she shouted. "Don't run; I'm coming."

"Rose!" I yelled. She didn't hear me, or didn't want to. I climbed over the stile to go after her, but I just wasn't dressed for it. My heel sunk straight into the mud and I almost fell over backwards. I just managed to grab hold of the fence to stop myself.

My hair was blowing in front of my face. Rose marched determinedly into the distance. I couldn't stop her; probably nothing could.

I pulled myself out of the mud and climbed back over the fence. I'd done my part, done my best. You can only do so much. If they're that fixated on the abyss, you can't keep them out of it. Some people are just too determined to tie their own rope.

I stumbled back to my car, my ankle twisted and aching, and drove back home. The gale blew all afternoon and into the evening. The rain came down around six o'clock; it came down heavy but for not as long as they'd predicted. It was running in streams down the gutters and down the sides of the street.

It fell harder further north. _____ was not so badly flooded; the banks of the river held.

But many of the roads into town were flooded; that's why the shop shelves were so empty. This wasn't a hurricane, but the country roads flooded so easily. The town could so easily be cut off.

I watched things progress on the news between soaps, sitcom repeats and predictable detective shows. Of course, if this had been the Home Counties there would be hours of coverage. But as this was the highlands, bad weather wasn't big news. The local news was of course more keyed-in. There were road accidents, real flooding in other areas; some rural communities stranded. All train services had been cancelled past Edinburgh and Glasgow. A caravan had blown down a hillside at a campsite 50 miles away, killing a man and his two children.

From my window I watched wheelie bins get blown down the street. The rain wasn't coming down heavily by night time, but a fierce drizzle spat against the windows.

I drank heavily; my mind was on Rose – that stupid woman. Would she have the good sense to go home? Would she stay out all night in the cold and wet? If she didn't get herself killed, she'd probably die from the cold.

I tried my best to put my mind on other things, but the only other things I had to focus on were legal matters. I'd barely looked at the legal papers; a mixture of accusations, insinuations and gossip – they made me sick to my stomach.

I couldn't sleep. The roaring sound of the wind created an uneasy atmosphere. I tossed and turned beneath the sheets. When I closed my eyes I felt like I could see the storm in my mind – the wind rushing through trees, the rain hitting the puddles in the street, the people on the street struggling to get to shelter.

Then I imagined myself chasing Rose through the fields, arguing with her, pleading with her to come back home.

And little Chloe. She was with me, mocking me. "She's not listening to you," she would say with glee and a jolly little skip. "She doesn't have to do a thing you say. She's my mum. She doesn't have to do what she's told by you."

She laughed at me. I told her to go away. I told her she was dead; she kicked mud at me: "No – you're dead!"

I woke up with a start. There was a large crash outside. I listened cautiously for a time, hearing sounds of panic in the street. I went to the window and pulled aside the curtain.

Just a few houses away the wind had blown down a chimney. Bricks were lying across the garden. The family were in a panic, the neighbours were out in the road with them. I couldn't see much from my window and after a short while I pulled the curtains closed. A bit cold of me, but there wasn't much I could do for them. The arrival of the fire brigade a short while later made sure that I didn't get back to sleep that night.

I had breakfast early – the legal papers sitting on the end of the table, taunting me as I ate. I had no plans for the day. I took to staring at the wall in silence. I thought about doing many different things, reading, writing, listening to music, watching the television – but all of them seemed like too much hard work.

I got a call after nine from Joyce. Stick-thin Stephanie was in trouble. Part of her garage roof had caved in, and she needed help shifting everything out of there before it soaked with water.

It wasn't far for me to go, so I walked there. By the time I arrived, quite a band had formed. Various people's nephews, sons, brothers, cousins... all Stephanie's friends were old, so they had sent a variety of relatives to help. Her children were abroad, which is how all their furniture had come to be stacked up in her garage. A neighbour had kindly offered some garage space to store some of it for the time being, and Joyce said we could fit some in the back of the shop. I took the keys and supervised things at that end, making room amongst the assorted bric-a-brac in the stock room.

I had to wait quite some time while it was decided what should go in the back of the shop. No one had a large van, so things came in the backs of cars or in a mini-bus in one case. It was heartening to see so many people banding together to help out.

The shop got a dining room set and several boxes of plates and assorted bits and pieces. One of the guys – a nephew or cousin or friend's son – quite young, did his best to flirt with me and got me to make him a cup of tea. It was kind of nice, and he was good-looking. But I just couldn't imagine myself spending that kind of time with anyone.

Things were finished by just after lunchtime. I locked up and took the car the long way around to get back home. Deliberately I drove past Rose's, just looking for some sign that she had returned.

I don't know what I was expecting to see. Her house looked like any other house when you drove past. Unless there's anyone standing right by the window, you can't really see anything.

The legal papers went untouched for another night. I just couldn't face them. They'd be chasing me for them soon – nothing on the answerphone yet.

Another night of television and drinking followed. I was determined to go out on the Sunday – not just wallow indoors and drive myself crazy. The roads had mostly cleared and I drove out to a remote inn for Sunday lunch and ate it in near silence as everyone else seemed to be keeping away. And I so wanted distractions; any conversation, any overheard morsel.

There was no escaping my troubles. The only thing keeping my mind off Adrian's venomous relatives was Rose, and I feared for her safety. I should've done more to stop her, she could be dead already.

I cursed myself for driving away and enjoying lunch. Someone's life could be hanging in the balance and I was here stuffing my face. What was wrong with me? I fretted myself into a sweat and panic and rapidly paid for my meal and drove back to ____. I ran up to her doorway and knocked loudly. I knocked three, four times. No answer.

I peered into the windows, searched to see if there was a back alley to her back garden – there wasn't.

I waited outside, keeping vigil in my car. I sat there for four, maybe five hours. I fell asleep at one point, against my steering wheel – I had to explain to a concerned neighbour that I was fine and was just waiting for someone.

The sun started to set and Rose was nowhere to be seen. I thought about calling the police – but what was I to tell them? Some crazy woman who chased ghosts wasn't at home when I called?

I had no way of knowing where she was. I only thought – I only knew – that she had been out on the hills, chasing God knows what. But she could be somewhere else now; I didn't know what else she did during the day. I knew nothing about her. It was only a morbid instinct that told me something was wrong.

I drove home after it went dark. I got my senses back; she wasn't my responsibility and she wasn't my problem. I'd tried after all; what was I supposed to do?

Joyce was ill the next day, so I looked after the shop alone. It was quiet, the rain stayed away but the sky remained grey. I thought about putting the radio on, or putting on some music – but nothing seemed to fit my glum, foreboding mood.

The hours passed slowly. I made less than £50 for the whole day. I tried to read a book, but I couldn't get into it. It was some detective novel. I went around the shop looking for old stock to reduce as time slouched into the afternoon. Around about two o'clock, I was reducing some glasses that had been over-priced (they were chipped), when I caught a glimpse, the barest of glimpses, of a blue coat – a small girl – skipping past the shop window. Putting a glass down so carelessly that it fell off the shelf and broke, I raced towards the door, pulled it open, and found the street outside completely deserted.

Now I was seeing things.

I closed early. There was no point in staying around, although I couldn't summon up the confidence to tell Joyce. I locked up and went over to the Co-op to do my shopping. The shelves were still looking pretty bare; evidently supplies were still struggling to get there.

I filled up on what essentials I could buy, along with several bottles of cheap wine. I went to the checkout, paid, and carried the bags out to my car. I opened up the boot and lifted both bags into the back.

"Mum needs help".

I froze.

Slowly, fearfully, I turned my head. She was stood there on the edge of the car park, dressed in the same tatty blue coat. Her face was pale; her milky blue, washed out eyes stared at me with concern.

"She needs help, she's fallen down and I can't get her to wake up."

I was almost too frightened to speak. I swallowed and said: "What's happened?"

"We were playing and she fell over and now she can't move. You've got to come quick".

A cold sweat was gathering on my forehead.

"Come on," she said, pushing her way through the bushes that bordered the car park. I couldn't help myself; I couldn't possibly turn away. I closed the boot, locked the car and went after her.

Behind the bushes was a tall wire fence. There was a small hole in it, large enough to crawl through. She was on the other side already, skipping into a dense gathering of trees. I was dressed in no condition for this kind of thing: I wasn't wearing heels, thankfully, but my Ugg boots were hardly fit for purpose.

I bent down and squeezed through the hole in the fence, my coat's collar and hood getting stuck on the torn steel wires as I passed through as best I could.

I was in a dense gathering of tall, but young fir trees. Pushing through the branches I realised I had walked into an enclosed area surrounding an electricity substation, or whatever these stone power buildings were called. It was a small brick shed with a tall pylon next to it, flowing wires down inside.

I heard Chloe call to me; I saw her peer out from behind the building. I jogged after her. The other side of the small enclosure had a wooden fence, and she was squeezing through a gap between missing fence panels.

The ground at least was fairly firm here, but it was still hard to run on. I pushed through the sharp young branches and managed to squeeze between the fence panels.

When I was through I found myself in the forecourt of an abandoned petrol station. Closed for many years, the old looking pumps were rusted and smashed up; the shop was boarded over with steel panels. I'd never been out here before. Strange how you can so easily lose your bearings; I didn't know quite where I was.

I was on the edge of town somewhere. After the petrol station there were no other buildings, just open ground, field after field. Chloe was already on the other side of the forecourt, supernaturally quickly ahead. She climbed over a dry stone wall and disappeared into the adjoining field.

On solid ground I was able to move quicker. By the time I reached the wall there was no sign of her. But as I lifted my head, I could see her again, in the far corner of the field, jumping, waving her arms from side to side.

I wondered what on earth I was doing, but I couldn't give up the chase. I climbed the wall and I trudged through the long grass to the far corner, slowly and with difficulty. I didn't like the look of the sky: it was dark grey, the clouds thick, jagged and dangerously ominous.

I crossed from field to field, uphill, one into the next, each one more overgrown and more of a challenge. Eventually, the dry-stone walls faded; neglect had let them crumble. I was in rough, untamed landscape. I found myself struggling through thick heather, my trousers scratched and scraped by thorns. My boots, long-since soaked through, kept getting caught on branches and under roots. I was lucky not to rip my feet out of them.

Chloe appeared and disappeared like a phantom, unseen for short periods, but always making herself known to keep me on track.

I was sweating; the weather was cold, but I was sweating profusely. I was unfit and unprepared. I looked back towards _____. She had led me quite a way; over half-a-mile uphill, probably further – I'm not much of a judge of these things.

Finally, she led me to a footpath, although I had to pass through a muddy ditch to get there. I tried to jump it, but missed and ended up tripping and falling, my feet sinking into the mud and me striking down against a sloping bank of stones and wet soil. I swore loudly – but she was nowhere near to hear me. Whenever I shouted for her or cursed her she wasn't there.

The path was a mixed blessing. It was easier to walk on but it ran mercilessly straight up the hill, a tough ungradual ascent. It headed towards a patch of forest between two high hill peaks. Breathing heavily, I struggled on, the face of Chloe ever appearing at any moment when I was tempted to turn back and give up.

At one point, I stopped for rest on a tree stump. I was allowed less them a few moments of respite before she shouted for me: "Hurry, she needs help!" I almost screamed at her. I groaned out aloud. This was insane.

I followed the path finally to the wooded valley inbetween the hills. I yelled, "How much further?" to her as she led the way through the trees. As ever, she refused to answer. As I continued deep into the woods, I heard the sound of water, the rush of the river flowing from the peaks – had I come so far? I continued on for several minutes, keeping just ahead of sheer exhaustion and wondering when or where this might end.

I arrived at the river, here running wide across a slope of rocks. I wiped the sweat off my forehead, and scanned, full of frustration, for Chloe. As my eyes searched through the trees, I suddenly found her – Rose.

She was lying face-down flat on the other side of the river, her dark red coat standing out against the dull browns and greens. I shouted to her, but got not reply.

The frustration and anger melted away; I had to get across. Fortunately, the river was quite shallow, I was more afraid of slipping than I was of getting wet – every inch of my body seemed already to be soaked and soggy. I tried to step my away across some of the large stones, and was forced several times to simply go straight into the water – the shock of the cold went straight to my head, and now that hurt too.

Finally, I was across and stumbled down the slope to Rose. I shouted her name again. I pulled at her coat and shook her slightly, hoping for some sign of life. Jesus, she must have been out here for days, just slumped against the ground.

There was mud all over her clothes, and she was damp all over. She didn't speak, her eyes were closed. I was about to conclude the worst, when suddenly her mouth opened and let out a slight moan. She was alive, but maybe not for long.

"Is she alright?" Chloe was suddenly stood over us.

"I don't know," I said. "We need to get help." I felt my pockets. Damn it, I still didn't have a phone! I didn't know what to do. I had to find someone else. I couldn't lift her down the hillside myself. She might have broken bones; I could be making things worse.

"I've got to get help."

"Don't leave her," Chloe shrieked at me.

"You stay with her. I need to find someone who can get her down the hill."

I went back into the woods. If I followed the river down, I was bound to bump into somebody, arrive at one of the roads at least. I found myself gradually moving out of the woods, still keeping the river in sight. I couldn't really see anything from amongst the trees; I needed to be able to get a look at the landscape, see where I might be able to find help.

Finally, I came to the edge of the woods and found myself looking back across fields and hills. There was a footpath, I could see it. It led down towards an abandoned ruin of a barn and a farmhouse. And, yes! There were people there: two hikers. They were a long way from me though. I had to try, so I screamed. Screamed so hard my throat burned.

They didn't hear me at first. But there was a faint echo, and after some time I saw them look my way. I waved to them, jumped up and down, throwing my arms from side to side. They waved back at first – I had to convince them this was more than just an over-enthusiastic greeting. I threw my arms over towards the woods. Hoping they would respond to the summons.

They looked at each other, confused. Desperate, I screamed "Help me" with every bit of strength I could. That seemed to do it; they started moving in my direction and I started off in theirs. I careened down the hillside towards them, ecstatic with relief. At one point, I tripped and fell dramatically, both arms up in the air and down flat onto my chest. Fortunately, it was wet, soggy ground, but it still knocked the wind out of me. They ran quicker to help me, and eventually we met.

I explained that I'd found a woman, barely conscious and probably dying. They came with me up the hillside. I lied to them and told them that I'd been out walking. They didn't say anything, but they could tell something was wrong; I clearly wasn't dressed for it.

I tracked our way back to the spot quite well. Of the couple, he was a vet, which was sort of helpful. He examined her, said he didn't think she'd broken anything, but she was frighteningly cold. She'd been up here for quite some time.

They were proper hikers. They had an ordinance survey map with them; to get help out here they'd need a helicopter and they could tell them the right grid reference – I was so relieved.

Typically, however, there was no signal for a mobile phone. The vet's wife went off out of the woods to get a signal. He wrapped Rose in his jacket and took out his own mobile – on a different network – and started to spread out trying to get a signal himself.

When he'd moved away a little, Chloe re-appeared, walking out from behind a tree like she'd been hiding.

"Is she alright?" she said.

"She's very sick." I answered.

"But she's going to be ok?"

I suddenly felt myself getting very angry. "Why don't you leave her alone?" I cried. "This is your fault. Can't you see what you're doing to her?"

Her face hardened suddenly, just like her mother's.

"She's my mum!" she hissed, through gritted teeth.

"And you're destroying her! Just leave her alone. You're dead, you don't even exist!"

"She's my mum!" she screeched, stamping her feet. "You can't tell me what to do, you can't!" She jumped up and down in a fury and started to scream. The sound went right through my body; it made me shiver and tremble. The pitch could've shattered glass.

"You can't take my mum!" She reached down to pick up a stone and threw it at me. If flew towards my face with uncanny force and accuracy – I barely had time to dodge it. It flew over my shoulder and smacked into a tree, making a deep dent in the bark.

I looked back at her; she was gone again. She'd been so benign before, but now I was frightened. I looked suddenly at Rose and a horrible thought occurred to me: what if she'd done that to her? If she'd have hit me with that rock, she'd have knocked me out cold; little girls just couldn't throw like that...

There was a sound behind me. Taken off-guard, I turned and screamed.

It was the vet. I felt faint suddenly; this was all taking its toll. He could see I'd been through it; he took hold of me and propped me up against a tree. He gave me some water from a travel bottle. I told him I was fine even though I clearly wasn't.

It was almost an hour before a helicopter came; we made awkward conversation until it arrived. By that time his wife had returned and the three of us watched as they hoisted Rose inside.

I pretended not to know her; I just couldn't explain all this, all that had had happened. Because I didn't know her, I didn't go in the helicopter with her. I wish I had, but I just wanted to get home, somewhere safe as soon as possible.

They took her away and the vet and his wife helped me down the hillside. They took me to their Land Rover and kindly took me back home. It was almost dark by the time we started back on the roads.

I broke down and cried. It was just as we passed over the bridge to town; I don't know why then. They looked into the backseat as I was pouring with tears. They tried to comfort me, tried to offer me their help. They knew something about all this wasn't right.

I just wanted to get home. They took me back, I composed myself enough to say thank you. They were such nice people, but I don't even remember their names.

I cried for hours on the sofa, and passed out at some point, I'm not sure when. I awoke, my body aching and tired, in the early morning. I was starving, I'd not eaten since the day before.

After some toast and coffee, I noticed there was a new message on the answerphone. It was the lawyers; it had to be didn't it? I called them back straight away, just for someone to talk to.

I received a polite telling-off and a stern warning about putting things off this long. I tried to tell them it was hard, and to their credit they were very understanding; they could tell I was almost crying. I could sense the discomfort on the end of the phone. The woman seemed to want to offer advice beyond her legal remit to me; I could sense her concern, but she probably knew better than to get too involved.

I promised I would get the papers back to her tomorrow. There could be no more hiding. I looked at the phone after I put it down. What about Rose? I needed to find out what had happened to her. But I dreaded what I might find out. She might be dead. Just because she'd been rescued didn't mean she'd survive.

I thought long and hard about it but decided to put it off. I didn't think I could take it if she'd died. To go through all that and not make it through. I washed and dressed myself in clean clothes. I took a long walk, something to get some fresh air in my lungs and some of the depressive weight off my shoulders. It was a bad idea; my body ached and groaned from the ordeal the day before. I went to a café not far away for some breakfast, bought some nice pastries – and then went back to face my past.

I sat over the papers with a glass of wine for company. Things didn't look good, but then again, it was the case against. Lots of gossip, lots of hearsay, lots of mud-raking... they'd dug up an old case of sexual harassment; an oily doctor who didn't want to take no for an answer. All the bitter old hags who worked there had always held that against me; thought I'd asked for it, done it all for attention.

Unexpectedly it strengthened me. The anger, the outrage. The wrongness of it all. I still had some fighting spirit. Weak spirit all the same, still fragile. But it was a revelation to me nonetheless. I wasn't ready to give in to despair.

But the depth of the situation I was in was still a heavy burden. I put the papers quickly to one side as soon as I was done. Things could still get so much worse.

I looked over to the phone. I thought of Rose and of her body slumped down on the hillside. Suddenly, in some strange way, that became the crux of the argument. If she could survive, pull through in spite of it all. Then maybe I could too. But then again, if she hadn't...

I got the hospital number from the Yellow Pages. I phoned up and spent a long time on hold before being passed from one receptionist to another.

I breathed slowly and carefully as I waited for the news. It didn't help that I didn't remember her last name. But not so many people get brought in by helicopter, so that narrowed it down.

She was alive. In a critical condition, but alive. She had pneumonia and a broken leg, but she was alive. I felt a weight lift from my shoulders; such relief, I can barely describe it.

I felt compelled to see her. The hospital was miles away, but I could make it before visiting hours were over. I had go back to the Co-op to get my car. Then I drove like a demon, smashing through deep puddles on still water-logged streets. I wanted to bring her something, but not really knowing what she'd like, I bought her grapes – a pleasant, well-meaning cliché.

It was even further than I thought. The nights were drawing in now; the clocks would be going back soon. I arrived with only twenty minutes of visiting time left and on the wrong side of the hospital. I had quite a way to go to get to Rose's ward; I had to stop and ask directions more than once.

I introduced myself to the ward nurses and they led me to her. She was fast asleep; they said she was coming in and out of consciousness and wasn't making much sense. Perhaps that was best, I thought. I didn't really want to know what had happened to her on that hillside. She had most probably fallen, but there was still that unsettling possibility...

A doctor checking on another patient in the quiet, half-full ward came over to ask me some questions. I couldn't help it; I kept up the pretence that I had seen her on the hillside for the first time ever. They were hoping I knew somebody that could help to take care of her. She didn't seem to have any relatives that they could find. There was her husband, but they couldn't seem to track him down.

They were hopeful that she would pull through. I sat with her a while; I wondered if she could hear me if I spoke to her. But I couldn't think of anything to say. I thought about saying something trite like "Chloe would want you to pull through". But I didn't want to mention her name.

She looked so sad lying there. Blankets tucked up to her neck, her tired face, wrinkled and wrought before its time. Christ, maybe it would've been better if she had died. What kind of life was she living here in purgatory? Even if she pulled through, would she ever move on? Could there really ever be more for her than her already miserable existence?

I thought about saying that too, something like: "It's time to move on Rose; time to live in the present." But what good would that do?

Perhaps whoever they got to look after her could help her. Finally get her to get over her loss. Anything was possible, even if it probably wasn't. I left the grapes on the side; the one futile gesture I was willing to make.

As I exited the ward, I saw through the windows that it was raining outside. A talkative nurse, one I hadn't seen on the way in, commented, in a typically British way, that that was all we needed, more rain. I stood for a moment watching the droplets break against the glass and then I asked her whether anyone else had been in to see Rose. She said no; it was like the doctor had said, she seemed to have no relatives, no friends.

I watched the rain for a few seconds longer. Perhaps ghost girls didn't like hospitals any more than the rest of us.

The drive back was much slower, the dark and the pouring rain making for a much tenser journey. I'd foolishly thought seeing Rose would bring me hope, some joy. But how stupid I was; how was seeing her in there, in that condition, going to make me feel better? Her life was a living death anyway; it was just going to continue instead of ending.

I had to get out. That was the only thing to do. I would call my landlady in the morning. Time to get out and never look back. Whatever happened to me now, it couldn't be worse than a lonely mourning life like this.

The rain was starting to get heavy and progress through traffic was slow. I let a couple of cars pass me on a quiet crowded residential street, lined with parked cars. It was going to be a long, slow drive home.

As I reached the end of the street, a shape appeared in the road. Leaping from behind a parked van, a child appeared in front of me.

I had no time to react; before I could even put my foot on the brake, they'd thumped against my bonnet and disappeared under the wheels.

I screamed; my head snapped forward as the car came to a sudden stop. I took both hands off the steering wheel and clamped them over my mouth. I was still for just a moment before I howled through my fingertips.

I ripped off my seatbelt and threw myself out the door. I tripped as I got out and had to grab hold of the window to stop myself from falling over. Back on my feet quickly, I swung the door back and got down on my knees to see under my car.

The road was wet and cold and the street-lighting poor – I could see nothing.

Frightened and desperate, I laid down, in the road, looking as far and clear under my car as possible.

There was nothing.

But I hadn't imagined it. I'd seen a child, felt them thump against the bonnet.

And then I realised, my memory coming into focus, that my victim had been a girl. A blonde girl, pale-faced, dressed darkly, probably in blue.

I got up and on my feet again – she was here. It had to be her. Normal children don't disappear. I didn't know why or what had just happened, but I had to get away.

I got back inside and slammed the door shut. My keys were still in the ignition – I twisted them and started the engine.

I took a second to breathe, trying to calm myself.

The passenger-side window smashed. I screamed; a shower of shattered glass sprayed across the seat; I turned my head instinctively away as fragments hit my cheek.

I put my foot down. The wheels spun against the wet tarmac – I had to get away. I drove stupidly fast; I didn't know what I was running from, but I had to get away. The falling rain was a threat – she only came out when it rained. And while I was outdoors, I was in danger. She was dangerous. Rose wasn't just trying to chase and love her lost daughter; she must've been terrified of her. Frightened of what she'd do if she didn't go after her. Tormented not just by loss but by fear. For all these years…

A car pulled out in front of me unexpectedly. I almost didn't stop in time; I skidded dangerously across the road.

I shrieked to a halt. They stopped, seeing just how close I'd come to hitting them they hit their horn loudly. I saw an angry face snarl at me in the glare of my headlights.

I couldn't take the cramped space any longer. I opened the door and got out, walked out into the road and onto the pavement. My heart was pounding; I had to get a grip. I paced around a little, trying to get my breath back.

After a few moments, I noticed something lying in the road, just by the open door of my car. I walked up to it and leant down.

It was a broken wooden toy train. I recognised it quickly; it was the one I'd dropped that first time I'd ever seen her. That's what had shattered the window; I hadn't even seen it. It must've gone through the window and hit the door on the other side, slipped down the side of the seat and fallen out when I'd got out of the car.

I picked it up. Two of its wheels were still missing – it had to be the same one.

There was the sound of a car horn. Another car had pulled up behind mine, wanting to get through. The driver side window was wound-down: "Are you all right love?"

I dropped the train and got back in the car.

I drove a little more carefully, but still with speed. I was glad to be back on the country roads, feeling that somehow the wide open space offered fewer surprises than the over-crowded town streets.

When I got home I ran for the front door and locked it quickly behind me. I didn't even bother to cover up the broken window. The next morning the passenger side seat was soaked. At least the car hadn't been stolen; but it had been visited in the night.

A message had been written on the back window.

STAY AWAY FROM MY MUM - the condensation was gone, but the words were still visible. It was written big enough to fill the whole back window.

Let it never be said of me that I can't take a hint.

My mind had already been made up. I phoned my landlady and told her that I would be moving out at the end of the month. I'd paid the whole month so I'd stay till the end, I didn't want to leave Joyce in the lurch anyhow.

I thought carefully about what to do. I didn't want to call one of my close friends or family, they'd only berate me for falling off the map and not keeping in touch. I called Kieran, someone I'd been friends with for a while, but had never been so close to for them to have been upset by my long stretch of absence. He was settled with a new boyfriend but happy to put me up and seemed very relieved to hear from me. I didn't give him too many details, but promised to fill him in when I got back.

I made an appointment with the lawyers. They wanted to see me sooner, but I insisted this was the best I could do.

Those last two weeks passed very slowly. With my life moving towards something, it really put into perspective just how lonely and empty and pointless those months had been. Just empty, devoid of anything. Better to live or die than live in purgatory. Whatever happened from this point on, I decided I'd never go back to _____. I felt truly sorry saying to Joyce that I'd be back to visit her, when I knew I wouldn't. I had made one friend, but I'd probably never see her again. I had her number, swore I'd friend her on Facebook where we could exchange empty pleasantries.

I still had pathetically little in the way of possessions. Packing my belongings took less than half an hour. Before I left, I sat alone in the house silently. Though I'd brought with me so little, with it gone, the house seemed empty, foreboding, dark. I sat uncomfortably on a low stool in the living room. Clouds were gathering once again in the sky. It would be raining again soon.

I walked slowly into the hall. I was supposed to return the keys to Mrs McMurray that afternoon. I undid the door latch and let the door hang open. The clouds lingered ominously; in my mind they rolled like smoke rumbling from a fire burning out of control. The rain would fall soon; I might not have much time.

It felt like now or never; if the rain came down again, I might never escape. What did it matter, Mrs McMurray could get the keys back by post; send the deposit back by bank transfer, if she knew what that was.

I closed my eyes tight, gripped hold of my suitcases and pulled myself out of the door. With purpose I marched towards the car and threw them on the back seat. There was no time to apply more tape to the cardboard patch that covered the broken passenger-side window. There was no time to go back inside and check whether I'd left anything behind.

I locked the front door, sat in my car and I drove away. For once and for all, I sat in my car and I drove away.

But before I left, before I abandoned purgatory, I had one last thing to see. One last silly gesture I had to make.

I took a detour via Rose's house, hoping, though I knew it unlikely, to glimpse her at home through her window. Maybe she was still in hospital. Maybe she was dead. Maybe she was making a cup of tea. I probably would never know; the chances of me spotting her, catching her in just that moment, in her front window, were so ridiculously remote.

But I'd run over a ghost girl only a few weeks ago, so anything was possible.

And despite the odds, she was there. To my disbelief, I saw her as I panned past in my car. She was sat by her window, right up against the glass.

She was in a wheelchair, her leg broken and supported, held up horizontally in its cast. She was looking out; not at me in my car, but up into the sky, the clouds, the threatening tumultuous grey.

I wondered what she must be thinking as I passed. Was she in agony, forlorn because she was trapped there and unable to see her little girl? Perhaps she was terrified, frightened of what her angry, destructive child might do without her to stop her, to calm her.

Perhaps all this was nothing new. Perhaps she'd tripped and fallen a dozen times, got sick and been forced into bed time after time with new colds and viruses brought on by the freezing temperatures. Perhaps each time she hoped that she wouldn't make it; that her and her baby would finally be reunited in death, to walk the storms forever, together. Maybe that was just her rotten luck, the same odds-defying misfortune that had taken her daughter from her in the first place.

Perhaps she feared death, because they might never be together again. Perhaps she thought none of those things. Perhaps sodden and ruddy, she just carried on because that's the only thing she knew how to do.

I reached the bridge over the river – I crossed it with surprising ease, as if I never quite believed I'd ever make it. The clouds kept themselves restrained, the rain did not fall. My way out was assured; you could leave purgatory if you still had the strength to do it.

One day I'll have the guts to find out; see what happened to old Rose. Find out if she died out on the hills or tucked up in bed somewhere. Maybe warm and cared for, probably just alone. This will sound cruel, but I think I'll do it one day when I feel at my lowest, to remind myself just how lucky I am. That whatever lies ahead of me, I can take comfort that at that moment I was able to escape.

I remember keeping my eyes firmly on the road as I drove, never allowing them to drift away to the sides. If she was there watching me as I went, I never saw her. Thank God, I never saw her again.

Case no. 76
CAT LADY

I used to be able to hear her through the walls. You'd hear her talking to them: "What are you doing? What have you got there? Are you being good?" You know, like they were her kids or something.

Used to get on my nerves. When I'm working, I'm up at around five or six. When I'm not working, I still usually wake up same time – can't help it. I'd try going back to sleep but she'd keep me awake talking to the cats. I dunno what was up with that downstairs bedroom. Soon as Chelle moved out I took her room upstairs. It was smaller but at least it was quiet up there.

I dunno how many of them she had. At least three; I mean, there was definitely a black one, a ginger one and a brown one, but I swear they weren't all the same cats – they had different spots and marks on their fur. Used to shit in the back yard. She had no one else living there and I don't think she ever had friends over. Least I never heard them.

Then he showed up. I'd met him a few times down the road in The Lion. He was a cocky prick from the start. All swanky suits and sunglasses, and car keys – he always used to come marching in and slam his keys down on the table like he was cock of the walk just getting home. Tosser.

He was an estate agent or developer or something. Buying up all the derelict and shitty council houses and doing them up to sell on. Mostly for student landlords. You didn't need do anything fancy for the student houses; just paint the walls and put locks on the doors, that's what he used to tell me.

He used to talk to me cos no one else in The Lion wanted to have anything to do with him. Not exactly the most open-minded mob in there; they're the kind of thick-skinned old bastards who think giving women the vote was too much of a fucking liberty. They see a big black guy walk in, flashing his cash, and, well... if he hadn't have been built like a brick-shithouse's dad then they'd have glassed him and kicked his ribs in. Instead they just kept their distance and called him a nigger when his back was turned.

Me, I'll talk to anyone. In my business it's mostly Poles and Russian's these days anyway; they're the only ones desperate enough to do the work. Doesn't pay to be having a problem with where someone's from. Wouldn't get any work if I did. Anyway, what's so great about England anyway that makes us so high and bloody mighty?

Couldn't stand the bastard, but he'd talk to me anyway. I put up with it because I hoped he might throw us a bit of work, us both being in the same sort of business. And when you're out of work, it's not like you got much else to do. Believe it or not, there is only so much Sky Sports that you can watch before you start to go a bit mental.

I think he already knew me from somewhere. But he was like that anyway; he always acted as if he was your best mate, even if you hardly knew him.

So after seeing him down there a few times, suddenly he starts turning up next door. I thought at first that he was the new landlord and wondered whether he'd be paying me a visit too. But the old cat lady turned out to be his aunt; first we'd heard about her having any relatives. Me and Gregg had never seen anyone show up there before except for the postman or when her shopping would get delivered – they'd bring the cat food in on huge trays. I swear that's all they ever brought her; we thought that's what she lived on as well.

He showed up there a few times. It was a bad summer for me, recession and all. I was having to sign on and just had to sit around doing nothing, and it really drives me up the wall. Always like to be busy, you know? And you can't afford owt when you're skint. You search for pennies just to have a pint.

But he'd show up there every so often and a couple of times they'd have a row. You couldn't usually hear her talking to the cats, not in the living room during the day. But you could hear them two going at it. Dunno what about, I used to turn the volume right up. But it didn't take a rocket scientist to guess. And then when he was gone, she'd carry on with the cats. Telling them how she wasn't going to be turfed out of her own home.

After a couple of rows, he didn't show up for a while and he wasn't down The Lion either. Then one day – close to the end of summer I think, cos I had a couple of weeks working for me cousin Nick doing house clearances, but I was back on the dole – I came home and there was an ambulance parked outside our house. I was a bit worried at first; thought Gregg had maybe larged it too much once and for all. But it was outside her house, the cat lady. And I walked to the door, my door, just as they were wheeling her out.

She was zipped up in a bag – finally kicked it. The neighbours had found her – Polish couple. They'd heard the cats making a racket and had gone round to complain. They saw her lying face down in the hallway. Weren't sure how long she'd been there.

Sad way to go, on your own like that. I mean, if those two nosy buggers hadn't looked in she might've laid there for weeks.

You know it was only then that I realised that I had no idea what she looked like. Two years I'd been there. Didn't know what she looked like. Never looked her in the face once in all that time. Pretty sad really, but I suppose that's just what folks are like these days. I only know the Polish pair cos they're always complaining to someone about the bloody noise.

Anyway, he didn't waste his time. They were round there in days clearing the place out, loaded a couple of vans up with junk and then came over to renovate the place. I used to chat to the guy in charge when I saw him; still trying to find work. Apparently the place was covered in cat shit, took 'em days to scrape it all out. The cats were gone though, no sign of them unless Mr Flash took them away. I could imagine him going down the canal in his BMW to drop off a few sacks. He was a caring kind of guy.

Yeah, we all thought he might've had something to do with it. I mean, you're never sure and the police never came round and looked the place over. But he wanted the house, and he got it. And we all thought it was all just a bit of a coincidence, him showing up just a bit before she died. And what happened next... I don't believe in ghosts or any of that shit but that was pretty fucking fucked up.

The house was done-up, the builders had gone and not been back for a couple of days and I'd looked in and the place looked pretty cleaned-up. I was in The Lion and he was there having a drink with some guys who were trying to pretend he wasn't there. He came to talk to me as usual and he started talking about the place. They'd done a really good job getting it ready. No mention of his aunt or anything, nothing said about how devastated he was or anything like that.

He said I should go around and see it. He was pissed and I wasn't interested. But he wanted to go around there and he wanted me to go with him. So just then he starts talking about what I'm up to, what work I'm doing. And he knows full well I ain't up to shit. But he keeps on, there's some stuff I might be able to help him out with up at the house and he could use a guy like me to help him. I'm desperate so I end up going along with it.

He drives me there in his BMW, even though he's drunk. He leads us up the path and steps, keeps going on about how his guys are the best and that's why he pays 'em more. Seemed like the usual bunch of fuckwits to me, but what do I know?

He lets me in and goes on about how the house was in a terrible mess and they'd had to tear up the carpets and rewire the place. Just showing off. First thing I noticed was he'd put in panel flooring, which was going to mean shit loads of noise complaints. He showed me the front room; he wasn't sure whether it was going to be a student house or whether he was going to sell it as normal. So it was just empty, could be a bedroom or a dining room.

It was exactly the same house as ours, just the other way around. Fair play, they'd done a decent job of it mind. But it wasn't anything special. Attic conversion was quite good, and he'd redone the bathroom, new fittings and all. Nice enough – I didn't care, but nice enough.

Living room and kitchen were all right. He laughed about having found that the outhouse was still working, so he'd cleaned it up so they had a second toilet.

The last thing he wanted to show me was the basement. All these old town houses have basements; we had one – dark and filthy without a proper floor and a low ceiling. You couldn't do much with it except dump stuff down there. And the light didn't work, and it was too dark down there to find out where the light was without a torch, so me and Gregg we never went down there. No one ever did – they were all the same in all the houses we went to. The basement was just a dirty room you stored your crap in.

But his house was different. He'd lowered the floor, tiled it up, made it a proper laundry room with a chest freezer and shelves. It was going to be a proper room you could use. He was very proud of this for some reason – I suppose it makes the difference when you've got hundreds of houses that all look the same.

So he opened up the door and took me down the steps in the dark. It was late, so there wasn't much light from outside and the light cord was down at the bottom of the stairs.

He waited till I was at the bottom so he could have his taa-dah moment. He pulled the cord and the light came on.

And yeah, he'd done it up nice: tiled the floor, painted the walls, put in a separate washer and dryer, and the chest freezer like he said. He'd put up shelving units – but the thing we both noticed, the thing we noticed first, is that they were all covered in cats.

They were everywhere, hundreds of 'em; every colour and breed you can think off. They were lined up like a flock of birds, all perched along the tops of the washing machine, dryer and freezer, lined up on all the shelves, one on top of the other. And they were all looking at us, staring right at us.

"What the fuck?" he said, just before I could say it. They were all across the floor too.

They were hissing, baring their teeth. And then one walked slowly up to him, this big fat ginger one. The cat looked up at him for just a moment – then he went straight for his balls.

He screamed and he fell backwards. He grabbed the light cord as he went down and the lights went out – he tore the cord right out. He fell back in to me, pushing me and I sort of fell onto my side, down against the stairs.

They all went for him, hundreds of them – I could feel them crawling over my legs to get at him. It was too dark, I couldn't see much but I could see him throwing his arms about trying to push them off. But there were just too many of them – they were like a living blanket; he tried to throw it off but it just fell back over him. He was grabbing them and sweeping them away but they just came back, climbing over each other to scratch and claw at him.

This one cat – scruffy and mangy – it stood on his shoulders, belly over his face and sank its claws into his head. Went at it like a scratching post; tore up his scalp and drew blood. He shook his head, tried to roll over and then tried to pull it off. Its claws were dug in so far it took flesh off when he threw it away. But as soon as his face was clear, four more cats climbed over the cats on his chest and went over his head and face, covering him. He probably couldn't breathe from under them.

I got my senses back and tried to help him. He was lying across my legs, I couldn't quite stand up. Cats were falling into my lap, but they weren't interested in me; it was as if I wasn't even there.

I put my hands under his shoulders and tried to pull him up. He was screaming like a girl, he was out of his mind with fear, terror. I was able to push myself up the stairs on my heels; I pulled myself from under him and was able to get him part way up.

But the cats didn't give up easy. I could feel 'em moving around my legs, scrambling and jumping up, trying to claw him any place they could. I stumbled most of the way up, but before I got to the top I almost dropped him. They were still climbing all over him and he was still screaming, but he got one hand on the handrail to stop himself from falling. And they went for it; straight away they tried to loosen his grip, bit and scratched his hand and arm. But I got my footing back and got him back onto the landing and pulled him into the living room.

When we were in the light, the cats made a run for it and all piled towards the back door. I dropped him on the carpet – they'd done him up pretty bad; his shirt all torn, with blood soaking through. And his arms were pretty shredded as well. He only had one shoe on – there was just a torn sock with blood stains on it.

It was pretty horrific, but you know, I thought for a moment it wasn't that bad. I mean bad, but not like being cut with a knife, they were all small shallow cuts.

But that's before I saw his face. He had both his hands clutched over it, and you could see the blood running between his fingers. I called an ambulance while he rolled around in agony; he couldn't even speak, he was that traumatised.

They operated as soon as they could, but in the end they couldn't save his eye. He had to have a glass one put in; and you could tell as well, it didn't look very good. And the scars on his forehead didn't heal either, you could see them the last time I saw him. He wasn't driving his BMW then, I can tell you. He avoided me; he's not his confident old self anymore.

I suppose he got what he deserved. If he did what we think he did, that is. The cats certainly thought so.

I was always a dog person anyway. We've got one at home now. You know, just in case.

Case no. 104
IN A BOX

Here goes...

It was five or six years ago. We'd moved into this new house in Letchworth – me and Peter, and Benjamin. He was such a happy boy; so bright and so sweet. He had these big, wide open eyes, bright blue eyes, and this cheeky, enigmatic little smile.

He was only about three or four when we moved. Those were the happiest times of my life. After the difficult first few years of looking after him and struggling with money and work, everything was finally coming together. We were stable, we could afford things – the house, the car – Benjamin didn't need quite as much looking after. Things were so much easier.

You see, I'd been determined to keep up with my work after I gave birth. I wanted to do it, but also because we thought we'd struggle without the money. It was hard to work while Benjamin was little. But then Peter started to become more known, and his income helped to keep us afloat.

But then he recorded that album. It did so well. It changed his life; it changed all our lives. Suddenly we weren't always living on the bread line. We could afford to enjoy life more. We could afford to go away. We could afford a mortgage.

Everything was so perfect, for a time. Benjamin had been such a handful growing up; he was always so hyperactive – he got that from Peter; he could never stay still either. It had been such a struggle getting it all balanced before. When Peter had his breakthrough it was when we were getting Benjamin ready to start school. We moved closer to the school we wanted for him, we could afford the fees and I could spend more time working.

But more than that, I went back to painting; painting just for me. Just enjoying painting without any deadlines or clients or commissions. We all had our space, things were just... right.

Peter's career was going so well that anything seemed possible. We had holidays in the south of France, Italy, and Florida for Disney World for Ben. But success meant more work. Peter became very much in demand. Which was good, for a while...

The hours were long. You know what artists can be like; musicians even worse. Drunks, crack-addicts, hooligans, even schizophrenics. He was selective at first, but sometimes he was pressured into working with people he didn't want to. It's the freelancer's curse: no matter how hard you work, you're always terrified it could dry up at any time.

The late nights and hours were only half the problem. A lot of these kid bands they liked to imitate; they liked to 'pay tribute' to those who came before. Or copy, if you like. So they wanted to record abroad, at the Berlin studios were Bowie and Eno did Low, at Sun Studios where Elvis, Dylan, Cash and Carl Perkins played. And he wanted to go too; why wouldn't he want to work at some of the most iconic studios in the world? Never mind us...

I kept getting stuck alone doing all the work myself. He'd come to me and say "Come on, it's where Bowie did Heroes." So I'd have to go along with it and pretend it was ok for him to leave me alone with Benjamin. He'd be gone for months, maybe coming home a couple of times if he could squeeze it in. Of course, I could afford to get some help for Benjamin, but I didn't want to do that. I felt ashamed to hire a nanny; stupid, really, but I did.

Our parents lived too far away. His mother, Ellen, was very good and would come down from time to time, but my parents were old and my father needed lots of looking after.

And I started to resent his success. I admit that; his career had gone stratospheric and mine hadn't. I didn't care about the design work; I did ok with that, had some good clients. But it was my art I loved and I could never get any interest in my work. In some ways it was better when I wasn't doing it. When I didn't have time, I didn't have time. When I had some time, but not enough time, that's when I became frustrated. It's like I could never focus, never give it the time I needed. There was always something else to do; it's no small job looking after a house and looking after a child at the same time. Not that Benjamin was really much trouble; that was the strange thing, he got to a certain age and he was suddenly no trouble at all.

My God, I was so selfish. Sometimes I'd lash out, get angry and lash out. Poor Benjamin; it wasn't his fault, he was just a child. But it wasn't just that; even though we'd been in Letchworth for a few years I had no friends there, nowhere to go. We had friends in London, but it's not just a short commute. There was hardly enough time for me to go during the day and be back to get Benjamin from school and then of course I had to look after him on weekends too. I felt so isolated. Sometimes friends visited, but not often, they had lives of their own. And I never made a fuss, I felt embarrassed to really tell them how I felt.

We started to row a lot, me and Peter. We would have slanging matches over the phone. And I got so stupid, started to get paranoid about the people he was hanging around with. I didn't really think he'd have an affair or start taking stuff. I was just jealous and afraid that he was leaving me behind.

It all came to a head after he'd been in Jamaica with a band for months. I don't even remember who they were, their success was so short-lived. But at that time they were such a big deal. But they were always fighting and falling out. He wanted to can it, but the record label put so much pressure on him to bring them back something. He managed in the end – I don't think it ever got released.

When he got back he was barely through the door before we started to fight. Things had started to change. While he was away things weren't as they used to be.

Benjamin had gotten into a fight at school. His school was so damn liberal; kids get in fights all the time but they wanted to make a big deal about it. I had to talk to the headmistress. They wanted to talk to both of us. When only I turned up, well, they made such a big deal about that. Benjamin was too introverted; he didn't mix with the other boys, just played by himself. I got angry with them, told them there was nothing wrong at home. But there was something wrong, even if I couldn't explain it.

I couldn't even get Ben to talk about the fight; he said the boys had said bad things, but that's all he'd say. I couldn't make the connection; my Benjamin, quiet, introverted – that wasn't the boy I'd raised. That wasn't who he was.

But he wasn't the handful he used to be. He *was* quiet; he did play by himself and didn't make a fuss. I had the goodest, best behaved boy in the world – he was no trouble at all any more. Sure, he did normal things like sulk if I made him eat things he didn't like, or if we were in a shop he'd ask for toys or sweets or something and throw a tantrum if he didn't get what he wanted. But at home, when we were alone, he was quiet as a mouse. I'd be in the living room, painting all day, and I'd forget he was there. I'd just paint for hours and he'd be... somewhere. It sounds terrible; I hate to say it, but he just didn't seem to want me or need me.

He wasn't noisy, he wasn't loud, he never broke anything. It never occurred to me how strange that was. And then that became a problem – I got stressed because my son was too well behaved. It sounds crazy but I started to feel so distant from him.

We had a showdown, me and Peter; what was more important, his family or his career? He got so angry, as angry as I'd ever seen him. I made him feel guilty and he hated me for it, lashed out. He didn't understand that I was... I was falling apart. This wasn't what I wanted. I wanted us to be together, as a family. That's what it was all for, that's what we'd got married for.

The money wasn't that important. He kept telling me he was doing it for us. But he was doing it for him, for his ego. He liked the limelight, I know he did. He was getting the jet-setting lifestyle he'd always wanted and we were holding him back!

I couldn't make him see how much it was affecting me. He thought it was all rubbish this stuff about Benjamin. He was so damn arrogant; nothing could be wrong with his son – that stung his pride and he was furious. He knew I was jealous, but he didn't know I was holding something back...

I couldn't tell him just how much him being away was really starting to affect me. It was more than just the stress of him not being around, it was something else. I had started... I was beginning to think that something was watching me in the house. That something was following me.

It sounded crazy, and I thought it was. Once I started to notice how quiet it was, how quiet Benjamin was, it started to upset me. I couldn't stand the quiet; I used to put the radio or the television on in any room, just to drown out the silence.

I'd have to work hard to bring Ben out of his own little world, tell him we were going to the park or that we should play a game. Sure, he'd get excited then, start getting involved, but as soon as we stopped, soon as we got home or I'd get distracted from the game, he was gone again. He'd draw, he'd read, play with his building blocks or more often than not just silently wander off.

Sometimes I'd ask him, I'd say "What you thinking about sweetie?" – but he wouldn't answer, he'd just smile enigmatically, or just say "Nothing". Sometimes I felt like getting so angry, but I couldn't, not when he looked at me so sweetly.

One time, do you know what he said? I asked him why he was so quiet, and he said: "Silence is golden." I should've known then that something was wrong, really wrong, but I just couldn't bring myself to face it. I mean, what kind of five-year-old says that?

I became obsessive about noise; there had to be sound everywhere. But I couldn't fill the void; God, it was only a three bedroom terraced house, it wasn't huge, but it started somehow to feel cavernous, huge, empty, vast. And in that atmosphere, in those moments of silence, that's when I started to get the sensation I was being watched.

It could happen at any time, usually when I went out into the hall or onto the landing. I'd just be moving from one room to another, going from the kitchen to the living room, or up the stairs, and I'd get this feeling someone was watching me. I'd just get this sensation I wasn't alone. This, I don't know, shiver – this feeling. I'd turn, and I'd see nothing. And whenever I got this feeling, I felt cold. Dead cold, I'd get shivers all over my body.

I thought at first it must be Benjamin, playing a game with me. But he was never nearby, when it happened. He would always be outside, upstairs or in a different part of the house.

I couldn't admit it at the time, to Peter, or myself – I wouldn't even think about it between incidents – but deep down I couldn't ignore that something was wrong in that house. I couldn't put it into words, into ways he could understand. I thought he was so sensitive and open when we first met; what an idiot I was. What an idiot he was! He was oblivious right up until it was too late!

All the hysteria would come out during our arguments. He underestimated just how fragile I was becoming. I made him swear, made him promise that the travel, the long periods away, they had to stop. I just wasn't going to accept no for an answer. He had to stay around London and stay with us. I tried to convince him that we were better off together, as a family, stronger together. He agreed, but he wasn't completely on board; I could tell, I knew it. But I got his word and that was enough for now.

Things were more... normal, for a while. We got back to playing happy families. We were fine for money, we spent plenty of time together, family days out and the like.

Of course his resentment would bubble up from time to time. I was prepared to slap him if he ever said he felt 'cooped up'. This is what he wanted too – it wasn't just me! He asked me to marry him, start a family. Usually he'd bite his tongue and slip away for a sulk. I gritted my teeth and didn't rise to it, but things eventually got back to normal.

Benjamin was more his old self for a while. More lively, more in the world with the rest of us. He just seemed to connect better with his father, I don't know why or how. I wasn't any different with him, any less affectionate, any less warm, or fun to be around. Maybe he just didn't like me as much. I mean, I did everything I could with him. Everything. We got along fine; but he was never as affectionate with me. I don't know what I did wrong, because I was a good mother to him. I gave him everything I could.

He used to garden with me, that was the one thing we used to do together where I could see that he was having as much fun with me as he was with his father. Before we used to pay for this man to come over and do it. But I decided I was going to do it, because by that point I'd basically given up on my art, there was nothing, just a blockage. I'd lost my touch, if I'd ever had it. Couldn't get inspired, couldn't make anything I started come to life, so I just quit.

He seemed to like gardening and being outside. I think it was the digging and making a mess that appealed to him. Although he liked to see things grow; know that he'd planted something and then see it grow.

He got obsessed with making compost. We bought this compost bin for the outside and he was obsessed with trying to find things to put in. He'd leave some of his food and say he was doing it so we could use it to make compost. An excuse not to eat his vegetables.

Those were probably the last good times we spent together...

Things got so back to normal that when something strange happened, I didn't really notice. A clue to all that had gone on before came up, and I didn't even realise it. I didn't realise its meaning till much later, when it was too late.

This one time, during that happy time, I was putting clothes away and I heard him talking. His bedroom was next to ours and with him being usually so quiet, I went straight over to him to see what was going on.

He was hiding under his duvet talking to someone, but only he was there. I called out his name and he threw himself from under the blankets, like I'd walked in on something secretive.

"Who were you talking to sweetie?" I asked him.

"No one," he said, with a sly little smile.

"Oh," I said. "I thought I heard you."

"No" he said, and dived back under the duvet without saying another word.

Kids have their games; I didn't think much about it at the time. Things were happy again, I didn't want to dwell on the bad times, I'd put them to the back of my mind as much as I could.

You know how it is; you sometimes choose not to believe things you don't want to face. It was happy families again. Everything was supposed to be fine.

We went almost a year playing happy families. Things were truly blissful again. Me and Peter had started to connect like we used to. We even talked about having another child. It seemed like such a good idea, now that everything was back on track again.

It couldn't last though, could it? One day, he announced that _____, the band he'd helped go big, they wanted him for their new album. It was a big deal, could be worth a fortune. But they were recording in America – not England. He'd be gone for six weeks at least, maybe longer. I was livid; just as everything was settled he wanted to take off again.

We had this horrible row. He denied promising that he'd said he'd never go away again, that he'd just agreed not to do it for a while. The opportunity was too big to miss. He approached me as if this was already a done deal and there was no negotiation. We had such a slanging match, it was so bad, but he tricked me into agreeing to it, providing it was one last time.

I can't believe I let him leave us. He should've stayed. This all wouldn't have happened if he'd stayed...

Quickly things started to go back to how they were before. It was term time, so when Benjamin was away I never really felt alone. And then when he was there, his quietness, he was so quiet I wanted to scream. I felt alone when he was there and watched when he wasn't.

Sometimes he felt like a ghost, barely even there with me. I'd hear his creeping footsteps upstairs, just sparsely, like he was creeping around. It would drive me crazy. I kept it all back, I never went crazy mad at him; he seemed so innocent, so serenely in his own world. But when parent's night came around at school, I went to see his teachers and they commented with concern about how detached he was and wanted to know where his father was.

I could see how their minds were working. They were thinking he had a horrible home life, that his father was violent and that I was a drunk and that he had withdrawn from the terrible life he had. The questions they asked, the insinuations, I couldn't take it. I wanted to get up and throttle that woman; that look of fake sympathy and understanding. I did everything I could for that boy, my boy!

I was planning to take him to a therapist, to hell with what Peter thought. This just wasn't natural. At least if I got a therapist to bring him out of his own little world he might not come to hate me.

Then there was this one day I saw him out in the garden. We had these two trees growing, and he was running around them, and I could see him talking to someone. I watched him for a while; he was having a private little game with someone who wasn't there. Was that it? Did he have an imaginary friend? A friend so good that he didn't even need me?

I asked later that day. He was eating his tea and I was doing the washing up. He was quiet again, so I said to him: "Who was that you were talking to?"

He didn't answer, so I asked him again: "Who was that you were talking to outside?"

After pushing some food around his plate, he said: "Wasn't talking to anyone."

"I heard you. I saw you talking to someone outside. Who were you talking to?"

He didn't answer again. I got angry.

"Benjamin who were you talking to?"

"I wasn't talking to anyone!" he shouted. He slammed his knife and fork down, his food half-eaten, and just left. He stormed off upstairs and disappeared.

I was flabbergasted. My too-good-to-be-true, good little boy just didn't do things like that. I felt so guilty, I made myself feel ill. I shouldn't have shouted at him.

That night I really decided I was going to find a therapist for him. I was upstairs in the bedroom, looking through names on my laptop, writing down names, when suddenly, Benjamin was there in the doorway, in his pyjamas ready for bed – he was always so good about that too.

"I'm sorry I shouted Mum. Neil said I wasn't to tell you or anybody his name and I thought he would be upset with me. But now he says it's ok and I can tell you that his name is Neil and that he's my best friend and that we play all the time."

He grinned at me and I looked back at him speechless.

"He thinks you're funny," he said. And then he went back to his bedroom. I sat silently on the bed. I didn't know what to think now. Was I overreacting? Was I going mad? I looked it up online, imaginary friends. Apparently they weren't a bad thing, but a boy of Benjamin's age should be growing out of it.

I went to put him to bed. As I knelt beside him, I said I was glad that he'd told me about Neil. But I asked him, I said "Don't you think you spend too much time playing with Neil?" I said that he needed to be making friends with other boys and girls and that playing with them would be so much better than skulking around at home with Neil.

He suddenly got so angry. His perfect pretty face creased up into an angry, fierce little scowl and he cried: "Neil's my best friend, my best friend in the whole world. I like him better than I like you!"

He rolled over. I yelled at him. I screamed at him: "Don't you ever say something like that to me again. Don't you ever." I tried to roll him back over but he wouldn't move. I gave up, slammed the door and went back to my computer. I was going to find someone to talk with him. This couldn't go on.

The next morning I was adamant that I was going to call one of the names on my list. But early in the morning I got a call from Peter. He was happy, enthusiastic. Recording had been going so well, there wouldn't be any extra time needed. He'd be home within a week.

I wanted to tell him, wanted to raise hell with him. But I was so lonely; I just wanted to hear someone else's voice. And he was in such good spirits, I just couldn't tell him. I felt such shame, a mother who couldn't connect with her son... I couldn't bear the thought of being judged like that.

I just spoke calmly and nicely; he could tell I wasn't completely fine, but I just let it go that time, I didn't want to row. I just wanted him back home. It's horrible to admit you're going mad to someone.

I decided to put off calling someone for just a little longer. If Peter would be home in just over a week, I could discuss it with him. He wouldn't like it, but I wasn't taking no for an answer. He was going to hate me for it, but he'd hate me more if I didn't at least talk to him about it. God knows what he'd think about Neil – but of course Benjamin was all smiles and sunshine when he was there. Peter was so damn perfect; it was just me who was all wrong.

The next day was a Saturday, just me and Benjamin in the house. He was sulking, not talking to me out of anger and spite rather than his usual pretending I wasn't there.

I started to question him about Neil; he didn't give answers very willingly. I asked him about what he'd said the night before and why he wasn't supposed to tell me about Neil.

He said: "Neil said that you'd try to split us up. That you wouldn't understand."

I told him I wasn't trying to split them up, that I just wanted to understand. I asked him where Neil was now. What he looked like.

Neil was apparently a normal boy just like him, although he had blonde hair and freckles. I asked him how long he'd known Neil. Where Neil had come from.

"He's always been here. He's been here for years but only I can see him," he told me.

He skulked away into the living room, leaving me with a horrible thought. That damn feeling, that ominous fear that I wasn't alone. That someone was watching me. That maybe I wasn't just being stupid and paranoid and going mad, that maybe something was there in the house watching me.

The thought creeped me the hell out, oh God, I can't tell you. But I told myself it couldn't be true, that it was all stupid and that everything would be fine once Peter got home. And then maybe after we'd got Ben some help, maybe I should get some help too.

I had to get out of the house. I needed to do some shopping so I dragged Ben along with me, although he didn't want to come and made a sulky nuisance of himself the whole afternoon. Was it this imaginary friend that was keeping him so well behaved? I didn't know what to think, I was so confused; I was in hell.

One of the shops we went into was a charity shop. It was after I'd done the main shop; I'd dropped some old clothes off. I was looking through the clothes and the shoes and Benjamin was looking at the toys and the books. He'd been such a pain I was glad for once that he was quiet. Then suddenly he tugged my sleeve and said "Mum, have you seen this?"

He was all smiles and perk again. He pulled me towards this toy chest. It was about a metre long, painted white with clowns and balls and streamers – hand painted. Good in its way, the clowns were jolly, not frightening. It looked like something that might've come from a fairground. It had certainly been knocked around quite a bit though; the paint was starting to peel off. It wasn't new by any means.

"It's nice isn't it? I could fit all my toys into there and keep my room tidy. Can I have it please Mum?"

The old ladies behind the counter cooed. They loved that; a little boy who wanted to keep his room tidy. They thought he was an angel – I smiled awkwardly, unable obviously to tell them what a nightmare I was in.

The chest was ten pounds, but they said I could have it for eight. Benjamin stretched the word "Please" as long as he could and I... I just ended up being pressured into buying it. He didn't need it, I didn't really like it much. Kids can manipulate you like that, can't they? It was just a stupid chest, it shouldn't have meant anything. But that was the beginning, the beginning of the end...

...No it's all right, I want to go on. I just want to get it all out...

A few days later, just a few days before Peter came home, I was upstairs putting my clothes away. I knew Benjamin was in his room, I'd seen him. But when I came past his door a few minutes later, he wasn't there.

His room was empty, but I was sure he couldn't have gone back down the stairs. Even Benjamin, with his creepy quiet behaviour, wasn't able to shift around that silently, not up and down those creaky old stairs.

Some of his toys were scattered across his floor, so much for him being tidy! Then I noticed that the toys had been dumped right out in front of the chest. As if they'd just been emptied out. I had the sudden instinct to look inside.

I opened up the lid, and inside, half buried in stuffed toys, was Benjamin. He was lying on his back, his arms folded across his chest like a body in a coffin.

I cried his name: "Benjamin". His eyes flicked open.

"What are you doing in there!" I pulled him up by the arms and hoisted him out.

"We were playing hide and seek."

"Playing hide and seek, with who?"

"With Neil."

"Oh for God's sake," I said. I lifted him out and put him down on the floor.

"It was just a game," he shouted, getting defensive.

"Benjamin..." I said, trying not to shout myself. "You could've suffocated in there. Do you know what that means? Air

146

can't get inside and out, you can't breathe. You know about breathing don't you? They've taught you this at school?"

He looked at the floor, which meant he had learnt about it. Then he ran away, down the stairs. I found him hiding in the garden. He refused to come back in, even when it started to rain. I had to physically drag him inside kicking and screaming. He went to bed without his dinner that night; I wasn't afraid to punish him even if Peter was.

The next few days went by so slowly. Ben just had this face on him all the time, like there was a bed smell in the room. He hated me. My son hated me. I couldn't bear it; I never touched him, never laid a bad hand on him.

But I thought I could strangle him. I wanted to strangle my own little boy; what had I done to deserve this?

I just had to wait till Peter came back. His timing couldn't have been better. That day I had been to the doctors and had got caught in traffic on the way back. I called him and he agreed to get Ben from school. He was glad to and everything seemed fine.

Then, when I got home, I noticed something: the chest I'd bought Benjamin was sticking out of the top of the wheelie bin. There was a piece of it lying in the driveway. It had been smashed to pieces and then stuffed into the already overflowing wheelie bin.

I went in confused about what had happened. As soon as I was through the door, Peter came marching towards me ranting and raving. I asked him what the hell was wrong and took him into the living room, closing the door behind us, hoping Benjamin wouldn't hear.

I thought maybe he'd found the list of child therapists and thought I'd gone ahead and contacted one. But it was much stranger than that. He asked me, yelled at me, what the hell I thought I was doing buying that toy chest for Ben?

Didn't I know that he could get himself killed? Didn't I know that children often suffocated in chests like that because they didn't understand that air might not be able to get in? I couldn't understand what he was getting so angry about; I might've thought he'd gone mad if it hadn't already almost happened!

But I couldn't admit that, I was feeling already like I was a terrible mother. I tried to calm him down; that sort of thing had to be exceptionally rare. Death by toy chest; it's not high up on the child fatality list. It's hardly tuberculosis or... playing with matches.

He was sweating, I could tell something else was wrong. I thought maybe he'd found Benjamin lying in the chest again and had been scared witless. He told me that when he grew up someone he knew had died like that. They climbed into a chest and their parents had found them hours later, their face blue, their body cold and lifeless.

That explained it a little, but I knew there was more. Peter was usually so damn unflappable. We had a very frosty dinner; Benjamin was cheerful and talking again but he could see his father was upset so that didn't last long. We had pizza, usually a nice treat, but it wasn't fun.

After I'd put Benjamin to bed I made Peter tell me what had really happened. He didn't want to at first, but I could tell I'd stumbled across something terrible from his past, and I couldn't leave that sort of thing alone. I was his wife; he'd shouldn't be hiding things from me.

Eventually he started to tell me a story. When he was a kid, there were three children on his street and they used to play together. Having children roughly at the same time had made all three families very close and it was not unusual for them to have each other over to their houses or for them to play in the street and go on days out together.

There was Peter, Oscar and Nils – the Lundgren family were Swedish but had lived in England for over a decade. The three children played together all the time from when they were very young, but by the time they were seven or eight most of them had siblings too. Peter had his little brother Lance, who lives in Canada, and Oscar had brothers and so on. The Lundgrens had had a second child, after many problems. Nils had almost died in birth and they'd been told that they might never have another. That's probably what made Nils so shy and scared, Peter had said, that his parents were over-protective of him.

They'd had a little girl they'd called Sigrid and they were going to have a big party after her christening. It was being held at the Lundgren's house and all the three families plus relatives were there.

Out of the three of them, Oscar was sort of the leader, bossing the other two around. Peter was usually happy to go along with it, but Nils was shy and cautious and he'd sometimes get pushed around. Peter said he used to try to stand up for Nils, stop Oscar from picking on him. But often he would become impatient with Nils too and they both might pick on him, maybe bully him a bit.

On the day of the christening the three of them were playing together at the party after, along with Lance who was the oldest of the next generation of kids. They were playing hide and seek around the Lundgren's house, which was the biggest on the street, and somewhere where they didn't normally have the chance to play.

Nils wasn't good at playing hide and seek, despite living there. Oscar kept pestering him that it was because he was afraid of the dark. Nils was getting upset by this and even Lance was starting to tease him too. Peter was trying not to tease him, but he didn't want to defend him too much because he didn't want to look bad in front of Oscar or his brother.

After a while of teasing him, Nils said he could find somewhere to hide, somewhere where no one would ever find him. So Oscar told him to go; it was supposed to be Nils' turn to go look, but Oscar would let him have another go at hiding if he had such a great place to hide. So off he went, but instead of Peter and Lance going to hide too, Oscar thought it would be really funny if they just left him. That they'd pretend he'd found a place to hide so good, that they just couldn't find him.

Lance thought it was hilarious but Peter thought it was harsh. But then Oscar starting laying in to him, telling him he was a baby and that it was funny. Peter went along with it, but after a while, when Nils didn't show up, he went looking for him. He went all over the house looking, but he couldn't find him.

At one point he went into Nils' father's office. None of them had hidden in there, because they thought they might get in trouble. Nils' father was a lawyer and his office was full of paperwork and case files and in there was this chest. And Peter wondered if Nils was there inside. But when he went to the box he noticed there was a latch on the front and that it was on really tight.

He couldn't open it, so he thought Nils couldn't possibly be in there because it couldn't be opened. So eventually he gave up too and went on playing with the others. He had no idea something terrible had happened. So when, after more than half an hour, no one had seen Nils, their parents started to ask about him. And when they started shouting and he didn't answer, they started tearing the place apart looking for him.

Peter said it was almost an hour before they found him. He suffocated to death in that chest. They pulled him out and he was bright blue and ice cold.

His parents blamed it all on Peter and Oscar and their families were no longer friends. Nils' father started to drink heavily and he would shout and yell at Peter and his brother in the street. He and Peter's father got into fights. Nils' father said he'd take them to court but he never did. Eventually they just moved. But it drove a wedge between them and Oscar's family too. While Nils' family blamed both of them, Peter's family blamed Oscar's. He never saw them again after they moved.

Peter told me all this with tears flowing down his face, obviously he had buried these memories away deep and hadn't thought about them or faced them in years. He was less than ten when it all happened.

I listened sympathetically, held him as he cried. But while he told the story one question burned deeply in my mind. A question that had me all in a panic through what he was telling me. When he told me everything and he'd pulled himself back together a bit, I asked him about Nils' name. I asked him whether anyone had ever called Nils Neil?

"All the time," he said. People didn't get that it was a foreign name and people often called him Neil by mistake.

Apparently I fell off the bed and fainted. I don't think I was out very long; I woke up on the bed with Peter standing over me with his concerned face on. Peter wanted to know what had happened, was I alright?

I wasn't alright and I told him. I started to tell him everything about Neil and Benjamin. He didn't believe me at first. He started ranting and raving again about how there was nothing wrong with Benjamin and how he thought I'd got over all this. So I lashed out back at him and told him about the chest, and how I'd found Benjamin inside; threw it in his face to show him I'd been right all along. That our son was acting strange, that he was lost in a world of his own, that there was something else in the house with us!

I mean, what kind of kid has an imaginary friend called Neil? It's not very imaginative is it? And Benjamin had a wonderful imagination.

We argued all night. Peter kept trying to escape the truth; that the ghost of his dead friend had come back and now he was trying to take Benjamin away from us. I know that sounds crazy, but there was no other explanation. It all added up; insane though it sounds, it all made sense.

That next morning, the two of us sat Benjamin down and Peter asked him about Neil.

But Ben said he didn't know anyone called Neil; that he didn't have an imaginary friend and that he didn't know what I was talking about.

I practically screamed the place down; how could he lie like that? And straight away my loyal husband started to doubt everything that I had said. I shouted at Benjamin; he started to cry, tears pouring down his face. The perfect little manipulator.

I was livid, I was screaming the place down. Peter took Benjamin away to his room and then came back down to me and all hell broke loose.

He said I was going insane, that I wasn't the woman he married, that I was making it all up, that I was delusional. He couldn't see that Benjamin was lying to him. That his perfect little son wasn't so perfect. How would he know anything about him; he wasn't even there half the time.

But they'd played it so beautifully – I could prove nothing. Everything I was saying could be disputed. My word against Benjamin's; against the perfect little angel who did nothing wrong when Peter was there. Not a damn thing.

We argued for hours. Peter said I was the one who needed help, not Benjamin. And what's more, I if didn't get it, he was taking Benjamin away from me. He was going to take away my son because I couldn't be trusted with him any more.

I exploded; he said that there was nothing I could do about it. I said I'd call the police, he said he would tell them everything, about all the lies and delusions and about how unstable I was. I had a choice, either I could seek help voluntarily or he would report me to social services.

He was going to call his parents and take Benjamin there while I made up my mind. I was a wreck, bawling with tears, prostrate on the floor. How could he do that to me? My own husband, my own husband!

That bastard. He made me doubt myself again. Could I be imagining it all? Could I be making it all up? Was I really ill? Was it really all my fault? I just didn't know any more. I just didn't know.

All I know was that I didn't want to be alone. That I didn't want to be without my family. They were my life – I didn't have anything else. Without them I had nothing. I was nothing.

Peter couldn't get hold of his parents; that bought me some time. He could hear me crying my eyes out and I think finally he began to feel guilt, and shame. He came back into the kitchen and sat down with me and he tried to say sorry. Said that this was his fault, he should've known earlier that I was breaking down. He shouldn't have left me alone. He had plenty of warning signs and he was too stupid not to have acted on them sooner.

He didn't know what he was talking about, but I was so near suicidal that I would've taken anything. Any small sign of affection, from anyone.

We sat on the floor crying together for more than half an hour. We were going to get help together, we were going to get through this. Fucking idiot; he couldn't see what was staring him in the face.

After a while he said he was going to go upstairs and see if Benjamin was alright. I wasn't crying any more, I was fatigued and barely able to stand up; I had been that emotional. I washed my face and tried to look normal in the vain hope that Benjamin might be convinced that everything was going to be alright, that I was going to be alright.

Peter came back downstairs. He said he couldn't find Benjamin.

We both started shouting. Loud, at the top of our lungs, we yelled his name. We screamed his name. We couldn't find him. He was nowhere to be seen.

We both panicked. Frantically we started tearing the place apart. Opening cupboards, searching under beds, wardrobes anywhere. Peter searched upstairs, I searched downstairs. But there were only so many places to hide. I looked down behind the sofas, behind the television. I opened all the kitchen cupboards, under the table, behind the curtains. I searched under the stairs, pulling out all my canvases; he wasn't there.

I heard Peter pulling down the attic stairs. I checked my phone; he'd already been missing for more than ten minutes! I rushed to the stairs to help Peter.

As I put my foot on the bottom step I got that feeling. Cold shivers up my spine – I was being watched. I threw my head around. There was no one in the corridor, like always, there was nothing there.

But this time, I wasn't so sure and I was desperate, and in a state of panic, I yelled, "Benjamin" knowing, deep down, there was still no one there.

Then I saw it. Just the tiniest of glimpses of a foot, a child's shoe, just protruding from behind the kitchen doorframe.

"Benjamin," I screamed.

A child peered from inside the kitchen; he stood half behind the doorframe, just his left side visible to me.

His hair was blonde, his eyes were brown, his clothes were old and faded – it wasn't Benjamin!

He was smiling at me, malevolently, and then disappeared.

"Benjamin" I screamed and ran into the kitchen. The back door to the garden was wide open. It was pouring with rain outside. The boy was nowhere to be seen, but as I stood in the doorway I saw the door to the shed was not closed either.

I ran across the soggy wet lawn towards the door. I pushed it open and staggered inside. The shed was empty, except for all the tools and sacks of compost.

Compost – I looked towards the windows, below which stood the two compost bins where me and Benjamin used to toss our leftovers and vegetable peelings.

The lid of one of them wasn't properly closed; it was propped up like it had been over-filled.

I ran to it, threw open the lid – two feet pointed out at me from the soil.

I screamed and dug my hands in and pulled at Benjamin's feet. He was dug in so deep I couldn't even pull him out. I dug more, screaming, crying. I tipped the bin over; as it spilled out I was able to get my arms in and pull him out.

He was already cold, my poor little boy. His eyes were closed tight, I couldn't get them open. I tried to resuscitate him, but his mouth was full of soil. There was nothing I could do...

I picked him up and held him to my chest. He was already gone. I fell to the floor in tears, holding my beautiful boy so tight. I was in so much pain, I could barely even see, my eyes were so flooded with tears. The pain – my poor boy, my precious boy.

Benjamin, why did it happen? What did he ever do to deserve this? He was so young...

Peter came in. He saw me on the floor distraught, debilitated, in pain. That mother-fucker; he screamed at me and wrenched Benjamin out of my arms. He ran back across the lawn. I went after him but I got to the kitchen doors and found them locked. He locked me out to get me away from my son.

I banged on the doors, banged on the windows. He tried to resuscitate him. He beat his chest, tried to clear his mouth, but he could do nothing. He brought death into my home and now he could do nothing.

He called the police and ambulance on his mobile. He ignored me, didn't even look in my direction. I beat so hard on those windows that I shattered one of the glass panes but it was too late. Too late. I fell to the floor, onto the soaking wet doorstep.

I picked up a small piece of glass and tried to cut my wrists. I couldn't even do that properly. All the big shards of glass had fallen on the inside.

He did nothing to stop me. He just left me there. And when the police came he told them I'd done it. The mother-fucker told them I'd murdered my own son. My own husband told them I'd killed my own son.

They locked me up for a while. There was a trial, an inquest. That liar told them he'd done nothing, and when I told them it was all his fault, all his fault because he killed that boy all those years ago he flat out fucking denied it. Denied that he'd ever told me about Nils and that that boy had never existed.

They wanted to pin it on me; they all thought I was mad too. But they couldn't prove I hurt my boy. There were no marks on him. I'd have to have incapacitated him to get in there, but there were no marks on him. He'd just climbed in on his own. He just got in by himself and let himself be buried.

I've never seen that mother-fucker since. And I hope he rots in hell.

My beautiful little boy...

THE CALL OF THE SEA

When I think of her, the first thing that comes into my head is her staring out at the sea.

Thinking back, that seemed to always be the first place I'd see her; sat atop the high wall just above the beach. I never found out if she meant it like that, whether she meant for me to always find her there, or whether she was just always there; listening and watching the waves, both transfixed and terrified. Drawn towards the water, but petrified at what she might see beneath the surface. Did she feel it call to her? It's so hard to know what's real anymore. What happened and what didn't...

I've romanticised the past; I probably used to meet her in the dining room or at the arcade, perhaps just around the hotel, in passing. But that's just how I remember her; looking out to the water, always half in this world, half... somewhere else.

We used to take all our holidays in Morecambe. Dad was a man of habits, that's how we ended up going there eight years in a row. Before then, we'd gone to South Wales and stayed at this caravan park, but for some reason we'd stopped going there. Dad probably fell out with the owners; he had a habit of doing that. Morecambe was where his mum used to take him when he was a boy, so it was still old habits again.

This was the late 80s but the rot had not entirely set in. The era of the British seaside resort was coming to the end, but it was not over just yet. I can track the decay back in peeling paint and steel shutters. Each year we'd arrive and there would be more paint peeling from the walls, more concrete patches on the art-deco Midland Hotel; the crazy golf course looking that little bit less crazy; more shops closed and encased in metal. Even Dad, with his entrenched habits, was beginning to turn against the place in those last few years. If it wasn't for Lily we'd probably have stopped going.

Describe her? Her hair was black, over-long, past her shoulders – she just liked it that way. Her eyes were a deep chestnut, large and expressive. Her skin was white, but not pale or sickly; it had a luminous, vibrant quality. I'd go on to talk about her lips and body, but let's keep this sensible. As sensible as possible.

Of course, that was later. When I met her, she would've only been seven or eight. Hard to picture her now as a child, I only remember her as I knew her in those last few years. She always looks like that to me now, whether we're sneaking away to the changing rooms for a snog or building sand castles on the beach with buckets and spades.

I don't remember how we first met; we just became friends with her family. My dad would've met her dad in a pub or something. My dad and her dad, Steve, must've enjoyed drinking together because the following year we were at his hotel, The Bay Star. Quite a big place really, five stories, 40-ish rooms. Not the most attractive building: a square post-war concrete block, but painted a summery cream to fit amongst the seafront pastels.

My mum always used to tell me that whenever we went anywhere on holiday I was always guaranteed to come back with a friend. It's always puzzled me how this could be; I hardly had any friends at school. Yet vaguely it seems to be true, I have scattered memories of companions on camping sites and in playgrounds and in amusement arcades. And sure enough, I was quickly friends with Lily.

Hard to know when or how. There was a games room for kids at the hotel and there were sometimes other children around to play with. But we'd come up for potter's fortnight, which would be earlier in the summer before most schools broke up, so it was usually just me and her at the hotel. And I think her father offered to have me looked after so my parents could spend time together.

She was a bit spoilt at that time I seem to remember; prone to throwing strops when she didn't get what she wanted. I suppose it's natural she might be that way; her mother had died a few years before and her father was pretty protective of her. And he ran the place with her grandmother, and you know what grandparents are like...

Even then she always seemed to have her head in the clouds. Always so deep in her own world. That's when she was really bad tempered, when you disrupted her from one of her little dreams. She'd get really aggravated. But that would change as the years went by. She'd mellow, or sort of keep the dream going while you were around. Singing and humming to herself while you were talking to her or out walking with her, as if she wasn't really paying attention to you.

And I'd ask her, what are you thinking about? And she'd say something like, "I don't know" or "Nothing in particular." And if I really pressed her, she might say "It was just a feeling" or "It was just a moment." It was like she could tune in to a different wave-length to the rest of the world, and just feel it, live in it.

As the years went by, we got on better and I started to look forward to seeing her. It was what I looked forward to about going on holiday. My parents seemed perfectly happy to have me looked after, and by the third year we were going off on excursions to the beach accompanied by members of the hotel staff who weren't needed for an hour or two.

We'd play on the beach, build sand castles, play beach ball, fish amongst the rocks – but we'd never go in the sea. Never go near to the sea...

She was terrified of water. The rock pools were fine, but she refused to go even close to the sea, or the swimming pool at the hotel. I loved the hotel swimming pool, because at that age that was my idea of class – we were at a classy hotel because they had a swimming pool. But Lily didn't like it; she wouldn't even come poolside.

It was so strange because she always seemed so fearless. You know what little girls can be like, screaming and crying at anything. But not her; I never saw her afraid. Not when climbing the rocks, not when riding her bike down the hill. Me, I could get terrified. I was putting on the brakes all the time, but she'd zoom along like nobody's business. She used to terrify the staff at the hotel with her climbing. They'd go blue in the face at her as she scaled the heights of the rocks or the trees.

Never afraid of talking to people either. I suppose you just get used to that living at a hotel. I was shy about talking to strangers, but not her; she'd happily talk to anyone, although she was half in her own world anyway, so she probably didn't really hear them.

By the time we entered our teens we had free-reign to roam where we pleased. The summer we turned 13 I remember quite well; I ran down to her from the hotel, she was there, sitting on the stone wall, looking out over the sea as usual. We went that evening to the arcades, with a tenner from our parents, which seemed like riches in those days. We had chips down by the pier, or what was left of it after the great fire. A seagull came down and lifted a chip right out of her hand – we were so shocked. I went around swinging my coat at the seagulls to frighten them off. I felt so heroic, protecting her from the feathery menace.

Yes, by that time we were growing up and starting to feel like more than just friends. But it was all quite innocent. We were allowed out unsupervised; we hired bicycles to roam up and down the promenade and beyond; spent an afternoon building dams down on the beach – she didn't seem to mind the shallow water running down to the sea, as long as we never went near the wash.

We spent an afternoon at Frontierland – Britain's most decrepit theme park. Nothing ever changed there; same rides, same shows, only more tired and old-looking each year. They used to have this runaway mine train ride; it was done so all the carts made really sharp jolting turns, designed to make you feel like you might tip off the tracks. Looking back, perhaps that wasn't intentional; maybe there really was a risk of someone going over the edge! It's a shopping centre now I think. No great loss to the world.

I never said it, but by then I was really starting to think of her as being like my girlfriend. There was always so much unsaid between us. We'd have these late-night walks along the seafront: she, always in her world, humming along to her own inner-song; and me, desperate to say to her how I really felt.

My parents had already detected that we were becoming more than just friends, and I started to get some very knowing looks from Mum and Dad that made me embarrassed. But it could've been worse. They were very hands-off parents; I was never smothered growing up. Lily's gran, however, was a little more prodding in our relationship, and gave more winks and nudges than my folks did. Her dad on the other hand, he never seemed to really like me. He was never overt in his dislike, but I could tell he wasn't so keen on me. Especially as I got older. I suppose any father with a daughter is bound to be the same.

That was the last summer of my childhood. The next year, well... everything had changed. Although I suppose I hadn't changed that much, she had. She entered her terrible teens and suddenly she wasn't the Lily I knew. I came up for the summer expecting it to be just like it was before. But she was so suddenly different. Suddenly she'd gone all punk.

No wait, grunge – the early nineties... Suddenly she was fashionable, and I was... I was still a kid. Some dorky, geeky pre-teen who wasn't part of the in-crowd.

Suddenly school yard politics were here in Morecambe too. She wasn't there on the wall looking to the sea that year when I went looking for her; she was off with her friends. It wasn't like she hadn't had friends in all those years I'd known her, but for those two weeks she spent most of her time with me; we hardly ever had others join us.

Now she had a gang, three or four girls and a few guys. When she was nowhere to be found that first day, her gran directed me to where I could find her. She'd reached that age of growing up where you find yourself hanging around shops. She was by a late-night Spar with her new friends, pooling money together to try and buy cigarettes and then moving on to the next shop when they were turned away.

I was a nervous weirdo to them. I looked so square in my old jacket and jumper compared to their torn jeans and band T-shirts. She talked to me a little, but it was clear that I was now an embarrassment. She was desperate to fit in and in particular wanted the attention of this tall guy with a long face and spiky hair.

I sort of hung around with them, not saying much. They were too busy talking school gossip and listening to tapes on their Walkmans, pushing their heads together to hear the music on shared head phones. I didn't really know any of the bands; I never really paid much attention to music back then, at home all I had was cassette tapes of old Dad's Army episodes my dad had given me.

I would've thought she was an imposter, a completely different girl if it wasn't for the walk home. I went with her back to the hotel and for a brief while she was that same girl with her head in the clouds I used to know, humming along to a tune only she knew. In the past I'd found it endearing, but now it seemed like a barrier. I was dejected and disappointed; the girl I thought I loved was someone else now.

For the rest of that holiday I hardly saw her. She actively avoided me. I was embarrassing to her; I used to think of us both as outsiders together, but she was on the inside now. It was just me still looking in. I was so upset I moped that fortnight away. I spent virtually the whole time stuck with my parents, and they got pretty sick of my whining and complaining. But honestly, after six years what were we exactly going to discover in Morecambe that was new? All the same places, all the same attractions. I was getting pretty sick of it. The only thing I wanted was no longer within reach.

I think Mum was probably tired of it too, but my father wasn't one for change. Like all truly stubborn people, he'd dig his heels in for no good reason. That's why they divorced in the end. He became so inflexible that he wasn't just stuck in a rut, he was lost in one.

We were good friends with the hotel staff by this time and Lily's grandmother and I always seemed to get on. She was annoyed that Lily had been so mean to me; I don't think she liked Lily's new crowd very much, but I suppose it was understandable that parents might get a bit concerned when you start listening to Nirvana and Happy Mondays and start dressing like you don't wash any more.

By then she was becoming more of a parent to Lily; her father was drinking more and more. The business was struggling and his alcoholism was getting worse and his behaviour was rubbing guests up the wrong way, my dad included.

But Lily's grandmother, I think she must have told her off, because on that last night we were there, she invited me to go the cinema with her. I think she probably planned to go anyway, there were a bunch of her other friends there, she was probably just being charitable.

We went to see Robin Hood, Prince of Thieves, even though none of them seemed bothered about seeing it – generation X types, everything was so 'lame'. They were all older than us too, I hadn't noticed before, but this gang of hers were a few years ahead.

I can't stand to watch that movie now, but at the time I thought it was pretty cool. The guys we went with spent most of the time sniggering about it and making jokes, annoying everyone in the auditorium. I was more annoyed by the spikey-hair guy's arms around Lily. It was hard to follow the film and I wished I'd stayed at the hotel.

Most of the gang snuck out more than half way through, leaving me with Lily and spikey. Then, just as the film was reaching the end, they too snuck down to the fire exit at the bottom of the auditorium and bolted. They'd ditched me as well.

I stayed until the end and then moped my way out of there. Hurt and feeling betrayed, I planned in my head how I would say to my parents that we should stop coming to Morecambe, that it was a miserable and boring place and we should find somewhere else to go on our holidays.

But no sooner had I walked a few feet from the front entrance did I hear Lily's voice again. She shouted my name, or at least, she'd tried to. It had been cut off – she'd been stopped from shouting, abruptly. I turned my head and swore I saw someone disappear from view, hiding behind a wall, just down a driveway leading behind the cinema.

The drive led to a small car park for employees and deliveries. I knew I hadn't imagined hearing her, and although it was raining, I could hear movement; the scrape of heels on the ground.

I started off slowly, but ran as I realised there was a struggle going on. Just as I turned the corner, I spotted them tucked behind a metal skip bin, next to the ramp to the fire escape. I saw spikey-hair, pinning Lily to the wall with one hand clamped over her mouth and the other stopping her body from sliding from under his, telling her to be quiet.

He saw me and was about to tell me to back off. But before he did, I did something, to this day, I can't imagine myself doing: I went right up to him and lamped him one, right in the chops. I think he was as surprised as I was – he fell back and landed against the ramp railing. I didn't know what to do then, but I only paused for a second before I decided the safest thing to do was kick him in the balls and leg it.

Her top was undone and her bra was unfastened. After we'd run down the street and around a corner, we stopped to get her properly dressed. She was cold and shivering – she'd left her coat there, behind the theatre. Neither of us wanted to go back for it. She cried. I put her head on my shoulder and held it there for as long as she wanted. I gave her my coat and took being soaked on the way home like a gentleman.

We walked back home along the seafront, just like the old days. Only this time she wasn't quiet because she was in her own world, it was because she didn't want to talk about what had just happened. I didn't know what to say either, so we walked back in silence.

We got back to the hotel and I asked her if she was going to be ok. She nodded and thanked me for lending her my coat, which she gave back to me. After another awkward moment of quiet, she asked if I was going tomorrow. I said yes and then she said goodbye and that she would see me again next year probably.

We waved sheepishly to each other and parted. It felt like we should've hugged or said something more meaningful, but neither of us could think of anything to say. But as I turned to walk away, I heard her call my name again. I turned back and suddenly she was there in front of me.

She kissed me.

My first kiss.

I don't want to get cheesy but it was... it was like moving to Technicolor. I felt like I drifted inches up off the floor and didn't come down again for about an hour. She didn't even say a word; she just kissed me and went swiftly through the door to her room.

As we packed to leave that year all I wanted to do was stay. Lily didn't seem to be around that morning and I was so desperate to find her and say how much I didn't want to go. But my father wasn't going to let me interrupt his schedule and I couldn't let him know how desperate I was for us to stay longer because of youthful embarrassment.

We packed up, paid and left. But just as we were leaving, I got one final glimpse. She was there, climbing the steps to the hotel with some shopping.

She waved to us as we left and I waved back. I carried that image with me for a hundred miles home with a tear in my eye. The thought that I wouldn't see her now for a whole 12 months hurt so bad; it dug right into my soul and made my chest ache. But what could I do?

She was forever on my mind for the rest of the summer and into the new school term. I wanted her. I wanted her to be mine.

But how could I do it? I wouldn't see her again for a year, how could I stop someone else from making a move on her during that time? What if spikey-hair apologised and weaselled his way back into her heart? I didn't think she was that foolish, but who knew? I sometimes wondered if I really knew her at all. I only saw her for two weeks a year.

I decided after much fretting and worrying that I would write to her. It took weeks; I had to pluck up the courage to do it and then I had to decide what to write. Then it took weeks to write it, draft, redraft, tear up, throw away, start again... it was months before I had something ready to post, but I didn't want my parents to know, so it took me ages to find the address of the hotel. There was no internet then; I had to do my research and visit the library to find a listing and address for the hotel. It was almost the end of October by the time I finally posted the letter.

I'm not even sure what I put in the letter – something probably cringe-worthy about longing and wanting to see her every day. I didn't want to put her off by going too far, but I tried in a clumsy way to tell her just how much I loved her and how I hated that it would be so many months before I would see her again. Most importantly, I wanted to know how she felt about me and whether she cared and thought about me as I thought about her.

I almost chickened out before I sent it; I was so afraid of rejection. I had forgotten how dismissive she had been of me during those two weeks. How she'd been part of a new crowd that would look down on someone as terribly unfashionable and gawky as me.

Weeks passed, then months. Getting an answer was frightening enough, getting no answer was worse. By the time Christmas approached, the chance of getting a response looked bleak and I had already resigned myself to the fact that we would never be together.

My parents' marriage was falling apart; they were barely on speaking terms. Normally my aunt and uncle and cousins would come over and we'd spend Christmas together. But my cousin

Aaron had already suggested that they might stay away that year; that my parents' arguments had already almost spoilt it last year. There would have to be a reckoning between them before the big day. I made myself almost sick with worry not knowing when the explosion might come.

And then the letter came. It was just as school was breaking up and I was still wary about what might happen at Christmas.

I wish I still had that letter. It was just... I was so unhappy and so low and it was exactly what I needed. It brought me comfort and hope and a glimmer of happiness.

Lily thanked me for writing to her; she was happy to receive my letter which had 'shone some light on a dark time'. Her handwriting was so beautiful, so elegant, it practically danced across the page. I'd never realised she was such a gifted writer. It was as if for the first time we were really talking. All the awkwardness, the half-gazes, the things unsaid during those brief visits... suddenly we were communicating honestly, fully, completely...

Though the letter gave me hope, it was far from happy reading. Her father had become worse: he was drinking far too much and now he had suffered from a small stroke, followed by a serious fall down some stairs, breaking his leg.

He'd spent many weeks in hospital and she had worried that he might die. She had already lost her mother and was terrified of losing him too. He was home now, but needed constant care as he was still out of sorts and not fit to run the hotel. She was having to help out more and was struggling with her schoolwork but was managing to get through it as the hotel was not busy. But this too was a problem; her gran and cousins were afraid because they just weren't getting enough guests on season to cope with the quiet off-season.

After going through all her problems, she finally came to my letter and to my utter excitement said she often thought of me too. She was sorry for how she had been when I last visited. She had been fighting with her father and had tried to make new friends and tried to be like them, but realised that it was a mistake and that she would never really fit in with them.

She was sorry she had been cruel to me because, really, we were more alike than she was with any of them. And that, in fact, was one of the things she liked best about me; that she could just be herself and didn't need to worry about what anyone else would think.

She was sorry that we couldn't see each other more often, but now, more than ever, she had little time to herself, having to look after the hotel and do her coursework. We were both heading towards GCSEs and the pressure was on.

She said she would look forward to me writing again and I duly started on a new letter that very night. We became confidants for each other. Each revealing our true and honest thoughts through our letters. I wrote of my worries about my parents, how they were, apparently, starting afresh, giving their marriage one last chance and my doubts that they could ever really change things, my dad especially.

She wrote of her father's loneliness and his struggle with drinking. She thought he had never gotten over her mother's death and that he blamed himself for it, and that had stopped him from ever remarrying. Now his business was failing, she worried too he might sink deeper into depression, because of the years he'd put into the hotel. That summer would be decisive, if it did not make money it would not, in her opinion, survive another year.

We wrote to each other every month. By Easter a great plot had been hatched: our exams were around the corner, but after that we would have months before we had to start college. What if I were to come to Morecambe to work for her father at the hotel? We could spend the whole summer together. I could live there at the hotel, get paid a small amount, as they couldn't afford much; it would help her father and most importantly, we could be together.

I floated the idea to my parents and they said yes. As long as I revised hard, they were all for it. Her father gave the go ahead too – although I bet he needed some convincing.

So I revised hard and did my best. My parents were on their best behaviour, for my benefit, although you don't need raised voices to be affected by that kind of tension.

I couldn't wait to get away. And within a few days of my last exam ending, I was on a bus up to Morecambe. My parents were going to join me mid-August, as was our tradition now that potters' holidays were no longer observed.

I worried a great deal on the way there, self-conscious and nervous as always. I knew her now better than I'd ever known her. But still, seeing somebody for only a few weeks every year made it difficult. Everything had changed so much; we weren't just occasional friends any more. We were something more. Both almost 16 now; there was pressure and my mind was not unexpectedly on sex, although that still seemed like a far-off possibility.

My friends at school, what few of them there were, had spent the last few school weeks joking about it, teasing me about it. I had tried not to listen but I had high hopes and expectations, naturally. But I was more nervous than anything, and the fact that both of us were young for our school year – both with our birthdays in mid-to-late August – meant that I needn't worry until the legal age had been reached. I didn't think either of us wanted to break the law. I had most of the summer to work myself into her affections and make us both ready.

For the second year running she was not there at the sea front, staring out to the sea. She was a little closer to home, cleaning some of the patio furniture on the hotel terrace. It was just a long-lingering hug when I got there. No kiss, but I wasn't disappointed. The smell of her and the warmth of her smile and the sweet timbre of her voice was enough.

She showed me to my room – all staff rooms were on the ground floor. It was a touch dark because the room was just below ground level. It was clad in plasticy fake-wood panelling, giving it a boxy quality – it wasn't very big, but I was just glad to be there.

I didn't arrive till late in the evening, but dinner was still being served in the restaurant and I had a very nice fish and chips. That evening we took a long walk along the sea front. I realised then how much she had grown up. She looked so mature, so adult all of a sudden. She was more confident, more assured, more – I don't know... she looked taller; I remember thinking that she had grown. Perhaps that was just her standing on her own two feet now; all the responsibility had changed her.

She was more with me then than ever before, not drifting on to her own wavelength like the old days; no long mysterious gazes at the sea. But she was still the girl I had known, all smiles and knowing glances. We ducked into a bus shelter on the way, one of those old concrete shed types. We had our first proper snog there. It was worth the wait...

Those first couple of weeks were perfect. We were inseparable; even the early morning starts weren't so bad. Laying the breakfast tables at eight, serving, clearing and washing up until eleven, and then cleaning the rooms and making the beds. That was the best time; we were alone together in bedrooms... No prying eyes, just us together enjoying each other's company, and each other's bodies...

We had to be careful though; her father was suspicious and would come looking for us if we were away too long. He was on his feet again and working, although he did nothing very physical. He was more bad tempered now than ever; he wasn't allowed to drink at least, although that didn't exactly make him any cheerier. Both Lily and her gran were determined to keep him away from the front desk where his attitude might do harm. Bookings were ok, but not stellar, and they couldn't afford to make a bad impression on potential guests. Everyone who seemed to stay there was elderly, there were hardly any young guests. If the commercial decline of the seaside didn't threaten the business, the march of time certainly did.

They really were the best times I think I ever had in my life. We had each other, we had some money to spend; we worked during the day and had the evenings to ourselves. Neither of us, strictly speaking, were old enough to work, so we didn't work when alcohol was being served in the restaurant, just in case there should ever be trouble about it.

The nights we spent in the arcades, at the cinema, the bowling alley or at the cheap bingo halls, trying our best to win tacky souvenirs or knock-off toys. By then, things were getting pretty bleak along the sea front. There were more closed businesses than open ones, and the walls with the peeling paint now had coatings of graffiti and cheap pasted-on posters advertising club nights and local DJs.

It didn't matter though. Those long walks along the promenade, through the parks and gardens, or along the beach – those were my favourite things. They were when we were closest, when we were at our most happy and in love. And they always held the promise of an illicit detour, on a park bench, in a phone box or on the beach.

Everything was so perfect – trust me to throw a spanner in the works. Sometimes I don't think I know how to be happy...

The things was... she was my boss. And after a while, I started to get frustrated. Emasculated, a bit. She worked hard to keep that place running, and sometimes I was pratting around too much and she'd get on at me. It sounds so stupid, but I'd get wound up. It was supposed to be a holiday for me, but it was seven days a week, no time off. It got busier as the schools broke up and her father couldn't or wouldn't hire new staff. So there was so much work to do and she got stressed and started to get impatient and everything started to become less fun and... well... more like work.

I admit I could be a bit lazy sometimes, or slack off a bit. And she'd get annoyed and sometimes just tell me off. And sometimes in front of others and that chided me and got on my nerves. This was the girl who used to sometimes get lost walking in a straight line and now she was telling me off for not paying enough attention to my work.

And she was so confident now. She could talk to anyone, not like me; I still fidgeted and didn't know how to react if a guest started to get annoyed with their room or their breakfast. And guys would flirt with her. We didn't have many younger guests, but she was a good looking girl and guys noticed that. I suppose I felt a bit threatened. No guy likes to feel weak in front of their girlfriend, or to feel that they're weaker than their partner. It was pathetic, but I let my lack of self-esteem get the better of me.

One weekend, I was asked to clean the pool. I had to go around it with a big fishing net and scoop out all the leaves. She came looking for me and stood by the patio doors and asked me to help her put away the food delivery that was due in the afternoon.

While she was giving me her instructions, I noticed that she was stood in the doorway, that she hadn't set foot on the poolside tiles. It suddenly occurred to me – she was still afraid of water.

I pretended I couldn't hear her as she spoke. She spoke louder but I still couldn't hear her, so I told her to come closer. She hesitated but came out onto the tiles, slowly, arms folded. She told me what she wanted, but I think she noticed the slight smirk on my face. She knew that I had remembered her fear.

If we had any free time during the day, it would be on a Tuesday, after guests had been checked out from the weekend and preparations for new guests had been completed. We were still being a bit ratty to each other – we'd been spending too much time together – so when she asked me what I wanted to do that afternoon, I said I wouldn't mind having a swim.

She wasn't keen on the idea; she said her father wouldn't like us swimming when there were guests at the hotel. But there weren't that many, the place was quiet and her dad was away all day, so why would he care?

I asked her if she was still afraid of water. She denied it; neither of us wanted to admit weakness or fault. So I said she should come out with me and take a dip. It would be quiet and relaxing, not like the beach, which she suggested, but I said would be too noisy and too crowded.

So I went to the pool in the afternoon and waited for her. After I'd been swimming for more than half an hour she turned up in shorts and a t-shirt. She had it in mind that she would relax on one of the loungers and maybe read. But I chided her: "Why not just come in for a swim?"

She said she didn't feel like it. I asked her again, "You're not afraid are you?" She said again she wasn't, but she wasn't a good liar and I knew the truth.

"There's nothing to be afraid of," I said. It was just like being in a large bath – which it was, the water was shallow, you'd have to be a midget with weak legs to drown in that pool.

She said again that she wasn't afraid and that she just didn't feel like it. I got out of the pool, and walked over to her. "Just a dip, a quick dip" to show me that she wasn't afraid. I don't know why I had to tease her so badly; I just felt good being in control. And it was just water after all, nothing wrong or difficult about having a swim. You don't even need to swim in a pool so shallow.

She said no and got quite aggressive. I put my arms around her and started to move towards the pool's edge. She started to shout and scream; I didn't take her seriously. I moved my weight over to one foot and let us both topple into the water.

I didn't realise... I thought, at least for a moment, that I was doing her a favour. Showing her that there was nothing to be afraid of. Christ, like there was anything noble about what I was doing to her, tormenting her, wrestling back control like that.

She hit the water and screamed. She became hysterical. Her face was panic-stricken; she howled between breaths. She looked like she was drowning, even though she was swimming – I assumed she couldn't, that she'd never been in water. But she could swim and as I tried to help her, put my arms around her, she pushed me sharply away.

She swam frantically to the side and hoisted herself onto the tiles, slipping on the way and bashing her elbow on the pool's edge. She lay there gasping for air, like she was hyperventilating – I'd traumatised her.

I climbed out quickly and went over to her: her eyes were wide open, her mouth desperately drawing in air. She was shivering, lying on her side like a wounded animal. People from the hotel started to gather around us. I tried to comfort Lily, but she kept pushing me away.

Her grandmother came out. I passed her my towel to wrap her in. "I didn't know," I protested, I didn't know this would happen.

Her grandmother was furious with me. With the help of some of the staff they carried her inside. They didn't know whether to call her a doctor or not. Her gran didn't think so, she'd just had a shock and she'd be alright.

They left me standing there feeling like the biggest bastard in the world. And then he showed up. I was stood there face to face with her father – he hadn't left at all.

He went for me; put both his hands around my neck to throttle me. I couldn't stop him, he was in a frenzy. I couldn't move his hands from around my throat.

I was lucky any of the staff noticed, they were so busy fussing over Lily. It took three people to get him off me. He let go and I went crashing backward over a lounger, hitting my head on the tiles.

"I'll kill you," he shrieked at me. "You won't take her away from me. She's mine, she'll never have her. She'll never get her hands on her."

I was terrified, frightened out of my wits. I swear to you, without exaggerating, that he would've killed me. He was out of control; if those people had not been there he would have strangled me, I know it.

I was so frightened, I just ran. I just took off and found myself running along the beach. For hours I sat amongst the rocks, hating myself, hating her father. But thinking that maybe I'd deserved it.

What had I done to her? I felt like smashing my brains out against the rocks. She was the most important thing in my life, the only thing I had, the only thing I loved. The thought that I'd harmed her, hurt her... it made me feel like taking a knife to myself, cutting my body, ripping out great chunks of flesh as penance for doing such a vile thing.

I was out there for hours, not knowing what to do. I was so scared to go back – and I didn't know what I would find. I was so scared Lily might hate me, that I had done her great harm, that I had really hurt her. And I was scared that her father might kill me; that this time he'd have his chance and would honestly murder me.

I had to go back. I had only my swimming shorts on, by the time it was dark I was utterly freezing. I must've looked a real sight going into the front entrance, dressed at night in my shorts, shivering.

Her grandmother was on the front desk. She looked at me with a mixture of disapproval and pity. Like a pet that's knocked over a priceless vase; foolish, but innocent.

In fact, after a moment, she started to laugh. I did look a right state.

She took me to the kitchen where she gave me a hot drink and reunited me with my clothes. I told her how sorry I was, but she wasn't quite forgiving. She said I should've known better, especially considering how her mother had died.

This was news to me – as far as I knew her mother had died of illness. Her grandmother cursed herself, realising Lily had deliberately withheld the truth. I would've probed her more, but then Lily came in...

Her grandmother left us and I quickly broke down into tears, I felt like such a miserable, spiteful monster. She hugged me and told me that it was all right, that she was fine, she was ok. She had had a bad shock, but she was fine now. That she forgave me, which only served to make me feel more ashamed.

We went out walking along the waterfront and down by the beach. She wanted to tell me the truth. Something she had never talked about before – the reason for her fear of water. How her mother had died...

Her mother had been unwell, that was true. She suffered badly from depression, and after Lily was born, even more so. She was on and off tablets for most of Lily's childhood. She would have bad spells where she would unaccountably become hysterical and unhappy and break down into tears. The pressures of running the hotel would often be too much for her.

When her episodes became worse and more frequent, her doctor recommended changing her medication, because after so many years, her current medicine might no longer be effective. But depression medication is habit-forming; coming off it was no easy task and adapting to new pills was no easy thing either.

Her mother lost all her energy, became very tired all the time. To help her, her father hired more staff so she wouldn't be needed to work at the hotel at all. This was good for a while, but it produced an unexpected new side effect. Her mother became jealous, deadly jealous, and resentful. He was spending more time looking after the hotel than he was with her. She began to feel like the hotel was more important than her.

They would have these blazing rows. She started to hate him talking to other women. Whether they were guests or members of staff – they were all a threat. It was weeks before she was herself again. During this time she would never let Lily out of her sight; whatever else was happening, she could feel happy together with Lily.

For a while it all seemed fine. Her mother seemed back to normal and was helping her father run the hotel again. Then one afternoon, they were supposed to go to a wedding party. It was out of town at another hotel; a cliff-side place near the coast, by a small secluded beach. Her parents had been arguing that morning and no one was in a very good mood when they arrived at the reception.

No one is sure exactly what happened that day. It's thought that maybe Lily's mother saw her father talking and laughing with another woman and that she might have got jealous. Whatever the reason, she took Lily out of the reception after only an hour or so and threw her in the back of the car. She then drove the car down the hillside towards a small private jetty. And drove that car off the end and into the water, with Lily still on the back seat.

She could still remember what happened vividly. Water started to pour in through the doors. She screamed, tried to get her mum to let her out. But her mother wanted her to stay, told her to sit still and stay quiet. It was a miracle that she got out at all, that she somehow found the strength to push open a door and not be swept back inside by the water. She swam her way out of the car and managed to drift up to the surface.

By the time she put her head back above the water, people were running down to the jetty and the wedding guests pulled her out. But it was too late for her mother. They pulled the car out of the water hours later, but her mother's body was gone. They never found it.

That was how she had become so afraid of water; she had almost drowned. And worse, because it was her own mother that had almost done it to her. The person she had trusted most in the whole world. That more than anything must have amplified the trauma.

I felt like such a bastard, putting her through all that again. She said no, that actually, somehow, she felt stronger now. That some great weight had been lifted from her shoulders. That her fear of the water had always preyed upon her mind. Like some great elephant in the room – living by the sea meant it was forever there. A reminder of a tragedy she had always tried to put to the back of her mind.

She forgave me and in that moment I felt more like I didn't deserve her than ever before.

We walked then to the sea front. The tide was not so far in; the waves, not too fierce. We took off our shoes and socks and paddled into the water. We rolled up our trousers to our knees and with our hands held tight we walked that bit further in. The waves lapped at our shins, it was cold, but not so cold.

There were tears in her eyes, but she was not upset. She was emotional, but not afraid. She had faced something horrible from her past and she felt a great relief.

We made love that night. Spontaneously, amongst the sand dunes, where we hoped no one would see us. We were caught up in the moment; we did it without protection – that was so stupid. God knows what we would've done if anything had happened...

But at the time we just felt like part of each other. We'd faced something together and that we were now forever entwined, emotionally locked together in both past and present.

We entered a new phase of peace together, more happy in each other's company than ever before. A new understanding lay between us, a true bond, like we could finish each other's sentences and know what the other was thinking. She didn't have her own strange wavelength, she was here, with me, and in-sync, together.

Her father clearly had not forgiven me and he did not apologise for his attack. I was past caring now; I had a new confidence, more self-assurance. I would not cower to him and we mainly avoided each other's company. And then my parents arrived, still pretending to be happy together. I was glad to see them, but I barely noticed they were there. My mind was only on Lily; she was everything to me now.

A week passed before Lily said she'd like to go into the water again. Though she'd always been afraid of it, she'd always been fascinated by the sea and she'd like to swim in it. We went shopping for her first swimsuit; it was black with pink contoured lines – her two favourite colours.

We went down to the beach late afternoon, just as it was becoming quiet and the tourists were going home. We changed under our towels and made another slow walk out into the waves. We progressed slowly, walking with our feet on the ground, swimming a little, and then gradually moving deeper until she could no longer feel the sand and seaweed beneath her soles.

She was scared but excited. Her breathing was fast, I splashed her in the face playfully to distract and relax her. She splashed me back and we laughed together.

We kissed, kicking gently to keep ourselves afloat.

As we swam a little further, untroubled by the mild waves, I dared her to stick her head under the water. It was a big step for her, more of step than I realised as I jokily dipped my head beneath the surface. As I saw her hesitance, I said she didn't have to and she smiled a little. Then she looked down, pinched her nose and just dipped a little beneath the water.

She popped her head back out just a few moments later, taking a deep breath and smiling. There was nothing to fear in the ocean, in the water.

I said we should try midnight swimming, and always the romantic, that appealed to her greatly. We would have to sneak out though, her father would not care for her being out so late, even though we were both a matter of weeks from turning 16.

Despite her age, she'd never actually snuck out before. Neither of us had. We felt too old to being doing it; we weren't kids any more, but the little thrill made the trip that bit more special.

We went down to the sea front, the waves were a little more rough, but the air was calm and the steady roar was invigorating and exciting without being fearsome or frightening.

We bought our swimming kits but decided, spur of the moment, to go out naked. Skinny dipping. The beach was deserted; there was no one to see us.

We didn't mean to go too far out, just a little. We bobbed and flowed with the waves, kissed under the moonlight. I told her I loved her; she kissed me and said she loved me too.

I teased her, said she was much too slow, and would have to work hard to ever get as good at swimming as me. She said she had a swimming pool and she'd get loads of practice in.

We splashed each other playfully. A big wave roared over us, a bigger wave than we'd expected. I broke through to the other side, wiped the water out of my eyes and saw she was not there with me. For a moment I worried, said her name nervously, until she appeared again above the surface.

I smiled, relieved. "That was a bigger one than I expected," I said.

She nodded: "For a second there..." she began, but then she bobbed back beneath the water.

I swam closer, right to where she was. She came above the water again: "I'm caught on something," she said. "Something's pulling me." And down she went again. Her face, looking upward, barely broke the surface of the water. Water poured into her mouth as she cried "Help!"

I reached in and tried to grab hold of her body, but it was already slipping through my hands. I managed to grab hold of one of her arms and found myself pulled beneath the surface. I pulled back and she came towards me. But then she was tugged back again, her arm almost slipping from my grip.

We sank deeper into the water. She wasn't just caught on something, something was dragging her down. It was dark; opening my eyes, I could barely see anything in the water except the white of Lily's skin. I couldn't see or tell what was pulling her.

I kicked with my feet, giving it everything I'd got. But I could barely pull her back at all. I could see bubbles escaping from Lily's lips; I too could barely hold my breath.

Then for a moment, I thought I'd won. Whatever it was that held her seemed to have slipped. I could feel her coming towards me; she was safe. I was going to rescue her.

But as I looked again to her pale body in the dark ocean, I saw another figure there with us in water. Within just a heartbeat this creature swept a great arm in front of Lily's face, locking its elbow around her neck.

Before I could tell what was happening, its other arm appeared, sweeping towards me, swiping at me. A sharp claw cut into my forehead. I felt its nails move into my flesh and in the moment of shock...

...I let go...

I couldn't help it. And in that moment, not only did I let go, but instinctively, I went up for air.

I gasped, drawing in oxygen desperately. I noticed red water dripping over my eye – I was bleeding. I didn't worry about that; I dived again beneath the water. But in the dark, amongst the waves, I could see nothing.

I swam deep; I swam in circles. I came up for air and I shouted: "Lily! Lily!" I went down again and swam. I swam and I swam, but there was nothing. She was nowhere. There was no sign of her, no sound. I kept swimming, kept diving, but in even my desperation I quickly realised that it was hopeless. That I couldn't find her, that I couldn't see her.

I looked out across the ocean. There was no one. Who could've pulled her under, there was no one there! There was no one there for miles!

I swam back to the beach; I could do nothing else. It was deserted and so was the road. Unable to find help, I went to a call box and called 999. In tears I told them my girlfriend had been washed out to sea and I could not find her.

They responded quickly. A helicopter swept its light across the bay, police and coastguard combed the beach for more than half a mile trying to find a trace of her. They found nothing.

Oh God, when her father came down to the beach... He was inconsolable; he went for me again. He was restrained by the police, but by then I was so far gone that I would've let him do it. The only good thing in my life, the best thing in my whole life was gone and it was my fault. If I'd never taken her into the water...

My parents tried to console me, to protect me, but there was nothing they could say or do. They tried to feebly comfort me by saying that they would find her, but I knew they wouldn't.

I was arrested. They might've assumed an accident, if it not for the cuts across my forehead. Four cuts, the mark of fingernails, long and vicious. An injury caused in self-defense?

And no, they didn't believe my story. How could someone else have been there in the ocean, unseen by either of us? I was at the police station until the following morning. I was not ultimately charged, but that was more for a lack of evidence, perhaps my age too. The scars across my forehead were not enough to convict me, but they all thought I was responsible.

I gave evidence at the inquest. Death by misadventure was the ultimate verdict, but the scars, still prominent, were an uncomfortable sticking point.

Those days were a blur. I was in such a deep depression that I didn't seem to know night from day or one day from another. I know after the accident, we stayed in Morecambe for a few days to help the police, staying at a different hotel. I never went back to The Bay Star again.

Her father didn't come to the inquest. I never saw him again. He, like me, knew what had really happened. It was as if he'd known all along, had a fear or premonition. I kept thinking back to what he'd said at the pool that day I let her fall in; that she'd never have her...

What guilt he must have carried all his life. But by then all kinds of questions were lingering in my mind; those times when she seemed to be half in her own world. The way she used to stare out over the sea. Could there have been something, something always there hanging over them, threatening to take her away? I'd say that was pretty far-fetched, if I'd not seen what I'd seen. If I'd not seen her snatched from my arms...

On that day of the inquest, back in Morecambe: her father wasn't there, but her grandmother was. I remember seeing her leave the hall; she stopped to look at me as I was leaving. I thought for a moment that she was going to come over to me. But instead she turned and left. Did she believe in this... supernatural force? Or did she think what everyone else was thinking? That I was a rapist and that I had drowned her granddaughter...

To this day I'm not sure what my parents thought. It's always hung over me the thought that maybe they might think I did it. They said they believed me, but then this look of doubt would wash over their faces. How could what I have said been true?

What's worse is that it seems like all trace of Lily has slowly disappeared. The letters she wrote to me were destroyed during a flood at my parents' house, soaked through and destroyed. What photos I had of her seem to have vanished; my parents never took many anyway, but Lily doesn't seem to be in any of them.

The Bay Star is gone now. Luxury flats were being built when I, during one lonely summer afternoon, decided to visit Morecambe. The place is looking a little fresher now, some of the peeling paint has gone, the wrecked pier demolished, the shops open again.

I don't know what happened to Lily's family, I never heard from them of course. Maybe her father is still with us. It's possible, but I don't know. The only thing l have left of Lily is my memories, it's as if everything else has been erased.

She was the greatest love of my life. Crazy thing is, I only knew her for about 24 weeks, over a period of eight years. Less than half a year accumulatively of my whole life. But she changed everything. She's an ideal I can't put behind me; none of my other relationships, my other girlfriends, they've never lived up to her.

Her body never washed up on the beach. Like her mother, she's forever lost amongst the waves. I've never been visited by her ghost, but she's haunted me my whole life. A dream that's too good to be true.

Actually, I lied – I do have one thing to remember her by. I've still got the scars; they're here, just under my fringe. That's why I have my hair like this. So I don't have to look at them too often.

ON THE SHOULDER

They told you to be careful coming over to me didn't they? Don't creep up behind him and whatever you do, don't touch him on the shoulder...

Well, yeah, I got a story to tell you; yeah record it if you want. I don't give a fuck what they think and I don't care what you think either.

No offence.

I suppose you'll want it from the beginning? Started in a place like this, only worse. The Crown & Anchor – that was boozer with character; you came off into the street smelling of it. Stained carpets, stink of fags, last year's flies still in the window – the only air that got let in there was when someone's head got put through the window.

Sounds like a shithole, and it was. But it was our shithole. The crew in there, we was close, real close. You didn't get strangers in there, at least not for very long. Used to call it the turning point, the spot on the doormat where, after getting a good look at the place, they'd turn around and go back.

There was a good crowd in there, mostly. There was a time when it were just us City fans. But then the landlord, can't remember his name, fucking gambler, fat bastard; he had to sell up half the place for his debts and then his brother in law takes over. He's a fucking Vale fan, so suddenly the place gets cleaned up and we get this other crowd in. I mean they're fine for a while, but you can't talk about the game anymore, 'cos after nine o'clock when everyone's had a few, it kicks-off.

There were punch-ups and the old bill started getting involved. The new landlord got a warning or some shit. He started having to bar and report folk who got in scraps. So we was all on our best behaviour for a while, but by then some of the Vale lot had already got scared off, so that helped.

But there was this one fucker. Terry his name was, Terry Coles. Fucking mouth-on-legs. Everyone knew Terry Coles, mostly 'cos he could never shut the fuck up. You didn't want to know him, he just started going on at you. On and on. And he used to like winding folk up too. Really funny guy, real funny piss-taker. Worse than that, he was a fucking United fan too.

He used to like needling me, cos I got bit of a rough streak in me. Can't help it, always been like that. You'd think that'd make him leave well alone, but no, it becomes like a bloody challenge. Can you wind Carl up tonight? Can you make him see red? It was like he had a death wish.

So we used to get leery over the matches and the like. It wasn't just that though, he'd always have something fucking funny to say about your clothes and shoes and stuff. It was like he was trying to prove something. You'd come in and he'd take the piss out of your jacket, you'd tell him to piss off, and then he'd have a go because you weren't over the moon that he was taking the piss.

So this one time I just hit him. Smacked him clean off his feet; he wasn't expecting that. Yeah, I could get lairy, but I didn't normally just lash out like that. Course, that put a chip on his shoulder because he couldn't get back at me. My mates and his, if you could call *them* mates - they probably couldn't fucking stand him either – they got in the way and stopped him from taking a swing back at me.

But I was already in trouble with new landlord over a fight a few weeks back. I didn't get in fights often, not like me to just lash out, like I said. But these fucking students had decided to come in, probably just for a laugh and those poncy fucks can rub a man the wrong way with their pants hanging out their trousers and their "We're the fucking bees-knees" future of mankind bloody smugness. I'd had one too many and they'd gotten too fucking noisy, so I told 'em where to go and they got mouthy with me so I lamp one of them. New landlord's son – how was I supposed to know?

So I was about to get barred, when his brother, old landlord and still half-owner – what was his name... He comes and stands up for me; bless him, he's known me for years. Sure I've got a temper, but mostly I keeps to myself, don't cause trouble. So I'm getting my last warning now, do it again and you're out...

I don't want to find myself another local; I don't want to lose me mates. Not over a prick like Terry Coles. He makes a big deal about shaking hands and "forgiving me", and biting my tongue I just goes along with it. But he still knows I can't stand his guts, so that's not the end. Like everyone else, I got to sing his tune and he has to have me licking his boots and hanging on his every stupid word.

I tries to avoid to him, whenever he's there. And he always gives me this look, like "here comes trouble", here comes a headache... I ain't doing nothing, just keeping to myself, enjoying a pint, chatting to me mates. But no, he still has to have his pops and jokes and what else. Can't leave me be.

Well this one night, he went too far. I just had this big fucking row with my lad and I'm in there blowing off steam. I walk in with my face red and he gives me that glance of his and I just shout "What? What's your problem?" He makes out all innocent like he doesn't know what he's doing.

My mates though, they know what it's about so they give me a wide berth. Keep the conversation light. But this tosser Terry, he keeps trying to start with me. Results are on the telly, he's making cracks about City and he's looking at me while he makes them, I know he is.

Then somebody tells him. I don't know who, but somebody tells him my boy's a queer. We've been rowing all afternoon, that's why I'm in a fucking mood. I don't like it and I've never fucking liked it; he's supposed to be a man. But now that he knows, he's got to come over and say something.

So he walks right up to me, while I'm sat at the bar. He slaps his hand on my shoulder and he says to me "Mate, I just heard your son's a poof. Fuck, I wouldn't have that in my family. If my lad turned out to be a batty boy I'd fucking chuck that kid out on the street."

I've had about eight pints and I just fucking lose it. Whatever my son is, he's still my lad and I just couldn't take anybody saying any of that shit about him.

So I pick up my pint and I glass him, smash it right in his fucking face. He goes down and I give him a good fucking kicking, as much as I can before they stop me. He doesn't get back up and the landlord tells me I'm barred so I tell him to fuck off and storm out the place.

Then I goes home and fall asleep in front of the telly. Then about two hours later I get a knock on the door, a loud banging. I wake up and see out the window that it's the fucking filth. I open the door and they tell me that I haven't just glassed Terry Coles, that I've fucking killed him. A shard of glass went straight under his eyelid and pierced his brain.

I'm pissed off my head and I say: "Well that wouldn't do much, cos he ain't got a fucking brain." I know I said that, cos they said it back to me at the trial. I'm pissed out of my head, I didn't know what I was saying, but they still used it against me.

I mean, look, I didn't like the guy. I hated his guts. But I wouldn't have killed him on-purpose. I'm no murderer. But the police have got it in for me and I go down for it, 18 months for manslaughter. Although they let me out after 12. Lucky, lucky me.

They say prison's too soft these days, like a fucking Butlin's holiday camp. But I'm cooped up there with these same tossers for 12 months, nowhere to go, nothing to drink. Can't even watch the game. I make the best of it, read a bit – yeah, I do know how to read.

But Jesus Christ that place did my head in. It was enough to drive me over, but I ain't no coward. No coward's way out for me, even if I did think about it. Thought about it real fucking hard.

So I lose me place and have to move in with my sister and her husband, who's a slimey prick, but I takes it 'cos Lisa's a good girl and she doesn't have to take in an old tosser like me. I gets back on my feet soon enough; if these haulage companies turned their nose up at thugs and hooligans like me they'd have no one bloody working for them. Not that they don't take advantage and cut your pay for it.

Getting me life back on track wasn't the big problem though. I mean, my lad, he ain't talking to me, but there was nowt unusual about that. No, the problem was Terry fucking Coles.

Yeah, I know he's dead. I fucking killed him. But that ain't stopped him from making my life miserable. That ain't stopped him from coming after me...

It happened first one night as I'm coming back from the pub. I've had a couple, not too many, on my best behaviour 'cos I could still get sent back inside. The street's empty, totally quiet, you can't even hear the wind or sound of traffic from the A-road. You could hear a pin drop's echo, that's how quiet it was.

And I'm just walking down the road, on my way home, minding my own business, when I feel it – this great big hand slapping down on my shoulder, just like it were some mate of mine.

I almost jump out of my shoes. I spin around, expecting to see some geezer behind me. But there's no one there. No one there.

The street's empty, but in my head, there's one face I can see; it's Terry Coles, he's just put his hand on my shoulder to express his deep fucking sympathy about my son being a poof. There's no one there, but I can't get that image of him out of my mind. His stupid big eyes and phony, friendly grin.

I run home, I'm that scared shitless.

Next day, I just put it down to the drink. You have a few and you can get strange ideas. I try not to think about it cos it freaks me out. But that next day I promised to take Lisa's eldest Candice up to Hanley for some clothes shopping. That's if you can call 'em clothes. There weren't enough fabric on 'em to blow your nose on.

So I'm walking around with her on a wet Saturday as she goes in and out these shops, none of which I've ever heard of, and then we're heading back to the bus station, and I'm walking down the end of the high street.

It happens again. Great big hand slaps down on my shoulder. I go ice cold and I spin around and I look at all the people and none of them are looking at me. No one's right behind me, they're just walking past me, wondering "What the fuck's wrong with this guy. He's mental."

And I'm going mental, I'm looking at all these people and I start shouting: "Who touched me, who was it? Which one of you put your hand on my shoulder?"

Candice is dying of embarrassment; she don't want me there in the first place. She asks me what I'm doing and I point right at her and shout "Was it you?" She says "Fuck no," – foul mouth she's got – "What the fuck's wrong with you?"

So I'm stood there looking like a bloody lunatic because I know, *I know*, that Terry Coles is there and that he's watching me. Laughing at me.

It was hard that first year. Any place, any time. Terry hasn't changed much; he knows just how to get under your skin...

Like when you're at the checkout, just as you're about to hand over your money. The woman behind the till will say to you, "That's nine-sixty dear", and the hand'll slap down on your shoulder... It's like getting ice-water down your back. It totally knocks the wind out of you. I used to drop me money, spill it all over the floor. He'd do it just then to make me look like an idiot. He likes to make me look stupid.

His other favourite is to do it when I'm playing a game and winning. Whether it was pool or darts or cards, that slap on the shoulder and I'd lose it. The game would be over, I'd be fucked. Couldn't hit a ball, couldn't hit the board, couldn't make a bet...

Bit by bit he started to ruin my life. Can't go for a pint without a slap on the shoulder, and then my pints all over the floor or I'm losing it in front of strangers and kicking off. I couldn't work because you can't drive when some fuck decides to pay you a visit from beyond the grave. I'd be driving and then he'd slap his hand down on me and I'd lose control.

There was this crash, I went off the road. I only took out some hedges, but the cops saw me. Then a few weeks later I stop on the motorway, couldn't help it – he put his hand down on my shoulder and I slam on the brakes. Car goes straight into the back of me, some guy gets whiplash and concussion. Probably lucky there wasn't a pile up. But I lose my license and I lose me job.

It got so fucking bad I couldn't leave the house for a while. Council put me in this dingy flat once Lisa and Nev-ille turfed me out. But I stopped going out, you see this hair, this hair was brown like wood before I went to prison – now look at it: I got fucking old man's hair.

It's the dread of it happening that's the worst. You don't know when it'll happen, you don't know when he's gonna put his hand on your shoulder. He picks his times, he knows exactly when to time it. This one time he even did it when I was taking a piss. Knocks me cock out of my hand and has me piss all over my trousers right before a game.

Big fucking laugh, eh? Sometimes I think I can hear him laughing. Splitting his fucking sides cos he's so funny!

I ended up on benefits; council thought I was agro-phobic – is that what they call it when you can't go outside? Had to go to see a psychiatrist, what a fucking joke...

It had to stop then; I was no fun if I stayed at home. He couldn't humiliate me if I was indoors. No, he had to leave me alone for a while. Let me get my shit back together, let me think maybe he was going to leave me alone.

He left me alone for a long time, maybe six or more months without a touch. He let me get my life back on track. I got a job with a cousin of mine, helping him run his betting shop. I knows my games and my odds and numbers. I get the council to come over and paint my walls get the dingy flat looking a bit brighter. I even talks to my kid a few times. He's happy, so I suppose that's something.

But it wasn't long before he decides to let me know he hasn't forgot about me. This time it wasn't to humiliate me or wind me up. I was just shifting some stuff downstairs from my flat to my storage cupboard on ground floor. I was unlocking the door when his hand came down on my shoulder...

It wasn't a big too-friendly slap like it used to be. It was just this slight touch, just a reminder that he hadn't done with me yet. And I didn't take it like I used to, didn't go ice cold. I was expecting him, if not then, but sometime. I know how this prick's mind works. I knew he'd be back. Pricks like Terry Coles can never leave well alone. That probably annoyed him; I'd got over it a bit you see, there's worse things in life than being tapped by undead wind-up merchants.

I should've pretended, played along. 'Cos now he knew that he had to up his game.

He was quiet again for a while, let months go by before he has another go. I'm at Stoke station, waiting to catch train down to see City away. I'm on my own, cos most people stay away from me these day 'cos they think I'm a nut job. But I'm still going to matches... Fuck the lot of them...

I'm stood on the platform waiting and I see train coming in from the distance. So I pick up my bag ready for when it arrives.

Then, just as it's pulling into the platform, I feel that hand on my shoulder. I go stiff, cold, that's normal – but then that hand pushes me. Shoves me right off the platform.

I land on the tracks, just an inch away from the electric line. The train's coming towards me and people are screaming and shouting and I can see it coming for me and I cover me eyes and I scream, very nearly pissed my pants – no joke.

But Terry, he knows what I don't. That this ain't the long train; it's just a short one, four carriages instead of six. It's already stopped well ahead of me. I'm there screaming on the track like a bloody girl when it's already stopped still.

Fucking hilarious, eh?

That's our new game. He's trying to kill me, but he hasn't decided when yet. So he's toying with me, waiting till I let me guard down. Last week it was the tram – I'm in Manchester for the away game and he gives me a shove just as the tram's coming into stop. I'm out the way fast enough before it can hit me, but if I wasn't on me toes it would've taken me down. Driver has a right go, people are laughing, saying I just jumped out. I don't rise to it; what's the fucking point?

He's had plenty of goes. I can't walk down stairs if there's no bannister. Can't walk down the middle, have to have my hand on the rail; he's had a go at me on stairs more than once.

Can't walk on the road-side of the pavement – he might shove me off. Got to be careful in the kitchen to. You see that? That's what happened when he pushed me against the cooker that one time. Treatment in hospital for second degree burns. Hurt to even wipe my fucking arse on the toilet for weeks.

One day he'll get bored and have done with it. I won't help him, but you know what? I ain't gonna put up that much of a fight either. I mean, what have I got? I got no friends, my family doesn't want me near them. I'm out of work again 'cos my stupid cousin fucked up his taxes. I got no friends and no boozer. No pubs around here will have me in them anymore. I'm trouble, a nutter, a fucking killer!

They only have me in here 'cos they think I'm funny. Fucking students. Crazy Carl, it's all such a fucking laugh to them. Buy Carl a drink and he'll tell you about the ghost that taps him on the shoulder. They have goes sometimes; creep up behind me and touch me on the shoulder to see if I go mental. Sometimes I do, sometimes I don't.

They ought to have barred me here too, but I think I actually bring the punters in. I've become part of the fucking furniture, because I've got nowhere else to go.

So you get it all down... you get it all down for your book so you and your mates can have a good old laugh at Crazy Ole Carl. I look forward to reading about it – I can read you know. Then one day, when you hear about me, how I got mowed down in the road, or pushed off a bridge or drowned in the canal... well, you can have a big fucking laugh then too, can't you?

BENJAMIN WENT TO THE WELL

It's a shame my uncle isn't still alive. He told the story best; he always said I made it sound too much like a film. He was more of a man of words; he could tell the legend so it made the hairs on the back of your neck stand on end. And it's all true, every word of it, at least as far as we know it...

It's become a sort of a family tradition; all of us know it off by heart. We've all been down to where the house stood, seen where the well once was... visited the graves...

My family have owned land here for generations. There was a time when Bullham Brook was a bustling, busy, growing town, but that was when the mine was open. Some people connect the closing of the mine with what happened with the well – all the accidents, though my father was of the mind that it was more to do with corner-cutting and corruption. But superstition might be what's kept it closed...

My father was the first in the family to really study the story, try to separate fact from fiction. I've got it all here, all his papers and it's all borne out. Well, most of it... we've got death certificates, and parish records, testimonies and diaries. And crucially, the police report. Whether it happened exactly how it's supposed to have, who can say? But did something strange, awful and wicked take place on that hillside that night? Of that, there is no doubt.

It was my father's ambition to dig up the well, see if he could find bones. Of course, the money it costs to maintain the estate meant that he could never get the funds together. There was a time when this estate used to make money, but those days are long gone.

It's surprising the story isn't more well known, but I suppose this is an odd corner of the country, not much here. But now, when we have heritage tourists coming up to the house, the Trust like to wheel me out to tell it every so often. My uncle was the master; he relished a chance to tell it. Milked it for everything it was worth...

They called him the terror of Bullham Brook!

From the end of the family estate to the Cliffside tin mine, he ran and roamed, tucked and rolled, tore and trod. He brought chaos to each sleepy corner, to each garden and house from one end of the village to the other. No one was safe.

Ladies cried his name as their well-kept gardens were trodden through; shopkeepers rushed to prevent the chaos of his clumsy fingers; farmers reached for their forks when they heard the squawks and grunts that signalled the terror was near and their livestock needed protection.

Yes, Benjamin Morris was a little monster; precocious, hyper-active and mischievous; forever in and out of trouble. But who could blame him? Bullham Brook had so little to offer a young boy with a fertile imagination and energy to burn. The town was so quiet; he had no brothers or sisters to play with, and there were so few children, and fewer close to his age. Perhaps he merely craved attention; his father was always so busy helping old Parson – Zachariah Parson, my great grandfather – and his mother was so fragile, so highly-strung, so vulnerable, and with her spending so much time in her bed, she could hardly care for the boy and see to all his needs.

Whatever the cause, Benjamin Morris somehow, someway, always seemed to be close to trouble. Yet it must be stressed that Benjamin Morris was not a bad boy. He had not an evil bone in his body. But if it had not been for him, Bullham Brook might be a thriving, bustling town, instead of the ghost town it is today. You can see, if you look down into the valley, where many of the houses used to stand. Though small, this community once thrived. The busy tin mine brought workers, the promise of industry. But within a decade, all that would be undone.

Benjamin Morris would uncover a secret so terrible, so shocking, that it shook this town to its very foundations. When the tin mine closed, beset by accidents and misfortune, the court records would state it was due to carelessness, neglect and corruption. But for those who lived in the town, every accident, every act of unpleasantness was as a result of what Benjamin Morris discovered. People can be superstitious, especially back then, and over time they would leave and desert Bullham Brook. Which is why today, as a village, it is less than a handful of houses and little else but ruins.

The year was 1890. Benjamin was a boy of eleven; he was independent, spirited, and an unwilling student. The law required that he should go to school, which was carried out in the village hall – which is still there – adjoining what was once the church, which is not. His father thought his schooling a waste of time, that he should be learning a profession. If not on the farm, with him, in the mine; a good man, but a little backward-thinking.

When not in school, the fields and hills were Benjamin's stomping ground. Where he ran races, hunted rabbits, fished, made secret hideaways, leaped hedges and climbed trees. He had the lay of the land; he could do virtually as he pleased. There was but one rule – he must never go to the well.

It was his mother's rule, a rule which she imposed with absolute strictness. He had heard it first when he was only five years old. His mother was taking his father his food for lunch when they crossed the hillside field where the well lay, the only mark on the otherwise unspoiled landscape.

Already a keen explorer, the young Benjamin ran toward the otherwise unremarkable stone ring, but his mother screamed for him to come back to her. Prone to hysterics, she shrieked at him and made him swear that he would never go near the well, that he must promise to her that he would never, ever, go to the well.

It was foolish of her. Had she merely warned him that a well was no place for a child to play, then he might simply have never thought to go there again. However, her overbearing insistance that he must never, *ever*, go near this otherwise ordinary landmark instilled it with a sense of mystique. And although he obeyed his mother, he would never forget that spot and over the years it must have preyed on his curiosity many times.

But he obeyed; whatever havoc he might have wreaked, he was at heart a good boy. His mother's warning was severe enough for him to fear the consequences he might face if he were to visit the well.

He kept his promise to his mother; he kept it until he was eleven years old. As I've said, he was not a good student, and at school he was the bane of the school mistress, Miss Claxton, to all accounts a nasty, rather spiteful old spinster. The children are said to have called her Miss Bones because of her emaciated, sinewy frame. She had under her tutelage about 20 pupils, all of different ages, which one imagines would not have made her job simple and might well have contributed to her legendary temper.

Miss Bones was one of the three people Benjamin hated most in the world. He hated her boring lessons and the way she appeared to pick on him. But there was one person in class who he hated even more, one person who haunted him and persecuted and bated him more than anyone else.

That was Penelope Lucinda Revile. Penelope was the daughter of one of the mine owners, a new wealthy breed who had come to town. She saw herself as above the other students in the class and Benjamin particularly, who was roughly her age and therefore a kind of, shall we say, competitor. Now we've all known a Penelope at some point in our lives, usually as children; the sweetest of sweet girls – butter would not melt in her mouth. But when backs were turned, a different creature entirely...

Now, the situation, as told, is that during one of the school break times, the children were playing in the yard. Benjamin was playing alone with a ball and Penelope decided she wanted to play with the ball too. He did not want to, but Penelope insisted and Miss Claxton forced him. But he could not play well enough for her; he wasn't throwing the ball hard enough or he was throwing it too hard. And Miss Claxton, being well disposed to the spoilt young Ms Revile – perhaps giving deferential treatment to one she saw as being of a better class – kept telling off young Benjamin, though all he wanted to do was play alone.

Penelope tormented him all through play time. He was giving up too easily; she wasn't having enough fun with him. He wasn't responding as fiercely as she'd hoped. So, as the children queued to go back to the classroom, she waited behind Benjamin. And when Benjamin went back into the classroom, she took the ball from his hands and threw it across the classroom, smashing one of the teacher's potted plants and spilling soil onto the classroom floor.

"Benjamin!" his teacher screamed – now she'd done it; he was in for it now. The shrill, shrieking Miss Bones decided that his behaviour was so bad, so intolerable, that he must be taken to the vicar for punishment.

Now Benjamin might well have hated the strict Miss Bones and the brat Penelope, but they were nothing compared to the vicar. Of him, we know a great deal. He had been a soldier before he had become a man of God. He had been in the first Boer war, where he is said to have killed more than 40 tribesmen, although that seems like hearsay. Nevertheless, he was proud of his war service and his rooms were full of tribal relics, animals and various foreign curiosities. He himself was a big hulking brute of a man – there is a photograph in the archive – 6ft tall, with wide shoulders and a slanted face, with a small scar on his cheek and a larger one across his forehead.

A certainly frightening vision for anyone, never mind an eleven-year-old boy.

On seeing the young Benjamin enter his office, the vicar threw down his pen and exclaimed, "What has the accursed boy done this time?"

Tugging the boy by the ear into the middle of the office, Miss Claxton spoke hysterically of Benjamin's supposed transgression. Apparently the plant pot smashed was a gift from the vicar to Miss Claxton, who doted on him and treasured this return of his affection. Benjamin protested his innocence: "I haven't done anything, she's lying." The vicar struck him: "You'll speak when you're spoken to!"

Refusing to admit to breaking the plant pot, and for calling his teacher a liar, there could be only one punishment – the cane! The vicar is said to have been merciless in his use of the cane, but in Benjamin's case, he would've been even more severe. For the vicar was in fact Benjamin's uncle!

"To think that the same blood flows through our veins!" is what he'd say to Benjamin. And not only would he deal the severest of physical punishments, he would also be sure to convey all that had occurred to his sister – Benjamin's mother.

Yes, there was no one Benjamin hated more than his uncle.

He quivered and cried as he pulled down his trousers and leant over the vicar's desk.

"Don't blubber," The vicar commanded. "You know full well what happens when you're brought into this office. I live in eternal hope that one day you'll learn to behave yourself and do what you're told. But until then you will be made to suffer the consequences of all the terrible things you do."

He ruthlessly gave Benjamin six whip-strokes of his cane, causing the boy's knees to buckle as he squealed in pain. But the vicar heeded none of his cries, and waited promptly for the boy to quieten down and straighten his legs before unleashing each following stroke.

Benjamin could barely contain his tears when he was led back to the classroom, returning to his seat with his bottom burning and forced to continue his lessons and then stay after school as further punishment. If the stinging pain was not enough, he now dreaded returning home and facing his mother, who could well unleash further punishment.

Desperately he waited; Miss Claxton made him clean the desks and sweep the floor and clean the blackboard as further punishment. He would ask, "Can I go now miss?", and she would clip him around the ear and tell him to wait...

Eventually she let him go – and then he bolted for it. The vicar would take a long walk in the afternoon; if he was at least to have a chance to give his mother his side of the story first, he had no time to lose. He raced over cobbled streets, leapt over walls, bounded through bushes, desperate to reach his home before the vicar.

He thought he'd made it. When he reached his home, all was quiet. He walked through the front door and called for his mother and she did not answer. He went through the living room, into the dining room and into the kitchen and there was still no sign. He thought perhaps he had been lucky; perhaps the vicar had come while his mother was away and had not had the chance to tell her.

He felt a rush of relief. He had escaped yet another thrashing.

But his relief was short lived; moving slowly past the kitchen window he saw the vicar – back on his bicycle! And then entering from the back garden was his mother, fresh from picking apples in the garden. Her face was taut and twitching.

"You've been at it again haven't you!" she said.

"I didn't do anything!" Benjamin pleaded. But he knew she would never believe him. Who would believe – at least back then – the words of a naughty boy over that of the vicar, especially one who is a member of the family?

His mother had a temper; she picked him up and she shook him. "Albie says I should send you away" – for that was the vicar's name. "Send you somewhere where they'll teach you some respect!"

This idea was more horrifying than any other to Benjamin. He was lonely out in the country, but it was his home and a place full of adventure. And however he might feel about his mother's temper tantrums, he had no wish to be taken away from his family.

"I won't go," he shouted.

"You'll do as you're told," she shouted back.

"Father won't let me go." Benjamin insisted. "He hates the vicar and I hate him too."

His mother slapped him: "Don't you speak that way about a man of God!"

His mother rarely struck him, not with her hand. For her to take her hand to him meant that she might be on the verge of one of her bad episodes. Frightened and upset, he felt he had only one course of action to take and that was to go for his father.

He ran from the house, down the driveway and leapt over the stone wall at the other side of the road – that wall is still there, should you want to see it. His mother shrieked at him to come back but he stayed crouched down behind the wall until he heard his mother slam the door shut behind her and it was safe to come out.

From there, Benjamin made his way into the woods, the place where he felt the most safe. That might sound strange to you and I, but there he was away from bad tempered parents and teachers and punishing men of the cloth. He had the freedom there to do as he pleased with no one to tell him otherwise. He probably knew the woods as well as anyone who lived in Bullham Brook. He knew the best places to fish, the best places to hide, the best trees to climb, the place where couples might meet to avoid the prying eyes of others – or so they thought.

He had little time to take in his surroundings; he was still going as fast as he could to reach his father, though he was by now naturally very tired, having already run so far to reach his home earlier.

Benjamin's father worked long hours on the farm; my great grandfather Zachariah was old, but a generous man of benevolent nature. He was good to those who worked for him and he inspired great loyalty in them. That was good for most, but for a boy with a highly-strung mother, it meant long absences and too much time spent alone with a parent who could be difficult to handle, especially for a boy of that age.

At some point during his journey to see his father, he got so tired he had to stop and rest. He approached the river, which runs through the forest.

He would've stopped to catch his breath, perhaps washed his face in the water, taken a drink to quench his thirst. He waited for some short time to recover; but he was not to have much peace in what was normally his sanctuary.

At some point he was approached by one of the last people he would've expected to see out there in the woods. His childhood nemesis, Penelope!

"What are you doing here Sourface?" – that's what she used to call him.

Benjamin wanted to get revenge on Penelope. Her turning up was a pain, but out here in the woods there was no teacher to protect her.

He said he would hit her.

"You'd hit a girl would you?"

"You're not a girl, you're disgusting!"

"You wouldn't dare," she goaded him. "You're a coward, a yellow-bellied stinking coward!"

Benjamin protested, but Penelope wished to prove to him that he was a coward and that he was not as brave as she was...

So she told him that she had been to the well – the only place in the valley she knew he had never been to.

Benjamin insisted she was lying, but she would not back down: "I have so been up there. I know you haven't because you're such a coward. A little yellow-bellied coward."

"I am not scared," Benjamin cried.

"I go wherever I like," she cried. "I'm not afraid. I think I might just tell my mum that I saw you up there, so she can tell your mum and get you into more trouble."

Angry, Benjamin chased Penelope away. If he had not been so tired he might well have caught her, but she got away.

Everything was going wrong for him that day. If Penelope's taunts were not enough, he also slipped on the stepping stones that he used every time to take him from one side of the river to the other. His trousers were soaked through to his knees, nothing it seemed, could go right for him.

It was quite a trek across the hillside to reach his father. A straight path would take Benjamin up to a high road which would take him to where he might expect to find him. But he was too tired to face the steep climb and ended up walking off course, gradually up the side of the hill, forcing his way through the tall grass, thick and heavy – it was an unwise path and even more tiring for him.

He was only eleven, not yet so tall. Lost amongst the tall stems he drifted further off course than he expected. But the grass thinned after a while and he found himself unable to quite gather his bearings. How far had he drifted...

He soon found out. As his eyes drifted across the landscape they found a landmark he had not expected to find...

...The well...

He had not seen this patch of land in years. He had never been this close to the dreaded place his mother made him swear he would never go near.

He was – unimpressed. Looking upon the dull stone ring he could not help but feel a sense of anti-climax, what was all the fuss about? Parts of the river, the wood, the mine – they were much more dangerous looking than this unremarkable landmark. What was so special about this place?

This stoked the fire of his curiosity once more. Why would his mother make him swear off going to such an ordinary place? He stopped to think for a moment. He had sworn to his mother never to go near it, that was true, but he was angry at her for striking him and for always taking the word of the vicious vicar. Also, there had been Penelope's threat. She made such threats often; she liked to toy with him. But she might follow through, tell her mother who might then tell his own mother. But would Penelope admit to going to the well too? Surely she wasn't allowed to go up this part of the hillside? If he wasn't, why should she?

If he was to be blamed for going to the well, he might as well have a look. And if Penelope didn't say anything to her mother, well, there was no one to see him out here. No one else to tell on him.

So he went to the well. It was not so far for him to go, but he was so tired by then. When he reached the stone wall, he slouched tired against it. The wall was still strong, it held his weight without strain. He felt the stone; it was cold and riddled with moss.

It was getting late in the afternoon now. The sky was beginning to darken. He wondered whether it was worth continuing on to his father; he might already be on his way home.

After applying some force to the well wall, to see if indeed it was strong, he put his head over the top to look down into its depths. Unsurprisingly, it was dark, and deep. It was hard to tell from where Benjamin was standing just how deep it went. To find out, he rummaged amongst the grass for a stone. When he found one, he went back to the well and dropped it down.

It fell without a sound and disappeared. There was no splash, no thud – no noise whatsoever except for the whistle of the wind in the air.

Benjamin was disappointed and thoroughly unimpressed. The well was such a let-down, what on earth could all the fuss have been about?

He wasn't sure what to do now. Go home and face his mother, or go on up the hillside and hope his father had not already left for home and that he could get his side of the story across first?

Tired as he was, he felt it better to take the chance and see if his father was still there at the farm. It might at least help him to avoid further recriminations from his mother.

He turned away from the well, taking but a few steps, when he heard:

"Is someone there?"

He froze cold on the spot. He had heard a voice, very loud and clear. He turned around, swept his eyes across the hillside. He could see no one there, although it would be easy for someone to hide amongst the tall grass. Yet the voice had come from someone near, and surely he could've spotted someone hiding so close. But he could see nothing.

Scared and unsettled, he dared to say "Hello," not too loud and not too quietly.

"Down here," said the voice. And then Benjamin realised – the voice had come from the well! He walked slowly to the well's wall and looked down within.

"There you are," said the voice. "I can see you now."

Benjamin was panicked: "Have you fallen? I must get help."

"No, no, that was a long time ago. I live down here now."

"You live down there?"

"Yes, it's my home."

Benjamin was confused. "You can't live in a well."

"I can, I'm special."

"But, it's so dark down there."

"I like the dark," said his new friend. "Do you?"

"I don't like the dark."

"There's no need to be scared of it. Not when there's strong walls around you. What's your name?"

Benjamin was still a little scared. But the voice from the depths was friendly; it was the voice of a boy, just like him, only, maybe, a bit older.

"My name is Benjamin. What's yours?"

"That's a good question Benjamin. I don't think I've ever had a name. I've been down here such a long time..."

"But what shall I call you?" Benjamin asked.

"Oh – nothing," said the voice. "I'm just the boy in the well. Can I ask you something Benjamin, my friend? I can call you that can't I? I don't have any friends you see, no one ever comes to the well."

"Yes," said Benjamin, with a touch of uncertainty. "I'm your... friend."

"Oh thank you Benjamin. I get so lonely up here. Do you have many friends?"

"No," said Benjamin sadly. "No I don't."

"Well then, that's even better. We can be friends together. I could tell you were unhappy, that's what I was going to ask you. Why are you so unhappy Benjamin?"

Had anyone else asked how he was feeling, Benjamin might well have just said, "Fine!" and then refused to elaborate. But for a moment he was disarmed by the boy in the well's friendly manner and he could barely stop himself from shedding a tear.

"Because everything's so unfair," he said. "I'm always being shouted at and beaten, and for things I didn't do! And my mum's always throwing tantrums and my father's never there to stop her. Then there's the vicar who hates me. Everybody hates me and I've done nothing wrong, nothing, nothing wrong!"

Benjamin cried. The voice was silent for a moment.

"You've had a rotten time haven't you?" it said.

Benjamin nodded; he wiped the tears from his eyes.

"Do you want to know something?"

"What?" he sobbed.

"I hate the vicar too."

"Really?" Benjamin cried. Everyone seemed to love the vicar, especially all the town's women.

"He's horrible," said the boy in the well. "I may live in the dark, but I can see so much Benjamin, more than you could ever know. I know what he's like, he's been terrible to you hasn't he?"

"He's always causing trouble. Father hates him too, he doesn't want him to come to the house, but he comes anyway, because he's mother's brother. I try to avoid him, but Penelope Revile's always getting me in trouble."

"Penelope Revile... she's that little blonde girl that everybody likes?"

"She's horrible, horrible! I hate her."

"Oh I know. I told you, I can see all kinds of things you wouldn't even know about, there are no secrets from me."

Benjamin had started to cry again.

"Don't cry Benjamin. Do you want to know a secret? A secret about Penelope Revile."

"What?" Benjamin's eyes became bright for a moment.

"She's a little thief. She steals from Mr Wittle's shop!"

"From Mr Wittle's?" Mr Wittle was the grocer, a fat, jolly man who Benjamin actually liked and who was kind to him and always gave him a few extra sweets when he bought them.

"Every week, her mother lets her spend the change from the shopping and she buys sweets. But while Mr Wittle turns to get them, she takes a bar of chocolate from the shelf in front of the counter and slips it into her coat pocket.

"Mr Wittle's such a nice man; stealing's such a horrible thing to do isn't it?"

"You shouldn't steal." Benjamin was deep in thought.

"You're going to catch her aren't you? Catch her in the act. That would be a just revenge, wouldn't it?"

"Yeah. I can make everyone see what she's really like". Benjamin could barely contain his excitement.

"That'll show her, won't it?"

"Yes!" Benjamin was suddenly full of energy again. He was almost jumping with excitement.

"You feel better now don't you?"

He nodded vigorously.

"Good. I knew you would. You see, this is what friends do. They help each other out don't they? I mean, if I needed you to help me with something, you'd do it wouldn't you?"

"Yes, of course I would," Benjamin declared.

"You're such a good friend Benjamin. We're going to be really good friends you and I. But you should get a move on. Your father will be leaving Parson's farm soon."

"How do you know?"

"I told you, I can see all kinds of things from down here. Who knows, Benjamin? Maybe one day I might show you how to see in the dark too."

Benjamin turned and began to run.

"Thank you so much."

"Don't forget to come back and visit me soon," said the boy. "Don't forget…"

It was as if from that very moment, things started to look up for poor Benjamin. His father was still there at the farm and he told him all that had had happened, or at least a close version of the truth. Even his father was taken in by Penelope Revile, so he had to alter the facts accordingly. His lie was that he had thrown the ball in class, but had meant it for one of the other children. He had not meant for it to knock over Miss Claxton's plant. That was just an accident...

His father might not have believed him in full, if it were not for his mention of the vicar, for whom his father shared a similar enmity. This swayed him to Benjamin's side. When they went home that night, Benjamin waited in the kitchen while his father calmed his mother and seemed to rectify the situation. Benjamin was sent to bed with only an apple and some stale bread for his dinner, but at least he was spared another beating.

The next day was a Saturday and Benjamin could not wait for his chance to see if the boy in the well was right about Penelope's stealing. He awoke especially early and snuck out to go down to Mr Wittle's shop and wait for her, though he knew not when she would actually appear.

He loitered outside the bakery next door, until he was chased off by the baker. He then stood waiting across the road in front of the post office for his quarry to arrive. He waited a long time before Penelope finally came skipping along, happy as pie. Benjamin watched as she went into the bakers before finally going into Mr Wittle's shop, right into his trap.

He went swiftly across the road and peered through the shop window. Penelope was reading her shopping list to old Wittle and he was showing her where the right wares were, or retrieving them himself for her.

Benjamin snuck himself into the shop quietly, not wishing for Penelope or Wittle to see him. He hid behind the end of some shelves waiting for his chance. Wittle rang up Penelope's bill and she calculated how much change she would have from the money her mother had given her. When she worked out how many sweets she could have, she asked Wittle for some sweets so conveniently placed on a high shelf. The shopkeeper reached for his stool, stood on it and reached up to the jar.

It was at that moment that Benjamin saw it; he saw Penelope silently lift a bar of chocolate from in front of the till and slide it behind her coat buttons into her inside pocket.

Benjamin leapt into action, screaming "Thief, thief!"

Penelope screamed at him, denying it. But she was caught red-handed...

Mr Wittle was horrified. Who would've thought it? Good little Penelope Lucinda Revile, stealing from him. He sent Benjamin to fetch her mother – stealing was a very serious crime. With his nemesis crying, Benjamin skipped to her home positively triumphant. Penelope's mother didn't believe him, but when she arrived at the shop, she had no choice but to accept her little angel was not so angelic.

Benjamin watched with satisfaction as his goody-two-shoes enemy was dragged away. He had won an important victory, and what's more, he had found a new friend. A very special friend...

So excited was he of his victory over Penelope he ran straight back to the well, to thank the mysterious boy: "It worked, it worked!" Benjamin cried.

"I knew it would," said the boy in the well. "No one is going to look at her in the same way again. Her disguise has been uncovered; she was not what she seemed."

"No, she's horrible and I hate her and she got what she deserved."

"Yes Benjamin, many people are not what they seem. They hide behind disguises and pretend to be what they're not. But we'll uncover those disguises won't we? Show the world what those people are really like".

Benjamin was so excited, but the boy told him he must run on home because his mother was looking for him. Benjamin asked the boy in the well how he could see beyond his home, but the boy said it was a secret he couldn't tell him yet. But soon he would. Soon he would show him the world inside the well...

In the meantime, Benjamin still had more scores to settle, and the boy promised he would help him to settle them. After horrid Penelope, the next on the list was Miss Bones, his horrid teacher. The boy had an idea how he could get his own back on her too, and Benjamin positively couldn't wait to put the plan in action.

It was but a few days after he had caught out Penelope that he put in practice the boy's new plan. It was on a rainy Wednesday afternoon that Miss Claxton was doing multiplication revision – barking sums at her assembled pupils, insistent that they must deliver the answer back to her almost instantaneously, or receive a ruler strike across the knuckles. That very afternoon, we know that a boy named Richard Price, a mere boy of seven, had his hand turned red from the merciless teacher – she did not alter the punishment, regardless of age.

Fortunately, Benjamin had a good memory, and like most of the class, he knew his tables well to avoid any punishment. Benjamin was fortunate that day that the rain was falling, otherwise he might not have been able to see Miss Bones get what she deserved. Because of the weather, they would not have to eat their sandwiches outside, or cross to the church hall. They sat indoors, eating their lunches quietly, permitted only to play the quietest, calmest of games.

As Benjamin opened up his lunch, he did not take his eyes off of his teacher, waiting impatiently as she fiddled around her desk, adjusted her hair, tidied away some of her papers...

Finally, she reached for her bottom drawer and lifted out the tin box where she kept her own lunch. Benjamin raised his head, gripping the desk in his palms with anticipation.

She opened the box distractedly, and placed her hand inside. But almost instantly, afterward, she withdrew it, and then her jaw dropped open. She stood up abruptly, scraping her chair against the floor behind her. She started to scream and gasp for air simultaneously, warming up for an almighty screech, one that raised goose bumps on all the children's skin.

She tried to climb out of the window behind her; she started to scratch at the glass, screaming "Get away, get away." She kicked at the desk from her place on the window's ledge, knocking it over. And then the children saw what she so afraid of: the lunchbox slid across the floor, and from its inside hopped a great big toad!

The girls in the glass screamed, scattering the desks and chairs as they ran away from the creature. Of course the boys were not afraid – they thought it was so comical. Still, none of them wished to take hold of the toad and they had to send for the caretaker to remove the slippery creature.

Benjamin tried not to get involved, but he must've struggled to hold in his glee. Her reaction was better than he could've possibly hoped for. He thought that Miss Bones wouldn't like finding a toad in her lunch box very much, but her absolute terror was something he could not have predicted.

But the boy in the well had told him so, said that she had been terrified of toads and frogs and lizards ever since a frog had jumped into her pram as a child and hid beneath the blankets. It had taken Benjamin two days to find one near the river, and it was no easy task to catch and keep hold of him once he had found him.

He relayed his delight to the boy in the well that very evening. "You should've seen her face!" he said.

"I heard her scream," said the boy. "I think half the valley did."

"How did you know about her fear of toads?" he asked.

"I told you, I can see all kinds of things from down here. See all and know all. It's amazing what you can see in the dark. There are no limits, or walls."

"Can you teach me? I want to see in the dark."

"One day Benjamin, one day. You must be patient; there is still much work to be done."

"But we got Miss Bones and we got Penelope – they really got it."

"What about your worst enemy? What about the vicar?"

Suddenly Benjamin was quiet. Getting his own back on Penelope and his teacher was one thing, but the vicar, he was something else entirely.

"I said I'd help you to get revenge on all those that had done you wrong. And he's the worst isn't he? The nastiest and meanest of them all."

"But what if he catches me?" cried little Benjamin. "He'll thrash me, beat me."

"Brave heart, dear Benjamin. You needn't worry about the vicar. In fact, he's the easiest of them all. All it will take is a letter."

"A letter?" said Benjamin, surprised.

"Yes, just a short simple letter. Have you got your school things with you my friend? A pencil and paper?"

Benjamin reached into his satchel and pulled out some paper and a pencil.

"Write this down for me," said the boy. "It's all you need to get your revenge on your uncle.

All you have to write is, 'I know what you did'."

Benjamin scribbled it down.

He looked at the words and then he looked at the well.

"Is that it?"

"Trust me my good chum. That's all you need to write. Everyone has secrets, the vicar more than most."

Though he trusted his new friend, Benjamin still felt nervous and unsure.

"I was right about Miss Claxton and Penelope wasn't I?"

Benjamin nodded.

"Then trust me again on this. Just write these words down, put them in an envelope and drop it off at his cottage. Then all you have to do is watch what happens."

Benjamin didn't understand what the boy expected to happen, but he did what he was told, trusting that his new friend knew what he was doing. He took an envelope from his father's desk and wrote down the message on a sheet of writing paper. He sealed the envelope and took it to the vicar's house early the next morning, being as careful as possible not to be spotted on the way there or back, should the vicar later enquire if anyone had been seen going up the path to his cottage. He posted the letter, feeling not too confident that it would produce the effect he desired.

As it turned out, he did not have to wait for long for the effect of the letter to be felt. That very afternoon, he returned home from playing down near the stream when he noticed the vicar's bicycle leant up against the wall by the front door.

Benjamin was canny – he knew that if he were to announce his return, he might well miss what the fuss was. He instead crept inside, and sure enough, heard raised voices coming from the kitchen. Instead of going straight there from the hall, he crept around into the living room and into the dining room, where he could listen without being seen.

His mother sounded distraught; "Someone could just be playing games with you!"

"It's blackmail, pure and simple," said the vicar. "You swore you would say nothing to anyone."

"I have told no one. Why would I want anyone to know such shameful things?"

"It was a long time ago. I was possessed of some evil. I was a different man, lost and confused."

"So I've heard you say, so many times. But it never goes away, does it?" Benjamin's mother started to cry, but rebuffed any attempt by her brother to comfort her. "Putting on a collar and preaching the Lord doesn't make it go away!" she shouted at him.

"Why shouldn't it?" he cried. "I have given him my repentance; dedicated my heart and soul to the church, I have done everything I can."

"But what you did after..."

"It was the right thing to do. Nothing good could have come of it, you know that."

"Benjamin!" his mother cried.

He had leant too far into the doorway to listen and had been spotted. Both of them marched towards him; he backed away into the dining room.

"Eavesdropping now," snapped the vicar. "Another sin to add to your growing collection!"

"How long have you been there?" demanded his mother, shaking fearfully.

"I only just got home," said a frightened Benjamin.

"You've gone too far this time boy..."

"Albie, don't!"

The vicar charged towards him and Benjamin ran.

"What did you hear?" the vicar demanded, knocking his way through the dining room furniture to pursue him.

Benjamin went through the sitting room into the hall, the vicar just inches from catching him, when they both stopped all of a sudden. The front door hung open and there stood Benjamin's father watching them. His face stern and serious: "By thunder, what is going on here?"

The vicar took a step back and tried to compose himself. "We were just playing a game," he lied feebly.

"Doesn't look like any game I know," Benjamin's father said slowly. "I had no idea you and my son were such firm friends."

"Water under the bridge," said the vicar. "Like God, I always prefer to be forgiving."

After an aching silence, the vicar said: "Yes, well, I only stopped by briefly."

"All your visits seem to be brief," said Mr Morris. "It's funny, every time I see you, you always seem to be on your way out."

"Well I'm a busy man, the parish does not run itself. But perhaps sometime soon you could come around for supper. I feel that we hardly get a chance to talk you and I."

"Perhaps."

"Let me show you out, Albie," said Benjamin's mother.

"No need Emily," said Mr Morris. "I think he probably knows the way by now."

Emily passed the vicar his hat. He snatched it from her and walked swiftly to the door.

"You're home early," Mrs Morris hissed.

"Young Harry can round up the sheep by now I think. I've taught him well enough... I think you should go to your room Benjamin. Me and your mother, we need to talk."

This was not what Benjamin had expected at all. For hours and hours his parents seemed to argue. Benjamin tried his best to listen, but he could not make out much, except that his father seemed to think his mother was keeping something from him. It was the first time Benjamin thought his father seemed more angry than his mother. It ended, as it often did, with his father slamming the door and going to the pub. Sometime later his mother shouted for him; he went downstairs to eat a cold, miserable supper she had left for him. She was outside, sat crying beneath the old apple tree in the garden.

No, this had not been what he had expected at all, and the next day, when he visited his friend in the well, he expressed his displeasure.

"It was supposed to upset the vicar," he cried. "Now my mum is throwing tantrums again. My dad is furious, he doesn't want to even calm her down."

"Secrets are dangerous things, Benjamin," said the boy. "If they weren't, they wouldn't be secrets now would they?"

"You knew that was going to happen didn't you?" said Benjamin angrily. "You knew he was going to come over and upset Mum!"

"Benjamin! How could you say that! I thought we were friends you and I? I didn't do this for me, you know. I was trying to help you get your own back on the vicar, but if you don't need my help..."

"No, no, I do," Benjamin said quickly. "I was just sad to see her upset."

"She doesn't mind upsetting you though, does she? The day you first came up here, she struck you after you had been told off by the vicar. I'm surprised you don't want to get your own back on her as well."

"I don't want to get my own back on her," Benjamin said, almost in tears. "I just want her to be normal. To be happy, so me and Dad can be happy too."

"Then you must trust me Benjamin," the boy snapped. "Once this secret is out in the open, the vicar won't be interfering anymore. You've said that he causes the arguments, causes the trouble. Once he's gone, everyone will be happier."

"I suppose so. But what is their secret? What was all the shouting about?"

"You'll find out soon enough."

"But why can't you tell me now!" Benjamin pleaded.

"I've done so much for you Benjamin," said the boy, raising his voice. "I'm upset that you're so ungrateful."

"I'm not ungrateful; I just want to know what it is."

"I only have my suspicions," snapped the boy. "I don't know everything! The only way to find out a secret for sure is for those who keep it to tell the truth."

"But what about my mum?" the young boy pleaded.

"Don't you think that a lie, a secret, is a heavy burden to bear? That your mother might be relieved, grateful even, to be unburdened from it? Have you not been taught about these things at school?"

"I don't know," Benjamin pouted.

"Of course you don't. You haven't thought this through. You need to be strong, Benjamin. I can only help you so much. Trust me my friend, when we are done, all will be uncovered. And you won't have to worry about your mother, the vicar, or anyone else tormenting you ever again.

Can you be strong for me Benjamin?"

Benjamin wasn't sure; the boy from the well had always helped him before, but now he was scaring him too. After a moment, he just said yes so that he would not be shouted at again.

"Then we have work to do. What I'm going to ask you to do next may sound a little strange. But it will be the icing on the cake!"

With hesitance, Benjamin listened as the boy in the well told him the next stage of his plan – he wanted Benjamin to go to the grocer's and purchase a birthday card.

"A birthday card?"

"Yes, a birthday card. It's quite simple. You can spare some of your pocket money for a birthday card can't you?"

"Yes... I think so."

"Good! The timing must be so precise for this to work. It should be a child's birthday card. Something you might like. Then you must deliver it to your mother on this coming Saturday."

"But I thought we were out to get the vicar...

"I told you to trust me!" yelled the voice, showing its impatience. "Once she has the card, she will give it to the vicar."

"But why don't I just give it to him then?"

"Because he'll be on the look-out at his home for any new messages! Why all these questions? Have I ever steered you wrong before?"

"You did upset my mother."

"Only as a means to an end. But if you don't want my help, then fine. Just go home as normal, go back to your life as it was with foul Penelope, horrible Miss Bones and enjoy your beatings from the vicar. That's if you don't need my help."

"No, I do, I do," Benjamin begged.

"Then do as I say – it will work!"

Benjamin nodded. "I'll do what you say."

"Good, you won't regret it, my friend."

Just as Benjamin was about to leave, something suddenly occurred to him.

"What shall I write in the card?"

The boy in the well was silent for a few moments. Eventually, he said: "You'll know what to write when the time comes. Just put down whatever comes to mind."

Frightened now about what would happen if he disobeyed the boy in the well, Benjamin went back to Mr Wittle's shop, telling the shop keeper he needed a card for a cousin of his. He had just about managed to scrape up enough coins to afford it, though he had to search the whole of his bedroom for each last half-penny. The card he bought was colourful and had the picture of a clown on the cover.

He walked home with the card, looking at the blank inside page, wondering what to write. Why had the boy asked him to write the message? Why was he even sending it to his mother?

He knew that the boy's requests were odd, but he feared disobeying his instructions. Besides, if the card did what he said, and finally got rid of the horrible vicar, it was probably for the best.

When he arrived at his home, an idea suddenly appeared in his head. He went straight to his father's desk in the living room, reached for his pen and wrote very quickly:

"It's my birthday today. Don't tell me you've forgotten. Come and visit me, I miss you xx".

Benjamin looked at what he'd written. He didn't understand why he'd written it, in fact, he didn't really remember even writing it. One moment the card was in front of him, the next, the words were there.

He wasn't sure what they meant, but somehow he knew they were what was needed; that they were the right words and that the boy in the well would approve of them. So he placed the card in the envelope and waited to deliver it in the morning.

The rest of that day seemed to disappear. Benjamin awoke the next morning, barely remembering how he had come to be there or even what he had spent the rest of the day before doing. He could just about remember eating supper with his father and mother and the two still not really talking. Besides that, he could remember very little.

It wasn't until he was dressed that he even remembered the card. And then he couldn't remember what he had done with it. But as he stood on the landing, he spotted his mother collecting the post from the carpet under the front door. Could that be his card, there? There were two letters; she took them both into the living room. Benjamin was confused, what had happened to the card? Could that really be it?

Benjamin crept after her, trying his best not to be heard. His mother walked over to his father's desk and pulled out a letter opener from the drawer and opened the first envelope.

It was his card – now he knew it! His mother cut open the envelope and pulled out the card. She looked at it curiously before opening it up. It seemed to take a moment for the words to sink in. She seemed frozen, motionless as she looked it over and read what was inside.

Then, suddenly, she fell. Collapsed down to the carpet with an almighty thud.

Benjamin ran across the floor to her, screaming "Mum, Mum!" He shook her, but she wouldn't come around.

Benjamin's father heard the commotion and stormed into the sitting room.

"What happened?" he demanded.

"She just fell over!" Benjamin was in tears. "She read the card and fell over."

"What card?" His father was shaking her now too. After a moment she came around and started shrieking and screaming.

"What happened?"

"My baby," she yelled. "He's dead, he's dead, he's dead!"

She started to cry, but more than that, she started to wail: "My baby, my precious baby!"

"Your baby's here," his father shouted. "He's safe, he's right here."

He pulled Benjamin towards her, but she wouldn't even look at him.

"He's wasn't evil. He was my baby, my little baby. Don't take him, don't take him from me..."

It was as if they weren't even there. Benjamin was terrified, frozen to the spot in terror – what had he done...

His father commanded that he fetch the doctor and Benjamin wasted no time in obeying. He ran faster to the house of Doctor Jenkins than he'd ever run before. He was fortunate because the doctor was at home and was able to come straight away to the cottage. He took Benjamin back immediately on his trap, questioning him all the way about what had happened. Benjamin could not bear to tell him about his role in his mother's condition; he said only that his mother had collapsed after reading a card in the post and had become hysterical, more hysterical than she'd ever been.

When they arrived at the house, his mother was still writhing, crying tears of torment. She had purged into the waste paper basket. Benjamin's father was standing over her, helpless as to what to do.

"She's gone mad, doctor," he said. "I cannot calm her down." As the doctor came in, Benjamin's father ordered him to his room, uttering ominously: "I will deal with you later."

Those words sent a chill down his spine. He ran up to his room and dived in amongst the sheets, crying his heart out for what seemed like hours. He was overwhelmed now with guilt, if he'd have known what would happen, he would never have done it. His mother was in agony and it was his fault!

But of course it wasn't really his fault. It was the boy in the well; it had been his idea – it was really his fault! He should never have listened to him. They were supposed to be getting the vicar back, how was this hurting the vicar?

After his mother had stopped crying, Benjamin waited tensely for his father to come to him, and in time, the moment came. He heard his father's heavy footsteps on the stairs and he trembled as he came in through the door.

"Is Mum all right?" he asked in a panic.

"She is sleeping," his father said. He held up the card and all Benjamin's hairs stood on end.

"Where did this come from?"

"It came in the post; she picked it up from the doormat this morning with another letter."

"This writing," with one hand he held open the card in front of Benjamin, and with the other, he grabbed hold of Benjamin's hand. "This writing looks to me to be a lot like your writing. Did you write this?"

"No, I swear, I swear. It was on the doorstep this morning, I never saw it before. I never saw it." Tears poured across his cheeks. He shook free from his father's grip and buried his head in his bed sheets.

"What did she mean? About her baby being dead?"

"I don't know, I don't know," Benjamin mumbled in amongst his tears.

His father was calmed somewhat by the sight of his son crying, but only for the briefest of moments.

"I know you know something about this," he said through gritted teeth. "If you know something you had better say so now young man or else there will be hell to pay later. I've been patient with you, by God, I've been patient. But if you are mixed up in this, whatever it is, you will be banished from this house. Do you hear me? I will be through with you once and for all."

Benjamin didn't say a thing as his father slammed the door behind him. Though he was still crying, in his head, he was already making plans. He would need to be patient; he knew he might have to wait hours. He waited restlessly and hungrily. He kept creeping out to the top of the stairs, listening in to hear the sounds of movement, of stirring. He listened carefully until he heard the sound he had been waiting for – the sound of his father snoring.

He walked carefully down the stairs and into the sitting room, and sure enough, in keeping watch over his mother, who was passed-out on the settee, his father too had fallen asleep; his head hanging over the back of his old arm chair.

Now he was sure he could get away, Benjamin took his chance and darted sharply to the back door and made his escape.

Tired, but determined, he made his way back through the fields, through the woods and back up to the hillside where his friend, the boy in the well, would be waiting for him. Or at least, it would normally be so. As he approached the stone circle, the boy offered no greeting. Just as well, as Benjamin was in no mood for pleasantries.

"You lied to me!" he cried. "You said I was out to get the vicar, when all the time you were trying to get my mother!"

Benjamin waited for the boy to answer, but there was no sound, no response from the well.

"Do you know what you've done? Do you know what you've done to her?"

There was still no answer. The well was silent. There was no voice.

Or was there... at that moment Benjamin suddenly heard a voice, not from the well, but inside his very own head. And that voice said to him: "Me? I didn't do a thing. You did it all. You did it to your mother. You did it all yourself."

"You're a liar." Benjamin screamed. "I hate you! I'm never coming up here again. You're not my friend. I hate you!"

He turned and began to run back down the hillside, when suddenly the boy in the well finally spoke. "I'm not done with you yet Benjamin," he cried.

Benjamin ignored it and did not turn back.

"You'll see me again!" the boy cried out to him. "You will see me again!"

Benjamin ran as fast as he could back into the forest. He did not turn around and did not stop until he was home. His father was still asleep; he awoke when Benjamin arrived, but fortunately he did not realise his son had been outside. Nevertheless, he was still unhappy with him and ordered him straight to bed.

Benjamin slept poorly that night; restlessly tossing and turning, reacting to his ambivalent feelings of anger, guilt and fear, constantly awaking and falling back to sleep.

He woke abruptly the next morning; his father was shouting for him from downstairs. Benjamin rushed down, still wearing his night clothes; he entered the living room and was horrified at what he found.

There was a message written across the living room wall; scrawled in big dark red, frenzied letters; the words still wet and dripping down the wall.

The message read: "No present? It's my birthday come visit."

Benjamin almost screamed himself. He had been here – the boy in the well had come to the house. But how? What was going on?

His father was looking at him, staring down hard at him. "Did you do this?" he asked, barely able to control his anger.

Benjamin was speechless, then his father pointed at him: "Look at your hands". Benjamin looked down; they were red – covered in blood!

His father grabbed his hands. "You did do this!" He slid up the sleeves of his night shirt and saw two long, bloody cuts on his forearms.

"It wasn't me!" his son swore.

"What is wrong with you! Why you did do this?" he began to shake him. "Why did you do this!"

"It wasn't me," Benjamin said weeping. "It was the boy!"

"What boy?"

"The boy in the well!"

The front door burst open; the two of them spun around to see the vicar standing in the doorway. He hadn't seemed to have expected them; he cried out "Emily" before even noticing them there.

"I must speak to Emily," he demanded, walking towards them.

"Why are you here?"

"I must speak to her on a matter of great urgency."

It was at that moment that Benjamin's father noticed that the vicar was carrying an envelope, an envelope and a card that he quickly recognised.

"What is that you have?"

The vicar mumbled, saying that it was a private matter. Benjamin's father struck him, hit him square in the jaw. He was taken by surprise and fell back into the hallway. He took the card from the vicar's grip and opened it, finding it to be exactly the same card his wife had received the day before and in the same writing.

"Where did you get this?" he roared. He wasn't taking any chances; knowing that the vicar was a soldier, he went quickly towards the fireplace and picked up a poker. As the vicar rose to his feet, he stood before him again, poker raised and ready to strike at him.

"I want to know what this is all about. For years and years the two of you have kept secrets from me. And this will be the end of it! There's always been something between the two of you and I will know what it is. I swear to God, I will be told!"

"You are imagining things," the vicar snarled.

"Liar – what does this mean?" he said showing him the card again. "And what does that mean? The vicar had not seen the message on the wall; he recognised immediately that it was written in blood. "My God," he said, stricken with panic.

"I will know the truth from you, even if I have to beat it out of you!"

"No wait," he cried, as Mr Morris swung back the poker. "You don't understand; years ago, while you were away, at sea. Emily was…" He struggled to say it. "She was taken against her will by another. A brute, a monster; he forced himself on her and she… she became with child."

Benjamin's father began to shake. His anger was so intense, he couldn't even speak. The vicar knew that his life was in the balance, that the man had it in him to kill him if he so desired it.

"She wanted to keep the child," the vicar continued. "But our parents wouldn't allow it. This man; he was despicable, evil; his issue would've been abhorrent and they would not allow it in the family. So he was taken away from her…"

Benjamin's father scoffed. "Well, well," he said, "That explains plenty. They didn't want me near her when she was pure. But suddenly when I was back from the sea they were ready to foist her on me. Damaged goods was she?"

The vicar took a chance and tried to take the poker from him. But Mr Morris had firmer footing and forced him back, causing him to fall once again to the ground.

"You killed the baby, didn't you? Drowned it in the well!"

"It wasn't my choice."

"You took her baby and you killed it. No wonder she was so changed when I came back. She never was the same old girl I used to know. I knew it, but I was too glad to have her be mine."

"It had to be done, it needed to be done." said the vicar, before he realised: "How did you know that? How did you know about the well?"

It was at that moment that Mr Morris remembered his son and what he had said. But when he turned his son was nowhere to be seen.

"Benjamin!" he cried. "Benjamin, where are you?" He yelled throughout the whole house, but his boy was nowhere to be found.

"What does Benjamin know?" the vicar demanded.

"He said the boy in the well did it. He said he did it all, the letters and writing on the wall."

"That's ridiculous!"

"Where is this well?" Benjamin's father demanded.

"You must know the one. The hillside well, near the south-end of the farm."

Both took off for the well almost instantly, running out the door and through the woods after Benjamin, shouting for him as they went.

Despite their years of living in Bullham Brook, neither the vicar or Benjamin's father knew the land the way Benjamin knew it and both struggled through trees and unkept fields surrounding the village and Parson's estate. Benjamin's father proceeded quicker than the vicar, the two becoming separated as they ran on.

When Mr Morris arrived on the hillside and started to climb, he found that the sky was dark. Clouds were blocking out the sun and the wind was racing into a gale. The tall grass rumbled as it was swept from side to side in the fierce gusts. He found it hard to look ahead, to walk forward against the wind's unrelenting force. But he marched on; he could see the well, and to his horror, he could see Benjamin, standing upon the stones, stood precariously facing him, teetering over the open well.

He shouted to him, but Benjamin gave no sound of recognition, though it would be hard for him to hear over the roar of the wind. He climbed higher, his son still stood motionless there, looking vacant down to the dark void below.

Mr Morris got himself to within just a few yards of the stone wall when there was suddenly a crack of thunder. And above that rang out the words: "Do not come any closer or your son will become mine forever."

"Don't hurt him, please," cried his father, frightened almost beyond his wits and looking around, desperately hoping the voice had come from somewhere else, and not deep within the well.

"Shut up and listen to me," hissed the voice.

But Benjamin's father kept on: "If you must hurt someone, hurt me. Do not harm him, he has done nothing."

"I'm not interested in you; you mean nothing to me." And then after a pause and another roar of wind the boy shouted out: "He on the other hand, means everything."

Benjamin's father was confused until he saw that the vicar had caught up and was now with them on the hillside.

"You've finally come to visit me. And after all this time..."

"By God," he cried. "What are you?"

"You know who I am," roared the voice. "You of all people should know me!"

"Please!" Benjamin's father begged. "Whatever he did to you, please, leave Benjamin alone. He's done nothing, he's just a boy."

"*I'm just a boy,*" raged the voice. "A lost boy, forsaken by his mother and his father, the two people who should've loved him the most! What's the matter? Are you ashamed of your son!"

"I do not understand you," cried Benjamin's father.

"*I am not talking to you,*" screamed the voice.

It took a few moments for it all to sink in, for Benjamin's father to realise the horror of what the boy in the well was saying. The boy laughed as Mr Morris looked to the vicar, his face a picture of disbelief, horror and disgust.

"He didn't tell you did he?" the boy laughed. "The monstrous brute, the man possessed of some evil walks amongst you, disguised as a man of God!"

"I am a man of God."

"You're a filthy disgrace. You disgrace the clothes you wear, you insult the almighty with your stinking fawning words."

"I repented," said the vicar, falling to his knees. "I have sought forgiveness and given myself to the Lord."

"You're a liar and a coward! And you don't deserve forgiveness."

Lightning struck, thunder rolled amongst the clouds.

"I give you one chance to redeem yourself," roared the boy in the well. "The life you chose for me has been agony. It has been lonely, it has been cold, it has been full of pain; but you can help me now Father. You can redeem yourself by giving yourself to me. Come into my world; join me in my unhappy home in the well so that we can be together forever...

Or else I take the boy. I will not be alone any longer."

The vicar was speechless. He looked to the ground open-mouthed.

"No. No!" he roared, as he rose to his feet. He pulled his cross from beneath his clothing; he raised the silver icon out in front of him: "I will fight you evil spirit, be gone! I cast you out, be gone!"

The boy merely laughed at him. Struggling to go forward, the vicar began to chant, "Our Father" – he struggled to be heard against the wind – "who art in heaven, hallowed be thy name..." He tried so hard to shout out the words that he did not even notice Benjamin's father come up behind him and grab him by the back of his cassock. He dragged him forward and flung him towards the stone wall, with the vicar landing just a few feet from it.

Before he could get back on his feet, Mr Morris had grabbed him once again and forced him up against the wall, his chest and head now hanging over the darkness within.

The vicar screamed; as Benjamin's father tried to force him over, he could see his son, hanging over them, lifeless and limp, as if with the slightest movement he would topple down into the abyss.

The vicar got his grip on the wall and pushed himself up, forcing Mr Morris off him. Benjamin's father fought back; as the vicar turned to move away he charged him back against the stones again, the two now face to face in their struggle. Benjamin's father raised his fist and hit him once, twice, three times. The vicar's feet scraped against the ground; he was losing his footing. Mr Morris grabbed his cassock with one hand and reached down with the other, hoping to sweep the vicar's legs from under him and push him over.

The vicar cried out; trying to strike back at him. Benjamin's father roared; he swept up the vicar's legs. The vicar screamed as he felt his centre of gravity tip – he grabbed desperately at Mr Morris' shirt sleeve, pulling Morris towards him and against the wall. But it wasn't enough to save him. He felt himself slip and fall.

The sleeve tore. With an almighty scream, the vicar disappeared into the darkness of the well; his screams echoing until ceasing, abruptly, leaving only silence. A sound of impact was never heard. He just disappeared.

Benjamin's father fell on his back, gasping for air.

"You should not have done that," said the boy, with almost a hint of regret. "I would have had him give himself to me."

"You got what you wanted," cried Mr Morris, rising back to his feet. "Now give me back my son."

"I wish you had been my father," the boy said. "You were the only innocent amongst them. But I would have had him give himself to me of his own free will; now you too have sinned."

"I just want my son," Benjamin's father was in tears. "Take whatever you want, just please, don't take my son!"

The wind roared and the boy was silent.

"I have no wish to harm the innocent. But there will be a price to pay."

There was a flash of thunder. Benjamin fell. His father cried out...

...But he did not fall – he leapt! His father caught him as flew from one side of the well to the other.

Mr Morris fell to the ground with his boy in his arms. With the wind so fierce, they were forced down the hillside, falling and rolling down the grass. The roar was incessant; Mr Morris could not get to his feet. Yet amongst the noise, he managed to hear, for one last time, the voice of the boy in the well.

And it said: "Father, I'm coming for you. Time to play..."

There was the most tremendous crash of thunder. Benjamin's father held his son to his chest, afraid to move.

They waited there, on the hillside, hidden in the long grass, waiting for the maelstrom to pass.

But as fast as it had come on, so did it go away.

It seemed after only a few moments, Mr Morris was able to lift his head and found that the sky was clearing. That there was little or no wind, and most importantly, that the sun was beginning to shine on the hillside again.

Benjamin was out cold. His father felt his pulse, placed his hand on his forehead, felt his breath. He was alive, but unresponsive. His father spoke to him and shook him a little; he stirred but he did not wake up.

He was about to race down the hillside, get away from there and find help as soon as possible, when he suddenly thought to look back. He scanned his eyes over the landscape. Where the well had once stood was now just a pile of stone. The walls had caved in; the well was now sealed.

He started off down towards the woods, moving as quickly as his battered body would allow. Benjamin seemed unharmed, but he would not feel safe until he was back within the walls of his home.

He was dripping with sweat when he finally made it back. The front door was lying open as he had left it. He struggled upstairs and placed his son down softly on the bed and pulled his blankets over him

Exhausted, his father let out an almighty sigh of relief. Despite the most extraordinary of circumstances his son was going to be all right.

"Emily," he cried.

There was no answer.

He walked slowly into their bedroom, expecting to see her still lying in a drug-induced sleep. She was not there. Suddenly he panicked – the writing on the wall. It was still there, what if she had seen it!

"Emily," he shouted, dashing down the stairs and into the living room, where the message remained.

He cried for her again and dashed into the kitchen where he found the back door wide open.

He ran out into the garden – and that's where he found her. Strung up and hung, from the old apple tree.

...Sounds wild doesn't it? When I tell people the story, they don't believe it. Why would they? Yet, when they see the police report, the transcripts from the inquests, the photograph of the writing on the wall – yes there's a photograph – then suddenly it doesn't seem quite so crazy.

The reports that do survive, they make for interesting reading. The authorities were dumbfounded; they didn't believe the man's story, yet where was the vicar? What about the words on the wall? The cuts on Benjamin's arms and the baby... yes, with some investigation they found out the truth; that Emily Morris did indeed have another child. It could well have been a real scandal, perfect food for the growing tabloids. But it was kept quiet, probably because of the involvement of the vicar. I daresay even my ancestor did what he could to keep it quiet, for a time at least.

So they see the proof and then people ask me, well how do you know how this happened or that happened? They question the detail. What they forget is that Benjamin Morris did not die that day and neither did his father. They both lived many years more and they both told the tale more than once, Benjamin especially.

They left Bullham Brook – understandably. His father died working at the docks in Bristol, trying to start a new life. As for Benjamin, we believe he grew up into a rogue, a drunk and a thief. He spent time in prison for theft, public disturbance and vagrancy. But he also tried to profit from his misfortune; he began to tell the story of what happened that day for profit, performing on-stage recitals of the terrifying tale. That's where the legend comes from, his performances, his scripts and notes, and the words passed from one person to another over the years.

It was never a popular act, people didn't believe him or worse, they ostracised him for the inclusion of a man from the cloth and the acts of murder and incest. The people of Bullham Brook didn't take much kindly from it either – he never performed it in the village. In the end he would tell it just for coins in the street or just for a pint.

He was last known to be in Portsmouth, arrested for vagrancy about the time the war broke out. Perhaps he died in the war, no one knows. Such an unfortunate boy; fate was forever cruel to him.

Case no. 47
WRONG NUMBER

I moved because she left me. Modest two-bedroom place in Croydon, only a mile and a half from my new surgery. I wasn't sad to leave Shoreditch; it was no surprise to find that my friends were really her friends. Can't say as I liked many of them anyway; unexceptional people trying so desperately to seem exceptional.

I knew it wouldn't last. She a guitarist: "What do you do mate?"; "I'm a vet"; "Oh right," and then move on. If you're not part of their world, you're no one. She was more beautiful and talented than I had any right to be with. Should've stuck with the slightly chubby girls. The smiling round-faced lasses; the ones who spend most of their life behind counters, at front desks or bars; who crave the Sex and the City life while stuffing their faces with pizza and chocolate.

My girlfriend, my ex, ended up fucking a singer from another band; a pretentious prick with no ideas of his own, but oh my, what a really interesting haircut he had.

Whatever; if someone surrounds themselves with twats, you can only expect them to adapt.

So I moved into the upstairs of a converted house and paid £675 (bit of a bargain) to Mr and Mrs Sodha each month. I shifted all my stuff in and discovered how little I owned. I went out and bought a new TV, stereo, Blu-ray and some other stuff. I couldn't afford it, but I didn't really care. My salary as a new vet wasn't great, but it would do. And at least I didn't have to commute.

There wasn't much decent to look at there, but I did my best to leer at the occasional young mum with a wounded puppy, or college student with a sick bunny rabbit. I was not very good at it, at least not without a couple of pints down me.

I got the place hooked up with a phone line and the net pretty quick; about a week after I moved in I think. It happened the very first time after that. Eight-thirty Thursday night, I was sat on my sofa, pizza on my lap, can in my hand, when the phone rang. I put everything down and got up to answer it. When I picked up, I couldn't hear much except static:

"Hello," I repeated.

Out of all the fuzz and buzzing came a voice. "Hello," it said. "Mum?"

"What?" I shouted. I could barely hear. It was a girl's voice, youngish I guessed.

"Mum, I need you to pick me up."

It sounded like she was holding the phone a few feet from her face. What I could tell was that she was upset. She had the cracked, dry tone of someone who'd been crying.

"I think you've got the wrong number," I said. Felt a bit cruel, but what could I do for her?

"I can't do it anymore Mum," she went on.

"Hello?" I said loudly. "Can – you – hear – me?"

"You were right, he's a lost cause." She broke into tears.

"You've got the wrong number, love!" I shouted.

"I only wanted to help him..." She was definitely crying. "Come get me please, I'm on the corner of Saxon."

Then the line went dead.

It shook me a little bit, but she obviously couldn't hear me. So there wasn't exactly anything I could do about it.

I went on with my happy little life as usual. Working during the day, drinking alone at night. I didn't give the call any more thought, but then, a few nights later, at around half-past eight, the phone went again.

I had no clue it would be the same call again, so I just picked it up expecting it to be a survey call, or my mum, the only other person I had given the number to.

"Hello," said the same girl's voice, from way far-off, like before, half-covered by static.

My first thought was that somehow, she had the wrong number programmed into her phone. Or that maybe my number was really close to her mum's number.

But that wasn't what was so strange about it. What was so strange was that it was exactly the same message:

"I can't do it any more Mum." I was becoming a bit freaked out. I said again: "I think you've got the wrong number."

There was a pause, a moment of silence.

"You were right, he's a lost cause. I only wanted to help him."

She wasn't ignoring me; she was having a conversation with someone else. It was like a recording, but a conversation I could only hear one side of.

I put the phone down. I was a bit unnerved, maybe a bit unsettled, but I just thought of it as one of those strange things, some kind of bug in the phone network. It was just weird.

So I just went on with things as normal. Got up, went to work, had some lunch, went back again, and then either home or down the pub for a drink or two. Or more if I felt like it, which at the time, I usually did. I'd put some distance between myself and my friends, the ones that cared at least, not that I appreciated it at the time. I was looking back at my whole life with disappointment and wasn't interested in seeing anyone or really doing anything.

Of course, most of my existing friends lived in or around London, so the world had to revolve around them. Always must go into London, no chance of them straying from their precious city life. So I thought, fuck 'em, and couldn't be arsed going to see them when they couldn't be arsed to come see me.

And then a few nights later, the phone rang again. I had just got home from doing some shopping, so it wasn't until I was just about to pick up did I realise it was eight-thirty again. And there was the sound of the crackling and the static, and the far-off voice again, calling for her mother.

"I can't do it anymore Mum."

I listened quietly, not saying a word; feeling very unsettled now. I listened to her talk for a moment, until I said: "Is this some kind of joke?"

After a brief silence she said again: "You were right, he's a lost cause."

"Fuck off!"

I slammed the phone down and went to put my shopping away. She'd definitely taken longer to say the next line after I swore at her, I was sure of it.

It happened again the next night. I was in the bath that time, so I didn't answer it. But it happened at around eight-thirty; I heard the time on the radio. When I was out, and still dripping wet, I went to the phone and tried to get the number back from 1471. The automated voice said that the last call was on the 18th of April. I sat down and thought about it; that date was almost two weeks ago, and it was my mum. This was at least the fourth time the phone had rung in that time.

I came home during my lunch hour and rang up the phone company to ask them what the hell was going on. Well, what I asked was if there was something wrong on the line, because I kept getting strange missed-calls. I didn't go into detail because when I tried to explain I kept feeling like I was a nutcase, and didn't want to seem like one.

They said they'd have a look at it. I don't know whether they ever did or not, but it didn't change anything.

I was caught off-guard the next time. I was just finishing a mundane chat with my dad and put the phone down for just a moment when it rang again. I picked it up thinking it would be him, having forgotten to tell me something. But instead I got...

"Hello. Mum?"

Now was when I started to become frightened. I felt shivers race up my spine, the voice was so much clearer this time, it was the same words, but they were different.

"Mum, I need you to pick me up."

They were more anguished, almost harsh, angry. As if – now stay with me – because I ignored the last call, I had somehow

233

upset her, even though each word, each breath, was just as it was before.

I slammed the phone down and tore out the phone line.

I couldn't get the words out of my head, the way she had said them. Who was she? Why was she calling me? What the hell was going on? I left the phone unplugged, but the call left me tense all evening.

I was off work the next day, and when I was coming home I got caught out in the corridor by Mr and Mrs Sodha. You know the type: very chatty, very friendly, very nice. But too nice; you smile and you chat, and get away as soon as possible because they'll talk at you for ages if you don't and not about anything remotely interesting.

But I got sucked-in, in part because I needed to sign something to do with the deposit scheme. They made me a cup of coffee, gave me a slice of cake and I ended up trapped out of politeness. I don't know why, but after a while of them jabbering on, I asked:

"Who lived up there before me?"

No one apparently. Of course, as they had said to me when I moved in, I was the first person to occupy the flat since the conversion. But their tone was awkward; they didn't like me asking these questions. I could tell they knew something that I didn't; it became more obvious the more questions I asked and I wasn't going to let them get away with it.

"Who lived here before you?" I enquired. And when they avoided answering I told them I had been getting some strange phone calls, implying that they had been for the previous tenant.

Mr and Mrs Sodha looked at each other, wondering what to say to me. They assured me quickly that they had not lied to me, or misled me. There had been no previous tenant in my flat.

But awkwardly, they conceded that someone who had lived in the house previously had actually been killed.

They were quick to point out that the accident had not happened in the house. A woman had lived there before; her husband had left her and she was forced to bring up the three

234

children alone. The eldest left school at 16 to help her mother look after the two youngest. She was described in near angelic terms; a self-sacrificing girl who got her family through the toughest of times and put herself second.

Years later, when her brother and sister were older, she was able to go back to school. She went to the local art college where she became involved with a troubled young artist. He was supposed to be really brilliant – they told the story like it was from the pages of a woman's weekly. But he was unbalanced, a mental case, and their relationship was always up and down. He was supposed to have hit her at one point. Then he got on drugs, and although she had kept going back to him, that was the final straw.

She left him for good one night. Then she was in an accident. A hit and run. Her mother was supposed to pick her up and found her lying face down in the road.

You could've knocked me over with a feather at that moment. Was that what was I hearing? The last words of a doomed girl? An innocent who put herself at the service of others all her life, struck coldly down in the rain, dead, like she was nothing to no one?

But there was more to come. In the aftermath, the boyfriend, the artist, whose name they could not remember, was accused of the crime. There was a big brouhaha locally; she was popular with those who knew her and commended for her social work. But the police could not prove he was at the scene, or that he had access to a vehicle. He was committed soon after and they never found the car, or another culprit.

The girl's family lived in the house a little longer. But apparently they started to get phone calls, strange phone calls. They always thought it was him; but nothing was ever proven. He lived in the area for a while after his release from hospital, but was forced to leave. They said this in a serves-him-right sort of way.

They wanted to know what phone calls I was getting. Could this maniac be back in the area? Pretty startled, I said it was

235

nothing, just silence at the end of the line. They looked at me bleakly; when they first moved in, they had been phoned a couple of times by someone. Someone who had never spoken, but they could hear them on the other end of the phone, breathing.

I was upset to say the least. And they could see it, despite my attempts to hide it. They were probably more afraid that I would use this as some kind of excuse to get out of my contract and move out.

I went back upstairs and tried to make myself some lunch. But I was too shaken, too upset. I logged-on to the web and started searching; I didn't trust second-hand tales told by old couples with nothing better to do with their life than gossip. I searched through the local stories on the BBC site; there were a horrifying number of hit and run stories there.

But the number in Croydon were few. And the story was there, 'Hit and Run on Saxon Road'.

I wasn't prepared to see her face. She was so young. I suppose now that I think about it, she was actually older than me, or at least she been when the accident happened.

Her name was Catherine. It was only then I realised that I hadn't known her name.

Catherine Holden. I put it into Google and narrowed my search down to the local press, which had followed the story in a big way. She was indeed painted as an angel. Left school to help her mother, worked as care assistant at a local old peoples' home. She was described as being caring and understanding: 'good with all the residents, even the difficult ones'.

And then there was him – all but accused of being the culprit. He was judged to be talented; by who, I don't know. But he had had lapses in the past. Catherine was described as being taken in by his mystique, and by her need to look after others. But he was 'troubled' and could sometimes be 'violent'. Catherine's mother was adamant that he had killed her.

But he was not trialled: 'Artist Not Charged with Hit and Run'. There was a lack of evidence. Anthony Smith – that was his name – did not have a car. They never found the vehicle responsible; there would have had to have been substantial damage to it. No vehicle Mr Smith could have had access to had that kind of damage. And no abandoned vehicle was found that exhibited any such damage. There were no witnesses; Smith did not have a 'satisfactory alibi' but had recently been committed.

There were no further stories. I tried to find something more about Anthony Smith. But the name was too common, and I couldn't find anything.

I started to cry. Properly cry, not just a few tears, full on weeping. Those words, those helpless words: "I only wanted to help him". A beautiful caring girl run down like she was nothing. I couldn't help but think back to my own girlfriend, who I too had supported and helped, only for her to piss off with some junky guitarist. Is that what I'd done? Been seduced by the mystique of it? A musician, a sexy, hot musician? Allowed myself to be taken advantage of? Let her walk all over me just because I thought she was out of my league? Had she been at it for years? Screwing other guitarists then coming home to safe old me to support her and to clap along to her rubbish lyrics and stolen cords?

Fucking artists. Pretentious tortured fuckers; they didn't suffer, just the people all around them.

Poor Catherine. She deserved better. We both deserved better.

It was then that I went back to the phone. I picked up the cord, plugged it back into the slot and then waited. This time I would know her name, could listen to her cry, somehow try to touch the troubled soul that was reaching out to me.

I watched the clock as darkness fell and it turned round to eight-thirty. But there was no call. I even picked up the phone to check the line was working. There was nothing. I called the phone with my mobile; it rang on queue. But it didn't happen every night. I didn't always get the call.

So I waited the next night, made sure I was at home. And the night afterward – but nothing. She didn't call. I felt like I'd abandoned her. That I was the last person she had tried to reach and I had rejected her. She was lost, wherever it was that she was. I had left her adrift.

Part of me knew that even if she had called back, I could do nothing; that she never heard my voice anyway. But some part of me wanted to do something, anything, no matter how small. Even if, in the tiniest of ways, just being there, to listen to her cry for help, somehow meant I could be there for her, then I wanted to do it.

But she stopped calling. A week went by – not a call came.

I sank further into depression. I would come home from work and sink into the sofa. And I do mean sink; I would bury myself in the cushions, sometimes for hours, with or without the TV on. I ate only takeout food, anything that required the least amount of preparation. I put on weight. I looked pale.

My work suffered. My colleagues saw me show up with bags under my eyes, my clothes scruffy, smelling of cigarettes and alcohol. I was eventually called in by the surgery manager, who gave me a very strict telling off. I didn't take it well; I was still drunk from lunch. He said I was on my final warning.

I hit a new low. That night I went to the pub and hooked up with the pub slag. You know the type: dresses too provocatively even for an 18-year-old, but is somewhere in her mid-forties, and that's if you're being generous. Bad permed hair, cleavage wrinkles, always stands as if she's holding a cigarette. I was so pissed I staggered back to her place, a dirty dump down a back alley with fag burns on the furniture and mould in the coffee cups. I remember waking up next to her and wanting to vomit. That sounds excessively cruel, I know, but bear in mind that I had also drank enough to floor a heavy Irish wrestler.

I tried to tidy myself up for work that morning, but everyone, including myself, knew I was in no fit state to be there. I told the receptionist that I was going home ill at lunch. She didn't believe there was anything really wrong with me, beyond the obvious.

I went home, and after a short period with my head amongst the sofa cushions, I started to drink again. It was the only thing I wanted to do.

I passed out sometime late afternoon. I don't know when, all I know is that I awoke when it was dark.

The phone was ringing. It was a few moments before I realised what was happening. It was half-past eight. The room was spinning; I stumbled to my feet. Barely staying upright, I went for the phone. I picked it up and dropped it.

I fell to my knees with a thump and scooped it up. It was her, the sweet, but frightened voice spoke out to me:

"You were right, he's a lost cause. I only wanted to help him."

"Catherine, I'm so sorry," I said, my eyes filling with tears. "I'm so, so, sorry. You deserved so much better. So much better…"

After a short silence, I heard "Hello?"

My jaw dropped open: she had spoken to me! I started to tremble. "Hello," I said back.

"Who's there?"

She was speaking to me; she was real, she was alive!

"I'm coming to get you," I said triumphantly. "Stay where you are!" I don't know why I said it, why I believed that anything could be done. But right then, I believed that I could save her.

I slammed the phone down and leapt across the floor. I took my keys, not my coat, out to my car. It was pouring down with rain. I started the engine without considering that, A: I was in no condition to drive; and B: that I had no idea where Saxon Road was. I took off quickly and drove on to the main road before considering this, but a copy of my trusted A-to-Z helped me find what I was looking for.

I found myself diverted down a series of quiet suburban streets, the last place anyone would expect an act of violence and death. Saxon Road was no different; old Georgian houses, now split into flats.

The rain was coming down thick. I drove slowly, looking carefully between parked cars and trees and lampposts. Where was she? Was she even there?

Then, as I approached the road's end, I saw her. I could not see her face, but knew it was her – it had to be. She was dressed in a thigh-length white coat, with a long cream-coloured dress with a ragged floral trim. Her head was shielded by her hood – her arms were folded, hugging herself for warmth. She stood under a street sign pointing to Selhurst Station. I stopped in the middle of the road, got out of the car, and ran to her.

"Catherine," I yelled.

Startled, she turned to me.

It really was her. Her skin was pallid, her eyes marked by smudged mascara. She was soaked, absolutely dripping with water; it was as if she'd been there forever.

"Catherine," I said again. I ran right up to her; too close, she took a step back in hesitation.

"Who are you?" she said, frightened.

"I got your…" I didn't know how to explain it, explain how I'd come to be there. So I said, feeling like some romantic hero from a movie: "I've come to take you home."

She stared at me. Her mouth hung open, unsure what words to say. But then in the distance, we heard the sound of tyres screeching across a road.

It was pouring down after all, hazardous conditions to be driving in. Yet, in that moment, to us both, it must've seemed like fate. Like time running out.

She looked towards the sound and then back to me. And then she said, after a deep breath: "Take me home."

I nodded. I dashed back to the driver's seat, quickly leaning over to open the passenger side door.

With a slow but determined walk, she came to join me inside. She really was soaking; her clothes squelched against the seat. I did my best not to stare at her as she sat down. It wasn't until I had turned the keys in the ignition and had started to drive away that she pulled down her hood and showed her face.

I could see it only in the passing glow of the streetlights. She looked tired; there were bags beneath her eyes. She was thin, her cheekbones prominent, unlike they were in the photographs in the paper; taken no doubt in happier times.

Yet she was beautiful. Maybe it was the all-white look, soaked blonde locks and ice-white complexion that made her look like an angel. Like someone who did not belong in this world with the rest of us.

A word did not pass between us as I drove. She stared blankly ahead, barely changing in her expression. And I, I could think of nothing to say to her. I kept glancing across at her, looking for signs of thought or feeling on her face, but she remained blank. How was I to find the words, find the words to describe how I felt? This bizarre mix of sadness, guilt and joy that she was here, here now with me, and safe. I was so confused; I barely paused to consider that all this was impossible, that what was occurring to me, to us, was a bona-fide miracle.

I parked in front of my flat, leapt out of my seat, passed around the front of my car and opened up her door. She stood like a woman in shock; her handbag clutched unnaturally in front of her like a child with a teddy bear.

I skipped to the front door and unlocked it swiftly. I held the door open as she squeezed by. She was briefly more animated, looking around at the walls and the fixtures before saying slowly:

"This is not my home..."

Breathing heavily, I said, "That's because you don't live here anymore." She stared at me icily. Maybe that had been too blunt. "You've been away a long time," I said awkwardly.

Her icy stare gave away to one of sadness, recognition that what I had said was somehow true. With head bowed, she walked inside and slowly ascended the stairs. I followed closely behind and brushed in front of her when we reached the landing.

"Let me take your coat," I said. I hung it up on the kitchen door and showed her into the living room. I felt ashamed of its disgusting state: the pile of dirty plates, the loose take-away packaging, and the scattering of empty cans and bottles. I did a very quick sweep of the room, gathering whatever rubbish I could, and then darted into the kitchen and stuffed the lot in the dustbin, recycling be damned.

I came back into the living room and found her sat uncomfortably on the edge of the sofa, her back straight and her hands crossed on her lap.

"Can I get you something?" I said like a hopeless fool. "Something warm maybe?"

She looked up at me accusingly: "Who are you?"

I had fashioned a footstool out of a plastic carry crate I hadn't put away after I moved in. I put a cushion on it and pulled it across the floor until I was sat in front of her.

"My name is Johnny, I got your phone call."

She opened her mouth to respond, but withdrew the words before speaking them.

"Do you know how long you've been out there?"

"W...what are you talking about?" her face twisted, confused. "What's going on?" she pleaded.

"I don't know how... I can't explain," I said, words just pouring out. "But I've been getting your calls for weeks. And I found out what happened; I know what happened to you. And when you spoke to me, when you finally answered me, I had to come, and I knew just where to find you. I had to save you."

"I don't know what you're talking about," she said with panic, shuffling back into the sofa cushions in discomfort. "Where's Mum? I want to speak to my mum!"

"I'm here to help you."

"You can't help me," she sobbed. She started to cry. If there was one thing I had plenty of, it was take-away napkins. Within seconds I had handed her a tissue.

"Everything's going to be ok."

"It's not ok. It's never going to be ok. I loved him," she cried. "I really loved him, but he's destroying himself and I can't watch him do that. I just can't."

I took the chance and lifted myself from the box stool and onto the sofa next to her.

"Do you know what it's like to love someone so much it hurts? That it tears you up to watch them kill themselves, so much, but you can't just leave them."

I reached out to hug her, but her head was sobbing into my shoulder first. Streams of tears running down her face, her whole body trembling with grief. I held her; I held her tight.

She wept. I cried too. Unavoidably thinking now of my own former lover. She who had taken my love selfishly and had not returned my affection. She who had betrayed me, betrayed my trust.

"You can't just take on other people's problems," I spluttered. "You have to have something for yourself. You've got to keep some of yourself for you, or else you've got nothing. If you give too much you just come out empty. You're a person too. You can't live your life like a... like a... like a dry sponge, you've got to soak up some love for yourself."

There was a moment of silence. She lifted her head to look at me. Our eyes locked on to each other, both in recognition of what might quite possibly constitute the worst metaphor ever uttered outside of a sixth-form college poetry class.

It broke the tension. We both paused to laugh.

"You know what I mean," I said sheepishly.

She looked into my eyes again. Her eyes suddenly seemed large, magnetic. I could feel her looking into me, right into me; the movement of her eyes was felt in the back of my skull. I don't know who made the first move, but our lips were suddenly locked, her arms were around my neck, her hands running through my hair.

It was all so spontaneous, smooth and uninhibited, like an edited motion picture love scene. I pulled off her soggy blouse and she lifted off my stained T-shirt. We fell back on the sofa; she gently caressed my back as I rolled her over slightly to unhook her bra.

We made love for a long time I think. It all seemed so slow, I can't remember it without blurred edges, a kind of surreal out-of-focus montage. It doesn't seem real now. I don't remember the feeling of sweat on my back, or the sound of her moans. I don't think I even thought for a moment about contraception – and I was normally so courteous about that.

And then, at the moment of climax... it wasn't like a fade to black, it was like a fade to white. Some great trippy hippy freakout. I must've fallen asleep then. You never remember falling asleep, but yet that's the bit I remember most. Fade out. And then sleep. Sleep like I have never had before or since. Uninterrupted, un-disturbed; I did not dream. I remember not dreaming. There was nothing more to say, nothing more to think. I was... whole I suppose. And for the briefest of moments, absolutely content.

I awoke sometime the next afternoon. I lay in my pants on my living room floor, smelling badly of sweat and with more than the slightest hint of a headache. My body ached; I pulled myself up. I was alone.

The cushions from the sofa were on the floor. I stood up slowly and looked around. I checked the bathroom, the toilet, the bedroom and the car. She was gone.

In fact there was no real sign she had even been there at all. I surveyed my home carefully. Her coat was not on the kitchen door; there were no wet drips on the carpet, no muddy footprints, even the car seat she had soaked into was dry. And the living room was as much of a tip as it had ever been.

But I knew I had not dreamt it. I had had no dreams. She had been there. I felt her, smelt her, touched her. And I was so sorry that she was gone.

I waited dutifully until eight-thirty for her call. I did not eat, I did not drink, I did not wash. I cleaned the place up out of boredom. I took the bin out, did my recycling, crushed the pizza boxes and cans.

But her call never came.

I put on clean clothes and did my washing up. Even Hoovered the place at 20 minutes to midnight. But she didn't call, and she never called again.

I was sad at first that she was gone, but I knew that, and I apologise if this sounds corny, but that she was now in a better place. I can't say that I had expected her to call again.

Having saved her, in my own way, I thought it only sensible that I should now save myself. On the following Monday I met with my boss and admitted to him that I had become an alcoholic. That this had affected my performance and that I was very sorry. He could fire me if he so wished, but I would be grateful if he would give me one more chance. He seemed impressed by my honesty, but I can't honestly say whether he'll really allow me to continue beyond the end of my probation. I started to visit alcoholics anonymous for a while, just to show my willingness to change. Although I didn't really think that I was a real addict, just acting-out.

I went on a diet, just briefly. A reduction in take-aways made a big impact. And I started to exercise on a semi-regular basis. I'd be lying if I said that my bizarre encounter completely changed everything. But it had made me start to care about myself again, and to care about what happened to me.

I had not completely had my fill of unexpected phone calls though. A week or two after my strange encounter I had a call from her – my ex. I was surprised to hear her voice; we had had no communication since I had left our home. She had heard some concerning things about me from my "friends". I'd forgotten that she cared. We talked for a little while, caught up as it were. I was amiable, if not a little difficult. But in truth it was actually good to hear from her. I did miss her, in spite of not wanting ever to see or hear from her again.

She invited me out for a drink sometime, said she'd missed me. I declined as politely as possible. I didn't really want to see her. Besides, I had only a day or so before heard rumour that her and him were no longer an item. And I did not want to be her crutch. I was better than that. Of course she may have simply only wanted to be friendly. I didn't wish to find out either way. Better just to let some things go completely.

There was also one more phone call of note – an uncomfortable epilogue for this story.

It was late in the evening when the phone rang. I picked it up without fear, knowing that it could never be her.

245

But someone was breathing heavily on the other end of the line. It was out-of-breath, nervous breathing. It was unsettling, and creepy. It carried on for just a few seconds when, just as I was about to say something myself, there was a sudden unexpected whisper. It said: "...thank you."

And then the line went dead.

You could jump to a conclusion and assume that this was some ghostly final acknowledgement of gratitude from beyond the grave...

But the time was eight-thirty-two pm...

And it was a man's voice.

I supposed whether you're in the right or you're the wronged, we all have our chance to suffer.

If you enjoyed this book, please support future releases by leaving a review online.

Also available:

FOURTEEN NEW GHOST STORIES

NEW GHOST STORIES VOLUME THREE